WEALDSTONE

A DARK CORNER NOVEL

by

David W. Adams

WEALDSTONE

~ 2 ~

Also available from this author

The Dark Corner
Return to the Dark Corner
Resurrection
Wealdstone : Crossroads
Frame of Mind

Available via TikTok Shop & Amazon

WEALDSTONE

For Mum & Dad

Shirley & Vince.

This is my way of showing you how much you both mean to me, and to thank you for everything.

Everyone should have parents like you.

FOREWORD

Hello, and welcome to The Dark Corner Universe.
For those of you who have been here before,
welcome back. To those of you that are new, I hope
you find the following journey as intriguing as I did
whilst writing it.

I never could have imagined how much support I
would get following the publication of The Dark
Corner in January 2021. When I started, it was
purely to have a copy of my own stories that I could
put on my bookshelf. Now I find myself writing this,
my fourth book, and my first full length novel.

While it is true that the characters and events in this
story are based on my previous works and the tales
so far, it has also been my aim to write this book in a
way that those who have not made themselves
familiar with The Dark Corner books can also
follow.

When this started, I had intended to write standalone
short horror stories, each with a different perspective
or setting, and then move on to the next one.

However, as I was writing those stories, I found that
the little nods I was leaving in each one to one of the
other stories, began to turn into full blown references,
and then another character from earlier in the book

would appear, and I realised I had written an episodic novel.

It wasn't until the end of the first Dark Corner collection, that I realised what I had done, and decided if Marvel can do it, why can't I? And thus began the true development of the Dark Corner Universe. Consider the first two Dark Corner books, as Seasons 1 and 2 of a TV show, and Wealdstone is the big screen adaptation.

And here we are two years after I formulated an idea for the very first story, White Dress, the story elements of which were conceived 20 years ago, seeing the final chapter of the trilogy come to a head.

UPDATE

I intended this to be the final entry in the series at the time of publication in 2021. However, once it was released, I had so many people messaging me on Twitter and other platforms asking why I wasn't writing another.

And the truth was, that I had so many ideas in my head for more Wealdstone adventures, but wanted to try my hand at sci-fi as I am a huge nerd, as you may have noticed in previous books.

And so Resurrection was born. And pretty much died. I loved writing that book, but I felt a disconnect when it was out in the world. I kept being drawn back to the Dark Corner. And then upon re-reading it, I noticed something.

I had set Resurrection in the Dark Corner Universe, without even knowing it. The Decimators, the loss of Earth, all of that occurred in the story 'Galaxy of Pain' in the first book, albeit an alternate version. And upon re-reading Wealdstone for this update, I noticed I had referenced the Deltarians. Another Resurrection nod… before I even wrote it!

So I'm here to confirm several things for you.

Resurrection is the fourth book in the Dark Corner Universe. Officially.

Wealdstone is NOT the final entry.

There WILL be, not just one, but several further entries including expanding the world out beyond Wealdstone, as has been started in Resurrection.

And finally, the next entry in this Dark Corner Universe will indeed be a return to Wealdstone.

Wealdstone : Crossroads is due for release in July 2023. It has begun development and I've already written the first couple of chapters. And a summary is included at the end of this book of what is to come.

So please enjoy the events of Wealdstone, if you've not read the original copy, and the conclusion, not to the Dark Corner Universe, but to what I'm now calling The Pain Wraith Saga.

David W. Adams

'While some monsters are born, others are created. But the worst monsters are those who believe themselves to be heroes.'

E.H. NIGHT

PROLOGUE

For a summer night, the air was fairly cool. As John stepped out of the movie theatre, a cool breeze blew across his skin, making the hairs stand up.

"Jesus, that was sharp," he exclaimed, as his goosebumps raised on his arm.

Giggling at yet another example of how John liked to make a big deal out of all the little details in life, Judy put her hand through the crook in his other arm and pulled him away towards the beach front.

"You know, I swear the phrase 'don't sweat the small stuff' was designed to be played on repeat to you."

John smiled at his fiancée as they walked. He couldn't believe how lucky he was to have her. She had been the one person who just made everything else fall into place. He remembered the day he'd proposed. So un-romantic, that it could have happened in the middle of a baseball game on the Jumbo-Tron. The bucket of KFC chicken with the ring in the gravy pot. Nothing like celebrating an engagement by going to the emergency room for third-degree burns.

But that was Judy. She didn't care. She seemed to love all

his weird little quirks, and mannerisms. That weekend would be a good example of *him* entertaining one of *her* unusual hobbies. They had spent the day shopping for costumes, and then on Saturday, they would be partaking in a line-dancing class.

"So, what did you think of the movie?" John asked.

"Putting Will Smith aside, who was awesome as ever, what the fuck was that?"

Judy was clearly not a fan.

"Seriously? Not even Jared Leto can convert you to the DC Universe?" he asked, surprised.

"You must be joking right? You spent the whole movie drooling over Margot Robbie, and even a *Batman* cameo couldn't save this train wreck."

John had spent the last few years trying to convert his soon-to-be-wife from her obsession with the likes of *Captain America*, *Thor,* and *Iron Man*, but apart from Henry Cavill, and apparently Will Smith, she had decided there was nothing for her here, and *Suicide Squad* wasn't going to change that.

"Okay, I admit *Civil War* was better. You win."

John's defeat seemed to gee up Judy's attitude, and she

swooped in for a kiss. There didn't seem to be anyone around by the time the couple reached the beach. The moonlight was shining high in the sky, the soft rippling sound of the water breaking gently on the sand, just soothed the soul.

As the two of them stood on the beach, they slipped off their shoes to feel the grains between their toes and headed towards the water's edge.

"You know, I had an idea about the wedding," Judy said.

John was interested in all things wedding related. If it was his choice, they'd have been married the day after she said yes to his proposal, burns and all.

"What's that?"

"How would you feel about having the ceremony on the pier over there?"

Judy pointed at the now closed structure jutting out into the sea.

"The view would be amazing," replied John. "But can we afford that?"

Judy thought for a moment. It may be stretching their budget, but the location was so idyllic.

"You wanna go take a look?" she suggested, biting her lip as the mischievous idea was put out into the atmosphere.

"But they're closed, and…"

John stopped his sentence as he caught on to what Judy was suggesting and changed his reply.

"If we get caught, I'm saying you kidnapped me."

Judy giggled, and grabbed his hand, as she dragged him towards the pier entrance, leaving their shoes behind in the sand to be swallowed by the tide.

As they reached the wire fence, and saw the padlock through the chain, John started to lose his enthusiasm for this venture. However, that was soon changed when he watched his future bride take a run up, and scramble over the fence with next to no effort. She landed on the other side and held her arms out like an Olympic gymnast sticking a perfect landing.

She turned around to see a sight which made her laugh out loud. John was stuck on the top of the fence, and the metal was jangling as he wobbled his way over. He landed on the wooden boardwalk with such a thud, Judy dived to the right, hiding down the side of the ring toss stand in case someone had noticed.

"Oh, thanks for the help!" called John as he crawled his

way across the floor.

Judy's laughter would have given her away regardless of where she was hiding. As she looked up, she noticed the clouds had started to amass, although she thought it was odd how they were only over the pier, the moon still shining brightly over the sea. Helping John to his feet, the pair sneakily made their way around the various fairground games, food stalls, and tables and chairs, heading for the open deck at the end, where the ceremony could be held.

"Weather's getting up a bit," John remarked. "Must be a sign."

"How do you mean?" Judy asked.

"Well, the storm clouds are only gathering over the pier. Must be a warning from the financial gods."

Judy gave him a stern look, and he backed down, and held his hands up to signal his second defeat of the night's discussions. When they reached the end of the pier, the view in front was perfect. Judy began getting a little emotional and held on to John's arm for comfort.

"This is it," she said through a rather wobbly vocal tone.

John had to agree, it was simply stunning. He was now having visions of having the ceremony later in the evening, as the sun was setting, for the perfect wedding photos. Above, the clouds were beginning to become thicker, and started to swirl. Judy saw a couple of silent flashes of purple light within and decided they should probably call it a night.

"This looks like it's going to get a bit wet in a minute, so can you take a picture of me with the gorgeous moonlit backdrop, and then we should head home."

"Yeah sure, hand me your phone."

Judy leaned on the railings, stretching out her arms, and attempted to recreate her milkshake cloud selfie she had taken on her vacation to the Florida Keys the year before, right down to the duckface. John aimed the camera on the phone and tried his best not to laugh at the sight of his fiancée and her overly puckered lips. As he went to take the picture, the phone began to fritz out. Seeing his confused face, Judy asked if he was okay.

"Yeah, the screen just keeps going frizzy, like static. Stay there, I'll try again."

But again, the screen continued to act up. A sudden grumble from the clouds above increased the urgency for them to leave, and the flashes of violet light suggested a wooden pier was not the place to be right now.

"Hey babe, let's just go. We're gonna be in the middle of a

thunderstorm in a minute."

John again held up his hand for patience.

"It's fine, just let me thirty-two."

Judy wasn't quite sure what she had just heard.

"What did you say John?" she asked.

"The council of thirty-two will pay," he replied.

Judy gripped the railings a little harder, her concern increasing with the flashes of purple.

"Babe, are you okay?"

John got a confused look on his face and lowered the phone. He looked like he was grappling with a thought that he couldn't really express.

"She's coming."

He now had a terrified look on his face, and Judy's emotions began to take over. Tears welled up in her eyes.

"John, we need to go, you're being weird."

John dropped the phone to the ground and raised his hands to his head.

~ 17 ~

"I... I can't... can't focus."

Judy moved forwards, her hand outstretched.

"John please, let's just go, you're scaring me."

She moved forward inch by inch, but a loud rumble on the deck behind John made her stop in her tracks. The whole structure now seemed to be vibrating, the plates and cutlery in the food stalls shaking to the floor. John's expression now turned to one of pain.

"She is coming. She is not satisfied. Five million gone, but she is not satisfied."

Judy lost what was left of her calm manner completely and began shouting.

"JOHN MARTIN! GET A FUCKING GRIP AND TAKE ME HOME RIGHT NOW!"

Suddenly, John spun on the spot, and let out a blood curdling scream as a bolt of purple lightning ripped from the clouds above and hit him directly in the chest. On impact, he flew through the air, past Judy, smashing through the railings, and flying into the ocean below. Judy scrambled to her feet, and ran towards the twisted metal railings, looking down into the water, but not seeing anything.

"JOHN!" she screamed.

But there was no sight or sound of her fiancé. The clouds above were now gone, but the huge amount of energy that had struck John, had sparked a fire in the cafe to the right of where Judy was standing. As the flames began to spread, she knew there was only one way out, and taking a deep breath, she threw herself over the side, and plunged into the water that had moments before consumed John.

Judy kicked herself to the surface, as above, a huge explosion ripped across the pier, and sent hundreds of fragments, debris and chunks of wood and metal cascading into the water. Judy ducked underneath the waves for shelter, knives, and kitchen appliances puncturing the water around her. When she again rose to the top, the fire was now at full force, and she pumped her arms and legs until she reached the sand once more. Stumbling along the sand, her eyes scanning the beach for any sign of John, her panic continued, and she kept screaming his name. Hearing nothing, she collapsed to her knees near one of the pillars of the pier and burst into tears. And then she heard muttering from beneath the now flaming structure.

"The thirty-two allowed it to happen, and they must pay the price."

Judy looked up and saw a figure standing in the darkness.

"John?" she asked, hopeful that this was her man.

"She searches for vengeance, she was sent away."

Judy moved into the shadows, now that she recognised the features of the man. It was indeed her fiancé, but the voice that was coming from the lips of this man, was not John's.

"John are you hurt?" she asked.

"Pain. So much pain. Nothing but pain."

Judy was now almost beside him, and as before, reached out her hand. He was still facing away from her, and he appeared to be hunching his shoulders, and leaning forward.

"John, we need to get to a hospital. Come with me, I won't hurt you."

"But we might hurt you."

The voice was sinister, and Judy felt a cold presence in the pit of her stomach. Despite this, she reached out and placed a reassuring hand on John's shoulder, and he turned around slowly. Judy looked into his eyes, but they were different. They had flashes of purple which seemed to glow in the darkness.

"John, what's happening to you?" she asked.

John's eyes began to tear up, as his own voice seemed to return.

"Please Judy, help me, I don't know what's happening. There's so much pain, and I can't stop it. Death and murder and blood, it's all replaying over and over in my mind! I'm feeling… pain and anger…"

John trailed off and began crying, but as Judy reached up and placed a comforting hand on his cheek, his face became static, and the emotions were gone. His eyes flashed bright purple, and flickered from side to side, as if he was trying to watch a million images at once.

With one swift thrust, John plunged a jagged piece of the metal railings into Judy's stomach. Her eyes bulged in pain and surprise. They begged the question of 'why?' but the man she knew could not respond. Her hands moved to rest on the metal pole now protruding from her body, and her gaze slowly lowered until she could see her shirt darkening with the blood. Looking back up at her fiancé, blood began to trickle from her mouth, and as John let go of the other end of the pole, she collapsed to the floor.

As the gurgled sound of Judy coughing up her own blood continued, John walked from under the pier, and across the wet sand. As the fire trucks arrived above on the main street, below, the waves carried Judy and John's shoes across to where she now lay, the sand dark with her blood.

1

The people dove into the bushes, screams echoing around the shopping district as debris was thrown through the air, chunks of cars and park benches flying through windows. The growls were so deep and guttural that the ground vibrated, as the creature tore down the main arcade. Its huge, wide feet cracking the concrete slabs as it thundered its way towards the cinema construction site. The size of this monster was not enormous, but the sheer strength it possessed meant that it was not to be trifled with. The scene playing out appeared to resemble the running of the bull in Spain, with anything in its way meeting a swift demise. As another bench made its way through a shop window, it took out two teenagers on its way, blood spraying across the window frame as the glass shattered.

As it let out a significant roar, it came to a stop, and began focusing more on the people searching for a way out. Overhead, the noise of a news chopper caused the creature some distress, and it raised its paw like hands to its pointed ears, and closed its red eyes, squinting through the noise. As the chopper moved slightly further away, the focus returned to the people directly ahead, and the monster locked eyes with the construction foreman, who was now standing at the entrance to the site, blocked in on either side by trucks which had been delivering materials. The fear in his eyes as the creature ran its tongue over its slowly extending teeth was immense. He had nowhere to go, and nobody to help.

The distant sound of tyres screeching reached the creature's ears, his head slightly twisting to the side, annoyance in the eyes, its face exhibiting a frown. With the attention briefly elsewhere, the foreman attempted to sneak by one of the trucks, but this was a highly sensitive being, and its head snapped immediately back in the direction of the man, and it charged towards him. Letting out a terrified scream, the foreman leapt into the cab of one of the construction trucks, and slammed the door shut, just as the creature hit it full force. The truck leered onto its side, the man rolling inside the cab, and the monster began bashing at the vehicle, leaping on top and trying to claw its way into the cabin.

"HEY!"

The voice came from behind, and the creature turned towards the source. Deanna stood where the bench once was, and she was stood in a defensive posture. The creature growled at her, and then returned to the shredded metal, seemingly mangling it more than intended through frustration, actually making it more difficult to enter the truck.

"I SAID, HEY!"

Deanna caught its attention once again, and as its head turned back towards her, the glint of the full moon shimmered in the red of its eyes.

"Why don't you try picking on someone else, huh?"

Deanna stood her ground, but she would be no match for such a tower of strength should it come for her. The shopping district was now more or less empty of people, the news chopper was keeping a safe distance, hovering over the car park, watching the scene unfold, and in the distance, the sirens of the police could be heard. They were never quite close enough when they were needed. But in this case, they would be a hindrance.

The creature slowly climbed down from the wrecked truck, and inside, the foreman shouted for help. Staring into Deanna's eyes, the monster before her once again licked its teeth, drool dripping from the mouth, forming a shimmering pool on the floor. It paused briefly, and squinted at her, almost a look of recognition.

"That's it big boy, you know me," Deanna nodded as she spoke to the creature.

It tilted its head to one side and squinted again. It was visibly considering her words and began to untense its muscles. Deanna spoke again, and slowly edged forward as she did so.

"You need to come with me, Duncan. It's not safe for you out here."

A slight whimper came from Duncan, his bulked up mass slowly beginning to shrink down its stance. In the background, the foreman was being pulled from the truck by Scarlett and Desmond, as quickly as they could. Duncan seemed to pay no attention, the red in his eyes becoming less intense. He began to edge closer to Deanna, and she reached out a hand towards him. The police sirens were getting closer, and their time was running out. They needed to get Duncan off the streets. As him and Deanna came to within six feet of each other, the search lights of the news chopper hit his eyes, and he cowered backwards, and tripped over his own huge feet, falling through the window of the Body Shop, shattering the glass, one large piece penetrating his side. He screamed out in pain, and roared at the moon, before clawing his way back to his feet. He charged at Deanna, and she attempted to dive out of the way, but was too slow. With one swift swipe, Duncan sent her careering through the air, slamming into a brick wall of another store, and falling ten feet to the ground with a thud.

Above, the chopper continued to shine the light directly at Duncan, and he raged and charged around smashing everything in sight, bewildered and tormented by the beam. He tore a planter from the ground, and launched it towards the chopper, thankfully falling short as it lurched backwards, falling and landing onto the roof of an ice cream stand. It was at this point, that Duncan noticed Desmond and Scarlett attempting to sneak around the edge of the perimeter with their injured foreman.

"Oh shit."

Desmond tried to hurry the others along, noting Deanna in the corner of his eye beginning to stir. He had known she would be fine, but there was always a small degree of concern for his mother. Duncan charged towards him, roaring the entire time, saliva cascading left and right, the pavement cracking beneath the heavy footsteps he was taking.

"Come on, where are you?"

Desmond's eyes were darting around, searching for the solution. In a matter of seconds, the beast would be upon him. Duncan placed himself on all fours, and with an immense burst of energy, propelled himself into the air, teeth extending into six inch points as he did so. An incredible crashing sound came from his left, as a truck tore through the remains of the Body Shop, bursting out of the shop front, and leaning out of the window, Daniella fired a series of shots, each striking Duncan in the chest and stomach, altering his flight path.

As Desmond dove to safety, Duncan's limp body fell from the sky and landed on the concrete with such a force, the shockwave shattered the paving slabs for a seven foot distance in all directions. As Daniella's truck came to a grinding halt just shy of a slightly shell-shocked Deanna, she climbed down from the driver's seat, and kept her modified revolver aimed at her husband. The beast that lay before her whimpered, with blood trickling from each of the wounds in his torso. His form appeared to be shrinking down. Daniella aimed her weapon at his head before addressing him.

"Duncan? Can you hear me?"

His head turned to face her, his eyes now blue, his teeth retracting.

"I... I can hear you."

His speech was gravelled and slightly slurred, and he winced in pain as one of his hands brushed one of the bullet holes, which along with the rest of his form, was now shrinking.

"Good."

Daniella raised her weapon and unloaded another shot into Duncan's head, and as he closed his eyes, she lowered the gun. Desmond and Deanna joined her, and they all stared down at Duncan's now limp human form.

"How many shots was that?" asked Desmond.

Daniella opened the chamber and checked her weapon.

"Five. And that was because of the angle. I'm not sure they would have penetrated his back."

Deanna looked around at the carnage, and the sight of red and blue flashing lights in the car park.

"This can't keep happening, if he gets any stronger, we won't be able to stop him."

Daniella nodded.

"Let's get him into the truck and get out of here. Max and Kristin reckon they've strengthened the restraints at the house."

The others nodded, and they picked up the unconscious body of Duncan, and slid him into the back of the pickup truck, covering him with a tarpaulin, and climbing back inside, Deanna started up the engine. Beeping the horn, Scarlett ran across the arcade, dodging the wreckage and leaping into the back.

"Is he okay?" she asked as the truck backed through the carcass of the Body Shop back onto the access lane.

"For now," replied Daniella. "But we need to find something stronger. The silver and holy water isn't working anymore."

Scarlett nodded.

"Could use some sort of special amulet," she joked.

Deanna smirked as she drove, but the others did not. Desmond knew that they needed more resources, and more feet on the ground. He turned to face Scarlett.

"Any word on Kathryn's newest recruit?" he asked. Scarlett shook her head.

"Nothing. She has sent him emails, and tried to call, but he's not answering. I think he might be a lost cause."

Desmond sighed.

"With all this recent activity, we need all the help we can get. Tell her to keep trying."

Scarlett pulled out her phone and began dialling. As the truck left the devastation behind, the police moved in and began pulling their way through the wreckage of the stores, people surrounding them, and the news crews clambering for details. None of them were sure what had occurred, the images from the chopper had somehow been distorted, and in the distance, a flash of purple light seemed to strike down from above. One thing was for sure. This was by no means the first challenge of the night, and it would not be the last.

2

Jack watched the news coverage with much less surprise than one might expect. Wildly strange occurrences in his home town were no longer uncommon. The report showed aerial footage of minor explosions, and people running for their lives. The voice of the news anchor was deadly serious.

'The ruptured gas main caused significant damage to the Silverton Shopping District, just months after a huge explosion tore through the cinema complex, killing several college students. As seen in this footage shot from our aerial copter, multiple explosions can be seen both within the stores and throughout the main arcade walkways. The gas was said to be of such potency, that people hallucinated images of werewolves and supernatural creatures, one eyewitness saying he hid in a truck from a monster that appeared to want to eat him whole. The gas even seemed to reach our camera crew in the helicopter who reported the same thing. Despite the investigation revealing the gas explosions, paranormal societies throughout the country are claiming Wealdstone is becoming a hot bed of activity and are wildly concerned. We will have more on this story, after the weather with Casey.'

In fact, paranormal experts were saying that Wealdstone was fast becoming the supernatural capital of the whole of the United States. Jack had been watching reports like this for the last couple of years, and the number of online articles were growing. Random flashes of lightning, sporadic periods of murders from formerly timid townspeople, creature sightings, hauntings, and most recently, the alleged video footage of a woman being shot five times only to rise and walk away.

Jack's own father and his actions in the town were the reason he and his mother had fled to San Francisco in January of 2016. In late 2014, Jack's father, Jack Marsters Sr. had gambled the entire family savings on a pyramid scheme run by a shady businessman and had been taken for a ride. The family had lost their home, the respect of their friends, and Jack Sr. had lost his job after lashing out at a co-worker.

The following Christmas time, he decided to take his revenge after Jack and his mother left him and torched the offices of the businessman who had conned him. However, unknown to Jack Sr., the businessman was asleep inside at the time, and the fire also spread to a nearby children's hospital, St. Vincent's, killing one-hundred and three kids. It was at this point, that Jack Jr. and his mother, Alice, moved out of Wealdstone, and to San Francisco for a fresh start.

Despite the events of that Christmas in 2015, Jack still

felt a tinge of sadness for his father. He had watched his mind unravel over the twelve months leading up to that disaster and couldn't do anything about it. After they left town, they heard that he had been sectioned under the Mental Health Act. Alice had told Jack never to speak of his father again, that he was a murderer, and was not worth the time of day. When he saw the report of his father's death in a fire on the site of the old hospital, he spent the rest of that night pondering if somehow fate had claimed his father in a twisted form of vengeance. However, in the months that followed, reports began to come out of Wealdstone that the toy store owner had seen Jack Sr. inside the store and watched as he burned alive in the presence of children. Most normal people chuckled and suggested the guy was looking for attention to publicise his store reopening, but Jack Jr. was more sceptical.

He had heard from his old college friend, Kathryn, that she had been the victim of a known serial killer's attack but had been defended by spirits. She had since opened a haunted museum in the very house that she was attacked in and was raking in the money. But Jack wanted nothing to do with it. After all he and his mother had been through in the last few years, all he wanted was to have a quiet life. After he lost his mother to cancer twelve months after relocating to San Francisco, he started dating the nurse who had cared for her, and they had been living together since late 2020. Jack was the happiest he had ever been. And yet, something wanted to pull him back to

~ 33 ~

Wealdstone. It was like a magnet in the back of his brain, telling him that he needed to return, but he couldn't figure out why. And then, every seven or eight months, he would see some report about another unexplained event in the town, and that desire would grow stronger.

Kimberly had always been a bit of a sceptic when it came to the paranormal, but Jack had more of an open mind. After he had joined the police department, Jack became known as Deadshot to his academy buddies. He would frequent the firing range twice a day, honing his skills to vent his inner frustration at wanting to go back to a place that was the source of all his pain. He had become quite skilled. Every year, his squad would win the firing challenge in his precinct and had won dozens of trophies from other contests.

Kimberley on the other hand, was not an avid fan of this activity. She was more of a gentle giant. Jack had always been intimidated by her five foot eleven frame, especially as he only came in at five foot seven. It had taken him quite a while to actually ask her out. After his mother's funeral, he had bumped into her at the wake, and finally asked her out. They had been together ever since, getting engaged nearly a year ago. This, though, was the sixth time Jack had watched this news on repeat. Something was ticking over in his brain. Was that a random streak of lightning in the background? Something wasn't adding up. His thought process was broken, by the sound of the front door opening.

"Hi honey," Kimberley said as she closed the door to the apartment.

"Hey, how was work?" replied Jack, switching off the TV.

Kimberley made a 'so-so' gesture with her hand and placed a bag of groceries on the counter top.

"You feeling chicken tetrazzini for dinner?" she asked.

"Yeah sure, sounds great, thanks."

Jack looked back at the blank TV screen, and his mind began to ponder again. A fact which did not go unnoticed by his fiancée.

"So, what happened this time?" she asked.

A process she had gone through dozens of times before. Jack flicked the TV back on, and Kimberley watched as the news cycle rolled around again.

"So… werewolves?"

Jack switched the screen off again.

"Apparently, vampire werewolves."

Kimberley raised her eyebrows, before continuing to prepare for dinner.

"Vampire werewolves? Sounds like a horror writer ran out of ideas and blended the two most cliched creatures for a B-Movie."

Jack looked at his phone, as another alert informed him, he had yet another email from Kathryn. Kimberley noticed that too. Being a nurse, she was trained to look for signs of distress.

"What's that, the fourth or fifth email?" she asked. Jack shook his head.

"Tenth. She keeps insisting they need more manpower to investigate the weird activity. To be honest, I feel like I'm being drawn back there every time something happens."

"But you're happy here, right? With me?"

Jack was concerned he had hurt her feelings, and walked into the kitchen, wrapping his arms around her.

"Of course, I am. It's just there are things I don't really know about my Dad's death. You know, he died in a store on the site of the kids hospital he torched. The owner saw it, then happened to turn out to be the brother of my… friend in college, who now happens to be part of a paranormal investigation group. Tell me that doesn't sound like a huge coincidence."

Kimberley placed the tagliatelle on to boil and turned

back to her future husband.

"You have a wonderful job, in a great city, with friends, and if I may say so, a simply amazing fiancée. You don't need to complicate all that by travelling hundreds of miles to hunt monsters and dredge up childhood pain."

She placed a series of kisses on Jack's lips, and then continued to chop vegetables and herbs, while Jack stared at the wall, deep in thought. The smell of chicken sizzling filled the air as Kimberley started to fry the meat in a pan, and Jack's stomach growled. He had been so engrossed in the news that he had forgotten to eat lunch.

"I guess somebody's hungry," she pointed out to him.

He chuckled and nodded his head.

"I skipped lunch."

Kimberley shook her head, and threw him a piece of chicken, Jack catching it in his mouth, and almost drooling at the chargrilled taste of the white meat sliding down his throat. Grilled chicken was his favourite meat in the world. His Dad had always loved to barbecue in the summer and bought Jack his first griddle pan so he could do it indoors when the snow was falling outdoors.
As he sat and enjoyed a delicious meal on the couch with his girlfriend, the windows open, and a lovely summer breeze blowing in, Jack thought about why he would ever

want to leave this place.

Kimberley was right. He had his perfect life. And yet he couldn't shake that feeling. And for every email Kathryn sent him, he had to seriously stop himself from replying to it. The TV was on, but he wasn't really paying attention. The news was now focusing on Tom Brady renouncing his retirement from the NFL, again, but the footage from earlier was playing out in his mind. Kimberley had fallen asleep on his shoulder, and his beer had gone warm on the table beside him. He was slightly disturbed by the sound of footsteps outside the door. Probably the neighbours again, he thought. They were a fan of a dinner party, and every so often, they would get a little too drunk, and end up having arguments on the staircase.

Jack carefully lay Kimberley's head on the cushion, and walked over to the sink, pouring away the warm beer, and popping the bottle into the recycling. Again, he heard commotion outside the door. Feet were shuffling around, backwards, and forwards, and he could hear whispering, but couldn't make out what was being said. As he approached the door, he thought he saw a flash of purple light under the door. Pausing for a moment, he noticed all the voices and shuffling had stopped. He heard Kimberley stirring and looked over at her as she shifted into a more comfortable position. A smile crept across his face, and he turned back towards the door.

The door smashed open with such force, it hit Jack in the face, and he flew backwards, cracking his head on the counter top, and falling to the floor. Through blurred vision, he saw four people enter the apartment and storm directly towards the couch. As Kimberley woke up, startled, she screamed and two of the intruders headed straight for her, while the other two headed into the bedroom, searching for something. Kimberley ran around the couch, and headed for the door, and Jack reached out for her from the floor.

But as he watched, the two intruders caught up with her, lifted her into the air, and slammed her down onto the counter, on her back. One of them withdrew a long serrated blade from his coat, and as Kimberley screamed her lungs out, plunged the blade directly into her heart. Jack watched the whole event unfold in slow motion, rooted to the floor, blood dripping from the back of his head, vision still distorted, as his love was murdered in front of him. The knife remained embedded in Kimberley's now lifeless body, blood beginning to trickle down to the floor from the counter top, and as Jack slipped further away, he saw purple flashes in the eyes of the offenders, now back to four as the other two emerged from the bedroom, having seemingly not found what they were looking for. He could just about make out what they were now saying.

"It's not here. She must not be here."

"All of the evidence pointed to this one, she has to be here."

"She is not here!"

"The dagger will tell us, we must wait."

The four stood in a line, watching the dagger sticking out of Jack's former partner, and waited. Just as Jack reached the edge of blacking out, the knife shot up from Kimberley's chest and stuck in the ceiling like a dart on a dartboard. A vast purple mist emerged from Kimberley's torso, splitting into four, and knocking each of the intruders to the ground, before merging back together, and flying out of the door. The murderers leapt back to their feet, and one of them yanked the blade from the ceiling, and all four headed out of the apartment in hot pursuit.

As Jack finally passed out, there was a faint scream of terror from one of the neighbours as they entered the apartment and saw the sight before them.

As Kimberley's blood continued to drip onto the floor, Jack's phone went off again. The screen illuminated.

'*Kathryn calling...*'

3

"It's three a.m. Kathryn."

Deanna was sat almost in a collapsed heap, on a chair in the far corner of the kitchen.

"Yeah, I know, but I must make sure Daniella is okay. Besides, I need to help Desmond make a fresh batch of the ammo."

Deanna rolled her eyes, as she climbed back to her feet and walked over to the refrigerator, opening the large silver door, and picking up another bottle of *Desperado* from alongside the five bags of blood hanging from the shelf above. She closed the door, and moved to stand beside Kathryn, who was now attempting to funnel holy water into the hollowed silver bullet casings.

"Kristin is going to wonder where you've been. You've worked late every day for two straight weeks. I can help Desmond with this. Go home to your wife."

Kathryn shook her head and squinted to focus on the bullets.

"We have had so much activity lately, she understands."

"I wouldn't be so sure of that. She didn't exactly sign on to run your museum," Deanna replied.

The front door to the mansion opened, the huge walnut wood creaking with the movement. Neither woman looked towards the noise, and the loud clunk of the door closing again didn't garner their interest either. The house had seen much better days, but there really had been no arguments when it came to a location for the team to base themselves. With 'Herman's Curiosities' out of bounds due to the unstable nature of what was going on there, and Highland Manor seeing way too much activity, the old Miles Mansion was the best choice. Nobody had occupied the place since Jonathan Miles' mistress had committed suicide, and Kathryn was able to pick it up at a property auction for less than she had bought the Martin house for. But it was still in need of a lot of renovation. For the time being, most of the activity was conducted in the basement of the house anyway. As Daniella entered the grand entrance hall, Grace joined her from the basement entrance.

"Hey Mom."

Daniella staggered over to her daughter and gave her a rather laboured hug.

"How is he?" she asked, referring to her husband.

Grace shrugged her shoulders.

"Not bad for a homicidal creature that just went tearing through a shopping district. Again."

The joke did not land well. Deanna and Kathryn joined them both, and between the four of them, Grace was the only one with any real energy left.

"Heard anything from Scarlett and Desmond?" asked Deanna.

Grace shook her head.

"Last I heard was just after one-thirty, and they'd managed to track the last vampire down to the old cinema at Wellsfield."

Deanna placed her left hand over her eyes, and rubbed them intensely, desperate to try and stay awake. Kathryn let out a huge sigh, and the four of them moved over to the library area, slumping down onto the sofa and chairs, Daniella resting her head on Grace's shoulder.

"We can't keep this up," Grace suggested, to the agreement of the group. "The amount of activity is just way more than we can handle."

Kathryn held out her arms but couldn't keep them there for long.

"I've tried my best, but I just can't seem to get hold of any extra help."

"Well to be fair, we need more than one extra recruit," replied Daniella.

Grace nudged her foot against Deanna's leg to wake her up from a brief slumber and agreed with her mother.

"This is the tenth straight night with multiple incidents. The intensity of it is almost constant, there are more purple hits than ever before, and we are spread thinner than baking paper."

The group agreed with Grace, as Desmond and Scarlett entered the mansion, along with Max. Deanna gestured towards them with what was left of her beer, but Desmond shook his head.

"Well, that's it for the night," he said as he too slumped onto the sofa. "I'm hundreds of years old, and tonight I feel every one of them."

"Amen to that my boy," replied Deanna, raising her bottle once more before downing its remaining contents.

"How's Duncan?" asked Scarlett.

"He's sleeping in the pool, but we've had to strengthen the harnesses by over a hundred and ten percent."

Grace looked at her shoes as she described the actions, they had been forced to take to contain her father. Max stood behind her and placed a reassuring hand on her shoulder. Her hand met his, and she welcomed the comfort.

"How are we on new recruits?" asked Desmond.

The group chuckled at the seemingly never ending loop of the same conversation.

"Sorry I asked," he replied.

The team consisted of just seven members, and one of those was permanently incarcerated in the empty shell of a pool in the basement, but the surges in activity meant that they could no longer hack it. And it was beginning to show. Over the last few months, there had been a massive rise in the number of murders matching the same modus operandi of thirty-two stab wounds, surges in vampire activity, and the intensity of hauntings was through the roof. Highland Manor was almost tearing itself apart with its undead occupants becoming stronger. It was part of the reason Kathryn had decided it was probably a smart idea to close her museum temporarily.

"I've been looking for help in all the paranormal investigation teams that aren't bullshitters, but to be honest, they're all terrified of what's happening here. And I can't say I blame them."

Kathryn stood up, and walked over to the window, stretching as she went. Desmond's voice followed her.

"And what about your friend in San Francisco?" he asked.

Kathryn shook her head.

"I don't think he's interested. We didn't part on the best of terms." Max suddenly perked up.

"Why? What did you do to him?" he said with a cheeky smile.

Kathryn snapped back around with an offended look on her face, as if to say he had crossed the line. It did not deter his enthusiasm.

"I didn't do shit, thank you very much," she replied.

Without opening her eyes, Daniella offered up the explanation.

"She fucked his best friend while they were dating."

That woke everybody up, and they all sent a judging look in Kathryn's direction, Grace could not have raised her eyebrows up any further if she had tried.

"We were not dating!" Kathryn replied in defence.

Max and Grace started chuckling.

"Is this the part where you go all Ross and Rachel on us?" asked Deanna, who had returned to a slumped posture with her eyes closed.

"We weren't on a break, Deanna, we were broken up. And besides, it was over fifteen years ago, he is engaged to a doctor now."

Raised eyebrows from the group suggested that she was perhaps still showing a little too much interest in Jack's life to know such a detail. She responded almost in an accusing manner.

"What? So, I keep tabs on his Facebook page!"

The others had a brief chuckle to themselves, as Kathryn's phone began to ring. She looked down at the display.

Kristin calling.

"Oh boy."

Kathryn walked up the grand central staircase and disappeared into one of the rooms on the first floor, closing the door behind her. Within moments, the rest of the group could hear Kathryn's raised voice.

"If she isn't careful, she's going to win the award for

shortest marriage in town," Scarlett said with a concerned look on her face.

Daniella nodded.

"They haven't been too solid since the honeymoon. Then again, not everybody celebrates getting married by being harassed by dead pirates."

Deanna stood up, placing her empty bottle on the end table beside her chair.

"Well, no offence, but I'm sick of the sight of you all, and I'm going home."

The others gestured a laboured wave of goodbye, and as Deanna left the mansion, Desmond and Daniella stood up too.

"I'm gonna go check on Duncan," offered Daniella.

Desmond followed her down into the basement, leaving Grace and Max alone. When they were sure they were alone, Max moved to sit beside Grace, and they shared a long and warming kiss.

"Have you told your Mom yet?" Max asked her. Grace shook her head.

"Not yet, although to be fair, I'm pretty sure she thinks

I'm gay."

Max looked taken aback.

"Why would she think that?" he asked, slightly offended.

Grace chuckled a little but tried to keep her face serious.

"Well, last week, she walked in on me holding Scarlett's boobs in each hand."

Max nearly choked on his own saliva, and Grace couldn't keep her face straight any longer. Max wasn't amused.

"What the hell, Grace!"

Grace composed herself long enough to speak and held her hands up in defence.

"I was checking for lumps. You know, monthly check for suspicious lumps?"

Max calmed down and understood. A few months ago, Scarlett had been concerned when she found two lumps on her breast and was concerned it had developed into cancerous tumours. The truth was in fact much weirder. She had been hexed when her and Deanna had hunted down a witch, and she began to form lumps in intimate areas. While the team had managed to cure it, she had been paranoid ever since, and Grace was her checking

~ 49 ~

buddy.

"You know, you can check me for things anytime you like," Max said, with what he thought was a James Bond style suaveness to his voice.

"Thanks sweetie, but your boobs aren't as big as Scarlett's."

"Very funny."

Suddenly from upstairs, came the sound of a slamming door, echoing around the empty corridors of the house, and the sound of quickened, heavy footsteps coming back down the stairs. Kathryn's face was red, and she had clearly been arguing with Kristin.

"Everything alright, Kathryn?" asked her niece.

Kathryn slammed herself down into the seat opposite and buried her head in her hands.

"I'm guessing that's a no," Max offered his reply.

From between her fingers, Kathryn gave him a very stern look, which he picked up on immediately.

"Okay… I'm gonna head home. See you guys later."

Grace watched her boyfriend walk away and got slightly

distracted in the sight. Max had started wearing skinny jeans. A change that Grace had most definitely noticed. As he walked through the door, and the huge walnut slabs closed once more, Grace turned back to see Kathryn smiling at her. Caught.

"So how long have you been dating?" asked Kathryn, the grin still visible on her face, despite her previous anger.

She was grateful for the distraction.

"About three months, actually," replied Grace.

"And you're keeping it quiet because?" Grace thought about it for a moment.

"Well with everything going on right now, people could probably do without the distraction."

Kathryn nodded.

"I hear that. Kristin just told me there have been four more purple strikes, and the police have their hands full with the deaths."

"How many?" Grace asked.

Kathryn took a deep breath before replying. "Seven so far."

The pair pondered that for a minute. In one night's, work, fifteen people had died, and none of them had even gotten to bed yet. Trying to get back to the sight of her angry Aunt, Grace delicately broached the subject of her troubled marriage.

"Did she call you just to tell you that?"

Kathryn let her guard down. She was way too tired to try and put a face on it again.

"Well… on the positive side of things, she agrees with me that it's time to shut down the museum for a while, you know, say it's under maintenance or something."

Grace waited, and when no second part of the reply was offered, she pushed for it.

"And…? The negative part?" Kathryn's eyes began to well up a little.

"The negative part is that she is wondering whether we need to take a break from each other, or whether we need to spend more time together. Whichever one it is, the current set up just isn't working."

Grace wasn't surprised by this. Kathryn had become so worried about Duncan and how the change had affected him, that she had begun to neglect the museum, and in turn, her wife. Their honeymoon had been a murderous disaster, and since then, she had basically been second in charge of the team behind Desmond. And now her marriage was paying the price. Grace moved to sit beside her aunt. She placed a reassuring hand on her knee and offered her wisdom.

"Well, now that the museum is closed, and Dad tore up the shopping district, maybe she can join us properly, and then you will finally be around each other more. This is kind of a family project anyway. Especially if I marry Max."

Kathryn laughed, and Grace joined in.

"And Scarlett?" Kathryn asked, in between giggles.

"Scarlett can be our side piece," Grace replied.

The two of them collapsed into giggles, and they shared a long hug, before both heading home. It had been a very long night, and had now passed four a.m. Pretty soon, the sun would be up, and the whole world would know about the carnage that had gone on that night. Luckily Duncan's rampage would go under the radar, with Deanna's ageless knowledge of technology, she had managed to hack the copter's live feed and blur the images, and the good old gas explosion scenario had been fed to the cops. Walking out of the mansion, they both headed down the long driveway leading from the house, with the imposing building towering behind them, and they hugged each other goodnight as they reached the bottom.

However, as the two of them headed off in different directions, there were two more purple lightning strikes in the distance, and Grace could feel like there were eyes on her. She paused for a moment, and looked around, but could see nobody. She gently caressed her gun under her jacket, just in case it was needed, but after a few moments of no movement, she carried on her way. She picked up the pace, and jogged down the street, completely unaware of Max's unconscious body lying in the bushes to the side of the road. As Grace's footsteps became more distant, Max's body was dragged away into the woodlands.

4

'The town police have detained four of the suspects but believe that another five may still be on the loose. At this time, they are not ruling out the possibility of a cult operating within the vicinity and are believed to be linking the killings to the mysterious purple lightning strikes within the last two weeks. It is suggested at this time that the cult members may be worshipping these freak weather occurrences. All of this comes in the same night as a gas mains explosion at the Silverton Shopping District which killed eight people and severely injured eleven others, with bystanders being affected by the gas itself and claiming to have seen a werewolf vampire creature. These claims were obviously ruled out. Coming up next, it's Karen with the sports news.'

Jack sat at the bar, surrounded by beer bottles, the TV on in the background, but he had already seen the reports. He'd been sat at the same point at the bar for four hours, ever since his release from questioning. She was gone. Kimberley had been murdered in front of him, and yet he could not help but allow his mind to move past that fact towards *how* she had been killed. The mysterious dagger, the four intruders, and the things they were talking about. A sharp pain in the back of his head, and his hand instinctively moved towards the source. The dried and congealed blood on the back of his head, was a stark reminder of the events of the weekend. The image of his fiancée lying dead on his kitchen counter, the blood pouring down the front of the cabinets. Jack would never be able to forget that sight. Was Kimberley even who he thought she was? And what the hell was that purple smoke that flew out of her body? Whatever had happened, Jack had been arrested on suspicion of murder by his own precinct. That had hurt more than the blow to the head. They were his friends, his colleagues. They knew him, and they still arrested him without even taking him to the hospital.

It was only after seeing the CCTV footage from the building's corridors, that he was released without charge. As he drained his sixth beer of the morning, bearing in mind it was only eleven a.m., his phone began to vibrate. He fumbled around in his pockets looking for it, and ended up falling off his bar stool, crashing to the floor, and taking the stool down with him in the process. Nobody came to help him, they just stared at him on the floor, and continued eating their breakfast. Jack finally managed to pull his phone from his pocket. The screen lit up, he was met with the picture adorning his lock screen. It was a picture of him and Kimberley at the hotel after last year's policeman's ball. That was the night he had proposed. He blinked away a couple of tears and swiped to unlock the phone. He was greeted by an email alert, and a familiar name in the sender bar.

'1 new email from Kathryn Silverton.'

Jack moved to swipe away the notification but paused. If Kimberley's death really was some kind of supernatural event, then there weren't many people around who could help him find out what it all meant. He recalled the items from the news, about random strikes of purple lightning, and wondered if there was any correlation between this and the purple smoke which left his fiancée's body. He tapped the notification and read the email.

'Jack,

Look, I know you've been ignoring my emails and my calls, but this is getting serious now. You must have seen it on the news. Things are getting incredibly active here, and there aren't enough of us to go around. Please call me back. We need you.

Kathryn.'

Jack read the email three more times, before he finally reached a decision. He needed answers, and he sure as hell wasn't going to get them in San Francisco. He pulled himself to his feet and paid his bar tab. Tapping the phone screen to reply to the email, he simply typed two words.

I'm in.

5

Duncan awoke from a rather hideous nightmare with a start, the chains attached to his limbs rattling like those of a prisoner trying to escape his shackles. As he realised where he was, he began to calm and relax his muscles, but his mind was still tense as he realised the reason why he was back in this space.

"Good morning sunshine."

A familiar voice came from the bar area of the former swimming pool, and as the daylight began to streak through the narrow basement windows above, Duncan saw the outline of his wife approaching, with what looked like a glass of cranberry juice. But of course, it wasn't.

"How are you feeling?" asked Daniella.

Duncan rested his head back on to the concrete base of the pool shell, and cleared his throat which was now dry, and raspy. He suspected this was due to the roaring he had been doing in his other form.

"Hungry," he replied.

He almost spat the word out, as if he was angry with

himself for needing to admit to his thirst.

"I wouldn't stick around that glass for too long, or you might be joining its contents."

Daniella was used to this kind of talk. Duncan had become much more withdrawn over the past twelve months, and Daniella suspected this was partially due to her actions. She had often wondered if he blamed her for his transformation. She did.

Duncan had been turned by a vampire when the family moved to Alaska for Duncan's new job. Daniella was a werewolf. She had been bitten by a former neighbour of theirs, with whom she had been having an affair. She'd managed to keep her condition a secret until the night of Duncan's change, when the family were attacked by a clan of vampires. Grace had been bitten and tortured, and Duncan was bitten trying to save his daughter. Daniella managed to reverse the effects in her daughter using her own blood, as Grace had not fully transformed. She only retained certain aspects, such as a higher degree of strength.

However, when Duncan also fed on her blood, he became mutated. He could walk in sunlight but retained the thirst for blood. He would transform under full moonlight into a hybrid beast, bent on carnage and bloodlust. And it was that behaviour that had led her and the team to contain him in the former pool of the Miles Mansion. Something which initially, Duncan had been on board with, but as he became stronger, he began to resent the arrangement, and had broken free on three occasions now.

"I very much doubt you would hurt me, Duncan."

Daniella set the glass of blood next to his head, which immediately lunged towards the crimson fluid. She took a swift step back as Duncan gripped the edge of the glass in his teeth and raised it up, tipping the liquid into his mouth. She cautiously continued backwards and sat on the edge of the pool. It didn't take long for Duncan to empty the glass, and cast it aside, the glass smashing on the concrete surface of the pool. His eyes glowed red as the blood began to quench his thirst. His breathing began to calm, and the tension in the chains eased.

As Duncan returned as close to his normal self as possible, he looked at each chain, and gave them all a firm tug, before turning to face his wife.

"They're stronger again, aren't they?" he asked.

Daniella nodded.

"The silver and water ammo isn't working properly either. I'm not sure how long we can keep you here."

"I'm not the one asking you to keep me here," he replied with frustration in his voice.

That, in part, was true. It had been Desmond's idea to keep him in the complex after the second escape. Duncan had woken from a brutal nightmare, as he often did, and broken the shackles. When he found his way out, the moon was full, and his hunger was at maximum.
Three people had died that night.

"You know we have no choice, Duncan."

Daniella raised herself to her feet and began to walk back towards the bar area.

"I'm getting stronger, Dani. Every day, I can feel the fire burning in my veins. Sooner or later, you're going to have to kill me. Or I'm going to kill you."

Daniella preferred to avoid conversations like this, particularly around her daughter, but Grace was actually the first one to suggest Duncan be put out of his misery.

"I've already said, you won't hurt me, Duncan."

"You can't be sure of that."

"Yes, I can."

"No, you can't, Dani. Right now, I'm fighting every urge to tear out these chains and rip your throat out. I can *smell* your blood. It's all I can think about. It's worse when Grace comes down here…"

"ENOUGH!"

Daniella was now red faced, and very angry. And yet despite this, Duncan's expression did not alter.

"I'm sorry that you've become some kind of mutant, but I will NOT murder my husband!"

"I'M NOT YOUR HUSBAND ANYMORE!" yelled Duncan, all four chains seemingly at maximum tension, even in his human state.

Daniella picked up her glass of water, and launched it across the room, shattering against the far wall, just missing Desmond as he walked in.

"Morning to you too."

Daniella stormed past him, and out of the basement area. Desmond looked towards Duncan, seemingly asking for an explanation.

"Don't look at me like that. This is your fault."

Desmond moved across to the bar and switched on the coffee machine. As the smell of roasted beans filled the air, Duncan's face twisted as if he had sucked on a lemon.

"Sorry Duncan, I know you like your drinks more metallic in taste, but I need a pick me up."

Duncan chuckled, seemingly for the first time in ages. He remembered how before the change, he had not been able to start his day without at least two coffees and a bagel inside him. Despite his transformation into a combination of monsters, he missed those days. Even the days that Daniella had been sleeping with another man, things were less complicated.

"Vanilla and coconut latte."

Desmond looked across at him with raised eyebrows.

"I'm sorry?" he replied.

"That was my favourite coffee. I came across it in a cafe once while I was on vacation in England. Couldn't get enough of it. When I came back home, I found out a local place sold the same one. Now I can't drink it, I miss it even more."

Desmond sympathised with him. There were many things that he missed. His first family was at the forefront of his mind most days. They had been gone for over four hundred years now, but he could see them in his mind as if it was yesterday.

"So, why don't you tell me what I'm supposed to do with you then," Desmond asked. "I heard you tell Daniella that you want her to kill you. Is that true?"

Desmond stepped down into the pool as he spoke and pulled a key from his pocket. Duncan was confused but replied all the same.

"It's the only way to keep everyone safe. You've seen what I'm capable of."

Desmond began to unlock the chain to Duncan's left leg, much to his bewilderment, but he continued to talk, as if this was an everyday occurrence.

"What if I told you, that I had a way for you to keep your thirst under control?"

"I'd say you were full of shit."

Desmond smiled as he unlocked the second leg.

"Yeah, and you'd be right. But I think I might be close to a solution."

Duncan was becoming more concerned at the ease and comfort with which his restraints were being removed. But he was intrigued, more than he was angry.

"How? What could possibly have changed since last night?"

Desmond removed the final chain and climbed back up out of the pool.

"I had chat with one of my contacts in England last night. She seems to think that there is a way that you can subdue your animal urges on the vampire side."

"How?"

"I'm not gonna lie, it's going to be painful. From what I can tell, most vampires that have tried this experiment have been killed."

Duncan sat up, rubbing his wrists. He was the most Duncan-like he had been for over a year.

"And you think that is the way to go?" Desmond smiled.

"I was thinking that your werewolf side, with the extra strength, will help you through it. If it works, you'll be a fully-fledged moon-howler like your wife."

Duncan climbed out of the pool and joined Desmond at the bar as he poured his coffee into his *Starfleet Command* mug. This was the first time that he had been allowed freely out of the pool base for months, and he was now highly suspicious.

"Why are you doing this?" he asked. Desmond sipped his coffee.

"Doing what?" he asked.

"Letting me out, trying to cure me."

Desmond sipped his coffee a second time and placed his mug down on the wooden surface.

"Duncan, things are getting worse. You're rampage is only the tip of the iceberg. Something is coming. Something big and trust me I've been around long enough to know the signs. We are not cut out for this. We don't have the people, or the resources. We need you."

Duncan didn't often exist outside of his own little bubble, but he could tell that Desmond was deadly serious.

"You really think it could work?" he asked.

Desmond chugged the rest of his hot coffee, which made Duncan slightly uncomfortable at the thought of him burning himself. He placed the mug back down and looked right into Duncan's eyes.

"I honestly don't know. But given what I think is coming, we can't afford to not try it."

Duncan nodded, and with this new information, his mind was beginning to turn away from the thoughts of violence and anger for the first time in quite a while.

"So where are we going?" he asked.

Desmond smiled at him.

"Not where, Duncan. *When.*"

6

The sound of the shower reverberated in Kristin's mind like a jackhammer. She had gotten next to no sleep, and her and her wife had barely spoken in the few hours they had spent together. Things were not going as smoothly as she had expected since they got hitched. Kristin had never been one to be tied down in a relationship. She hadn't always discounted them but having felt quite free to come out to her parents at a fairly young age, and have them accept it with warmth, had given her a stronger platform to be who she wanted to be. But when she met Kathryn, something changed. She knew that this was someone who was challenging and would push her to discover new sides to her own personality. She fell in love with the idea of that. But now she was wondering if it was that idea, or Kathryn herself that she loved the most.

Kristin looked over towards the bathroom, and watched Kathryn adjust the shower head to the full height. She hated that. Kathryn was pushing six feet, and Kristin was a mere five foot seven, and every time Kathryn got out of the shower, she forgot to lower the riser back to what Kristin often referred to as 'normal person height.'
And yet, she couldn't take her eyes off Kathryn's body. Every aspect of that woman kept her interested every minute of the day. The arguments and the tension that had

arisen between them with everything that was happening was disrupting their life, yes, but it didn't detract from the fact that she wouldn't want to be with anyone else. She was no longer sure, however, that Kathryn felt the same way.

Her brother was in a serious condition, and it was not exactly what you would call normal circumstances. If Kristin had been in that situation, she would probably be acting the same way. She was worried, and given their new found line of work, Kathryn was probably worrying that at some point, she may have to kill her own brother. Duncan had already suggested it on several occasions, but it was not a topic that was ever met with serious consideration. At least not in public.

As Kathryn switched off the shower, she stepped out of the cubicle, and reached for a towel. She wiped her hand across the misted up glass surface of the mirror, to see Kristin looking back at her. The shower had helped to clear her mind a little, despite the almost nonexistence of any real sleep. She smiled to herself. She knew Kristin liked to watch her in the shower. It's why she always left the bathroom door open. Kristin was the first person she had ever been with who truly appreciated both her body and her mind. But she too was worried that their relationship was not what she thought it was. She tied the towel around herself, and strolled back into the bedroom, sitting on the edge of the bed, hair clinging to her shoulders, and she let out a deep sigh.

"What are we doing here Kris?" she asked.

Slightly taken aback by this question, Kristin struggled to find an answer.

"What… what do you mean?" she stuttered.

Kathryn smiled, and reached over, placing her hand onto that of her wife's, twiddling the engagement ring around so the gem was facing forwards. Another little quirk of hers.

"The arguing, the fighting, the tension. This isn't what I want, and I know it's not what you want either."

Kristin felt a disturbance in the pit of her stomach. She was now unsure of the scenario she had been placed in. She began thinking that perhaps Kathryn had come to a decision without her, that this was it, and that was the last time she would see this woman's naked butt. That last part was more important to her than she realised.

"Kat, what are you saying to me?" she said, trying to stifle the emerging tears.

Sensing she had used the wrong tone to start this conversation, Kathryn took her other hand from her towel, and grabbed Kristin's other hand, clenching them both.

"I want us to just be together, like we were when all this

started. No more fighting. No more arguing. Let's just be us."

A huge wave of relief flew over Kristin. She hadn't known how she had truly felt about the state of her marriage until the sudden realisation that it may be about to come to an end. Now she knew. And she was relieved. More than she had ever been.

"Oh, thank fuck for that!" she exclaimed, to the wonderment of Kathryn. "I thought you were gonna say we should break up!"

Kathryn laughed out loud, and let go of both hands, to cover her face, letting out a little snort in between chuckles.

"Hey, I know we haven't exactly been a perfect couple lately, but this isn't '*Love Island*', I'm not going to vote you out! I love you."

The couple shared a long kiss, Kathryn not falling for the distraction as Kristin's hand attempted to pull away the towel. She slapped the hand away and smiled as she backed away.

"Hey, none of that, we have work to do."

Kathryn stood up and Kristin watched with great pleasure as the towel was dropped.

"Thank God I'm not gonna lose my access to that ass," Kristin said, with as much of a gruff New Yorker accent as possible.

As Kathryn got dressed, she laughed at just how bad Kristin was at copying any successful accent.

"You know, my little niece and Max are dating," she volunteered.

"Oh yeah, I know."

Kathryn seemed a little hurt that she hadn't delivered a piece of juicy gossip.

"How do you know?" she asked.

"Everybody knows. They aren't the most subtle. Besides, it's 2023. Subtlety has long gone."

Kathryn couldn't argue with that.

"True. Well come on Miss Lazy tits. Get some clothes on."

Kathryn threw a selection of garments at her wife.

"That's not usually what you say to me," she replied with another awful attempt at the New York accent.

"That is awful. You sound like Joe Gatto if he had a stroke."

Kristin faked a hurtful look on her face, as she pulled on her jeans. The laughter, however, was interrupted by the sound of the doorbell.

"Wonder who that is?" asked Kristin.

"Well, it could be Shaggy, or Velma. Any of the Scooby gang really," joked Kathryn. "Because God knows we don't have any friends outside of our haunted adventures."

Kristin watched her wife walk towards the door and stop. She turned and entered the bathroom, reached into the shower cubicle, and lowered the shower riser back down. Without looking back at Kristin, she left to go answer the door. Kristin smiled to herself.

"Guess we are okay," she said.

She pulled on her shirt, fastened up the buttons, and slid into her shoes. She bounced out of the bedroom, and when she reached the top of the stairs, she could see Grace and Daniella, both with very concerned looks on their faces.

"Hey guys, what's up?" she said as she descended the stairs.

"Max didn't make it home last night," Grace started, "and neither did Desmond, according to Deanna."

The seriousness of the situation was evident. But there was more.

"We were worried, given the level of incidents we've been dealing with, so we headed up to the house, and Grace found Max's bag at the side of the road."

Daniella was trying not to let her voice tremble but was gradually failing. She continued.

"When we went into the house, Duncan was gone."

Grace pulled her mother in for a hug, but she wasn't ready to show emotion just yet, and pushed her back. Kathryn continued the conversation.

"Any ideas on where they have gone?" Grace shook her head.

"When we went down to the pool, it looked like Dad's chains had been unlocked. They weren't broken. Which means Desmond let him out."

Kristin was now becoming more concerned.

"Why the fuck would he do that? It was his idea to lock Duncan down in the first place."

Daniella nodded.

"Exactly. He must have some sort of idea of what he's doing. But whatever that plan is, he didn't share it with me."

Kathryn saw that her phone was vibrating on the table next to the window and walked over to pick it up. It was Deanna.

"Hey, Deanna, any luck?"

"No, nothing yet. There's no notes, no signs of things going south, nothing. Wherever they went, they had no plans to let us know."

"Do you think there is a chance that Desmond is planning to kill Duncan?"

The question hit the others like a train. Kristin showed an expression of disbelief that she would openly ask such a question, but Grace and Daniella had a much more accepting look, as if it was a question, they had both pondered already.

"I really don't think he would go that far."

"Yeah, but to be fair, he did try and kill you and Scarlett when you first met back up."

Kristin gave her wife an 'I can't believe you went there' look. Kathryn held up her other hand as if to say, 'what?'

"Yeah, thanks for that little reminder. No, I don't think he would do that. Not without consulting Daniella or Grace first."

"Okay, well keep us posted, and take Scarlett with you. I don't want anyone working alone from now on."

Deanna hung up, and Kathryn placed her phone down on the table once more. She needed to formulate a plan, and quickly. But just thirty seconds later, there was a sound of an almighty explosion from just down the street.

"What in the hell was that?" exclaimed Grace.

The four of them ran out of the front door, to see flames emanating from one of the neighbours houses. People were running down the street, kids were screaming. Next door to Kristin and Kathryn's house, was another neighbour, frantically trying to explain to the emergency services the sight before her, and Daniella and Grace led the group towards the burning house.

"Was there anyone in there?" Grace asked a passing family.

"I don't know," said the mother. "I thought I heard

arguing in there, but nobody came out!"

The mother led her family away from the danger, and the four women ran towards it. As they reached the driveway, they heard what sounded like screaming coming from one of the open windows.

"Grace, go round the back, see if anyone is trying to get out. Daniella, you and Kristin try and get into that window to the side, I'm gonna try through the front door."

Kathryn barked her orders, like a true second in command, and the team nodded and split up. A familiar soundtrack of sirens sounded in the distance, but as usual, they were way too far away. The flames were coming from what looked to be the kitchen, and the back windows were blown out, so Kathryn kicked the front door in, but was blown back by the heat. She pulled her jacket up over her head and entered the house.

"HELLO?" she shouted, to no response. "HELLO?"

She heard more glass smashing and saw the outline of a person in the lounge. She batted away as much smoke as she could, and as she walked into the room, she saw a man, in his dressing gown, holding a knife. Blood was dripping from the tip, and he was standing over the body of another male. Kathryn took a step back, and reached for her gun, but she had left the house in such a hurry, she hadn't picked it up. Rookie mistake, she thought.

"Sir?" she asked.

The man turned to face her, but his face was not of a normal configuration. His skin had been burnt, and she suspected he was the one who caused the fire. But it was his eyes. They had flashes of purple. He turned the rest of his body to face Kathryn. Another loud pop from the kitchen startled her, and she stumbled backwards out of the room.

"Kat?"

Kristin and Grace were coming down the stairs, coughing through the smoke.

"There's three bodies up there, all stabbed to death."

Kristin spoke to her wife, but Kathryn's gaze remained fixed on the man with the purple eyes.

"I think we have another one," she said in reply, leading the other two to look in the same direction.

"Oh shit," came Grace's reply.

The man started to stumble towards them with a very pained look on his face, contorted now, with agony, his eyes darting back and forth.

"She is coming!" he shouted through the noise of the

crackling flames.

"Who is coming?" Kathryn asked in reply, holding her hands up in a defensive posture.

"The council let her slay them, and the council must pay. But she is coming."

"Sir, I don't understand, but we need to get out of here, right now."

Kristin signalled to Grace to go back the way they had come, and gestured to Daniella, who was now creeping in the broken hallway window, to back up and circle round.

"So much pain," the man continued, tears now mingling with the sweat on his brow. "So much pain!"

Without warning, the man lunged at Kathryn with lightning speed, dagger poised, and the two clattered straight through the table in the hallway, landing on the floor, splintered wood piercing her back. The man stared at her with fury and spat more words at her as they struggled.

"We will take back our realm! She will be stopped! The five million will be avenged!"

Kathryn punched the man in the face, the knife clattering to the floor. Pulling herself back up, blood now visible through her shirt, the man picked up the knife, and made another charge at her, and the two, entwined together, burst through the window at the side of the front door, and landed on the pathway, rolling down the hard surface. The other three ran around from the side as the man stood and made another statement.

"She will kill us all! She will destroy everything!"

Kathryn staggered back to her feet, and the man once again, with the knife in his hand, ran for her once more, screaming but not with anger, with an expression of terror. Three shots rang out, and the man's chest erupted with crimson in the three entry points. He dropped the knife and collapsed to the floor. As Kathryn and the others turned to look behind them, they saw Jack standing in the street, gun poised, the barrel smoking. He lowered the weapon and looked over at Kathryn.

"You're welcome. It's been a long time."

7

Max had never seen silver walls before. Well, outside of the walk in refrigerator at Sisko's, that is. It was a strange sensation to be staring at a wall and also be staring back at himself. The room was quite small, with the obligatory two way glass panel behind which he was sure people were looking back at him. He wasn't entirely sure how he had gotten here but given how tired he had been when he left the mansion, and the elevated level of events in Wealdstone, he suspected he'd been attacked, and then left behind when the police turned up. The handcuffs chaffed his wrists slightly, and the chair was hardly borrowed from a Hilton hotel. There was a clock on the wall above the glass panel, but the time was uncertain due to the fact that although Max could hear it ticking away, the hands weren't moving.

Movement could be heard from beneath the door behind him, and Max lifted his cuffed hands up on to the table, the metal reflecting the ceiling light off the shiny walls, and momentarily blinding him as the light hit him in the eyes. Seconds later, a man entered the room, and stood next to the glass panel for a moment, before sitting opposite Max at the table. The man in question looked like your typical procedural crime drama type. Imagine Booth in *Bones* or perhaps Steve in *Diagnosis Murder*.

That was the image which lay before Max. Shirt with no jacket, oversized belt buckle, shiny shoes, colourful socks, perfectly organised hair, and just a hint of a five o clock shadow.

"Interview commences at ten-thirty five."

Max looked around for a tape or recording device to which the man was speaking, but saw nothing in the room besides the clock, table and chairs. The man appeared to note the confusion, and pointed towards the as suspected, two way glass. Max nodded in understanding.

"Please state your name, and place of address for the recording."

Max cleared his throat.

"Max Power, 134 Portobello Close."

The detective did not look amused.

"Max *Power?*"

This was why Max usually asked people to just refer to him by his first name. He nodded, with a hint of embarrassment.

"Believe me, it wasn't my choice. I have what you might call, lunatics as parents."

Still unsure that he was telling the truth, the detective continued.

"Detective Sam Greenwood conducting the interview, no additional note takers present. Max, do you know why you are here?"

Max shook his head in the negative. The detective continued.

"At approximately three-twenty-five this morning, you were seen to be entering a large property on Brennan Hill with two other adults and appeared to be carrying modified weapons. Is this correct?"

Max knew full well that those facts were correct, but the more he looked at Detective Greenwood, the more he felt as if something was off. The eyes didn't match the voice.

"Yes, that's correct. Although I did not have a weapon myself, my companions did."

Greenwood nodded, and moved to write down a note, before forgetting he did not have anything to write on, or indeed, with.

"Moving on. Around twenty-five minutes later, several members of the public were seen leaving this house, and heading in opposite directions, just hours after several murders occurred within the town. Are you aware of those incidents?"

Again, Max nodded, but something about the detective and his behaviour was off. The ticking from the clock was now sporadic, almost ticking to the sound of a heartbeat, as opposed to the usual measurements of the workings of a timepiece.

"Can you tell me anything about the heightened activity within Wealdstone over the last few months?"

The stare was intense. Greenwood was obviously aware of something and was on the edge of playing his hand. Max had been training his observations, and his awareness for over a year, and had seen quite a lot of hauntings, possessions, demons, vampires, and all manner of creatures. But something about Greenwood, made Max feel like he too had seen his fair share. He decided to play it in the middle.

"I know that random purple strikes of lightning have gotten more frequent in the last eighteen months, and that they usually strike an individual who then begins to exhibit homicidal behaviour. This then leads to several murders before the suspect is usually taken down."

"And how do you know this?" Max smiled.

"Same way that I'm sure you do. I've seen it."

Greenwood was slightly taken aback by the suggestion that he was aware of more than he was letting on. Max noticed on the wall, the clock was now ticking faster.

"How many incidents have you been aware of in those eighteen months, Max?"

It was at this point that Max began to sense foul play. There was nobody else present, no notes were being taken, and despite the suggestion that recording was happening on the other side of the glass, Max believed this to be a lie.

"In terms of lightning strikes, the first one was as far back as 2016, before I became involved in investigating them. In the last year and a half? I'd say there have been roughly thirty, give or take."

Greenwood's eyes widened slightly.

"Are you okay… Detective?" asked Max.

"I'm fine. That's a lot of death. And pain."

Max switched the tables on him.

"It's funny you should mention pain, Detective Greenwood, because that is the recurring theme in all of these attacks. Each time, the speech from the attacker is garbled, but the thing they always seem to focus on is the pain they are feeling."

The clock on the wall was now ticking almost constantly with very few breaks in between. Max's eyes looked up towards it, and noticed the hands were now gone. His hunch appeared to be right.

"How did I get here, Detective?" he asked.

Greenwood leaned back in his chair and let out a sigh.

"I brought you here."

"And you felt the need to knock me out to do it?"

"I wasn't sure you would come willingly. And no offence, but of those in your group, I figured you were the easiest to subdue."

Max appeared hurt by that suggestion. He had spent as much time in the gym lately as he had done in the mansion. He had a girlfriend now, he had reason to up his game.

"So why don't you tell me what this is all about, and who you really are?"

Max had now fully become the detective, and Greenwood was momentarily on the back foot. Although it was indeed momentarily.

Greenwood stood up from his chair and walked back towards the glass. As he turned back to face Max, he raised his right hand, and gave it an almost ceremonial wave. As he did so, the walls and the ceiling appeared to cloud and melt away in a purple haze. The walls slid down to reveal wooden panelling, and the floor retracted to reveal the same. A window appeared next to a door, where the glass panel had been. When the entire illusion had been removed, Max found himself sitting, unrestrained, in a rickety wooden chair in the middle of the old cold store for the mansion, and Greenwood was stood in front of the door. Greenwood approached Max, and dragged a second chair from beside him, and sat down once again.

"I am not who I appear to be, Max."

Clearly Greenwood was expecting a more enthusiastic form of shock from Max than he got, but when he didn't, he continued.

"My name is Ariella. This body belongs to a detective in the Wealdstone police department. His name is indeed Sam Greenwood."

Max nodded, and then gave the surging question within him, another nudge.

"And *what* are you?" he asked again.

"I am what is known as a Pain Wraith. We exist in an ethereal state in our own realm, and our sole purpose is to experience all kinds of pain, of all varieties and intensities."

Max wasn't sure what he had been expecting, but this was not it. He couldn't form a sentence in reply, so allowed the explanation to continue.

"When we mature after a few hundred years, we are released and able to move into your physical realm to then begin to experience physical pain to further our understanding. And when that is over, we are set free to explore the physical world as we see fit."

This was a lot of information to get inside of five minutes. Max was now leaning forward with anticipation.

"Are you okay, Max?" asked Greenwood.

Of all the questions or statements that Max could have formulated, from all the information he had just received, the only question he could formulate was this one.

"So, you're not a dude, you're a girl trapped in a guy's body?" Greenwood was distinctly unimpressed.

"That's it? That's all you have to say? You're sat in front of a mystical being with the power to create an interrogation room and move through realms, and all you can think about it if you're looking at a *Freaky Friday* situation?"

Max held up his hands in apology. Or defence. He wasn't quite sure.

"I'm sorry! But this is a lot to take in. I mean I've become used to dealing with situations involving ghosts and demons, and werewolves, but it's a little bit different when you're sat in front of what sounds to be amounting to something from the *Q Continuum*!"

Greenwood actually chuckled to himself, as he reminisced.

"What's so funny?" Max asked.

"Oh nothing, just thinking of old times."

Max brushed the comment off and restarted his own line of questioning.

"So why me?"

Greenwood refocussed and explained.

"I've seen your group around town, and wherever there is trouble, you seem to be. I also have... dreams about you all."

"Dreams? About us?"

Greenwood nodded.

"You see Max, when whichever physical form we are in dies, we have a moment to choose where we move to next. Whether that is in time, or in location, we choose which body we occupy next. Usually, it is to further our study of pain, so we choose a person that we know is going to experience pain or death and move into that body. However, if we don't make that choice, our consciousness moves to wherever our energy is pulled. In the time in between, we experience what you humans call an out-of-body experience, where we observe from outside, memories of our past lives, those of other wraiths, or moments when a pain wraith has been present."

Max continued to nod, although he only heard one seemingly glaring fact.

"So, you're immortal, and you're everywhere?"

Greenwood pondered that for a second before nodding and shrugging his shoulders.

"Yeah, I guess we are. We have existed since the dawn of time, and I've lived at the end of human existence, and at several points in between. So yeah."

Max stood up and began to ponder around the cabin, in an effort to shake some of this new information from his head into his feet, and free up room for more.

"So, how old are you?" he asked.

Greenwood had a puzzled look on his face as he tried to work it out.

"Well, my race was born before your galaxy even came into existence, but me personally. I'm twelve hundred and three."

"Oh… so… you're a bit of a… teenager?" Greenwood nodded.

"Give or take."

"Can you leave the body you inhabit?"

Greenwood stood up from his own chair and walked away. His face had turned solemn.

"Yes, we can, but it's not good for the body we leave."

"Wait, what do you mean it's not…"

Max was interrupted by a sharp raised hand from Greenwood, who's eyes were now darting back and forth, head tilted, and he moved his ear towards the wall of the cabin. Suddenly, Greenwood launched himself at Max, and cleared him off the ground and into the corner of the room, as a vehicle ploughed through where Sam had just been standing, sending wooden shards, and glass everywhere. The van in question came to a sudden halt when it slammed full force into a tree on the other side of the cabin. With most of the structure destroyed, Greenwood helped Max to his feet, and looked deep into his eyes.

"Run! And don't stop until you find your friends!"

He shoved Max outside the wreckage and turned in time to block a knife being swung towards his shoulder. Holding the blade was a masked man, wearing black… with purple eyes. Greenwood beat the knife out of his hand, and punched him in the gut, sending him crashing to the floor, but was then set upon by a second and third person, same kind of outfits, both attempting to hold him in place. As the first person began climbing back to their feet, Greenwood noticed the dagger was still lying in the leaves on the ground. He pulled his arms together and delivered a swift kick to the back of each of the other men's knees, sending them both to the floor, before spinning around and punching them both hard in the face. From out of the back of the van, a fourth assailant leapt into the action, and immediately made a line for the knife. As Greenwood came within inches of the blade, the first attacker sideswiped him to the ground, and the fourth reached and retrieved the blade. Greenwood and the original attacker rolled around on the ground exchanging punches, each as strong as the other. The presence of the dagger was affecting Greenwood's abilities, and he knew it. He was fully aware of the purpose of that knife and needed to avoid it at all costs.

Despite his best efforts, Greenwood was pinned down to the ground as all four attackers regrouped. The original offender took hold of the knife and stood above him.

"Where is she?" he asked in a harsh, deep voice.

Greenwood was confused.

"Where is who?" he replied, continuing to struggle against his opponents.

"WHERE IS SHE!" the blade now just inches from Greenwood's chest, the eyes of the man questioning him were now burning purple with the intensity of the sun.

"I don't know what you're talking abo…"

Realisation then hit him. He stopped struggling, and his stomach sank. A unique experience for an ethereal being.

"Jasmine. She's here, isn't she?" he asked, his eyes glazing over as he left the moment.

"You really don't know, do you?" asked the attacker.

Greenwood shook his head.

"Some daughter you are."

The individual raised the blade high, glinting in the sun, and as he prepared to plunge it down into Greenwood's chest, shots rang out, and the man fell backwards, dropping the knife. With a new found alertness, Greenwood broke free of his attackers, grabbed the knife before it hit the ground, and swung the blade across the throat of the nearest man. The others turned to see where the shots had come from but saw nothing. Greenwood took the initiative and plunged the dagger into the spine of the second nearest, the blade emerging from their chest. With the removal of the blade, the same violet mist that had fallen from the walls of the cabin emerged from each body and disappeared into the air. More shots rang out, and a bullet shattered the tree bark nearest Greenwood. His eyes darted around the woodlands, and he spotted Max, waving around a hundred yards away. Another shot pierced the air and hit the third attacker in the shoulder, sending him to the ground. An opportunity which Greenwood refused to let go, as he slammed the blade directly between the eyes, the violet smoke erupting once more.

The fourth attacker took off towards the denser trees, but moments later, Greenwood caught a glimpse of a woman running at pace towards him, and as he watched, she charged into his side, and they both flew into a large oak tree, clattering to the ground. Max ran towards them both, as did Greenwood. Grace had the attacker pinned to the ground, a feat which seemed remarkable to Greenwood, as he himself had struggled.

"How the hell are you doing that?" he asked through bated breath.

Grace smiled at him.

"Let's just say I'm enhanced," she replied.

Max caught up with them.

"I kinda brought the cavalry."

Greenwood chuckled and responded to the high-five now awaiting him.

"So why don't you tell me exactly what is going on here?"

Grace seemed unperturbed by the fact she was pinning an otherworldly creature to the ground.

"First thing is first. This creature needs to be dispatched."

Greenwood raised the blade high but as he swung it downwards, a bullet ricocheted off the blade sending the knife away from him, and another bullet punctured his shoulder. The impact knocked him back, but the wound began to burn. Clearly this was not your normal ammunition.

"What the fuck?" he cried out.

As he looked up, Deanna, Daniella, Kathryn, Jack and Kristin were walking towards them, and the gun in question was being held by Kathryn.

"Step back from the knife," she ordered as the group reached them.

"He needs to be put down, or he will bring others!"

Nobody was listening, and time was not on their side. Distracted by the arrival of her mother and the others, Grace eased her grip too much, and the attacker pushed her away, and grabbed the discarded blade, plunging it into her side. Grace screamed in agony as the knife was pulled out of her hip. Greenwood wasted no time. As Daniella and Kathryn unloaded six shots into the assailant, Greenwood grabbed hold of the dagger, and plunged it into his chest. However, despite subduing the final attacker, Greenwood looked on in amazement, as Kathryn fired three shots into his stomach. He collapsed to the floor, shirt turning dark red, fast.

"Kathryn! You just killed a detective!"

Max's screams were loud and frequent. As Greenwood

felt himself bleeding out, Ariella's presence began to come back to the surface. She could feel herself being pulled away, but the dagger's presence made it impossible to simply manifest outside of the body.

"Get... the... dagger... away," she managed to murmur from Greenwood's now pale mouth.

Max realised what she was trying to say, and grabbed hold of the blade, surprised by how heavy it was. He gripped it tight and ran with it, followed by Deanna, while Daniella tended to Grace. The further away the dagger moved, the stronger Ariella could feel herself becoming. She began to resist the urge to move away, and as her strength gathered, she left Greenwood's body and began to manifest into her own form. The remaining gang members stood and watched in shock and a huge multi-branched form of violet ribbon swirled in the air before them, before folding in on itself, and expanding into a solid mass. Moments later, Ariella stood on the wet leaves, fully formed. It had been centuries since she had last taken her own choice of physical form. She was standing around five-foot-nine, with almost platinum blonde, shoulder length hair. The stares were warranted, and Jack and Kristin in particular were showing a lot of interest. After a few moments, Ariella looked down to realise she had failed to manifest any clothes. Reluctantly, Kristin nudged Jack, and he removed his jacket, and handed it over to her.

"Thank you," she replied. "I've obviously forgotten how to create myself some dignity."

Max reappeared, slightly confused at the sight of Greenwood's dead body, and the sudden appearance of a semi-naked woman, before rearranging his thoughts, and putting two and two together.

"Ariella?" he asked.

"Hi Max. Nice to meet you properly."

Max moved forward to shake her hand, but she held up her own.

"Maybe we can get me some clothes first?"

"Yes. Most definitely."

Kathryn spoke through gritted teeth whilst maintaining judging looks on both Kristin and Jack.

"Where's the dagger?" Ariella asked.

"I placed it in a containment unit inside the basement."

Max led the others away from the woods back towards the house.

"So… you're like a ghost assassin?" asked Grace as she

was carried up towards the house.

Ariella smiled.

"I guess you could say that."

"Cool."

Grace smiled as she passed out.

8

Two Years Earlier...

The key turned in the lock with a sharp 'click', securing the bar for another night. It marked the final property on the street to go to sleep, and the bar manager slid the keys into his coat pocket and headed off down the street towards his apartment. It wasn't much, and on the wage, he was on he was never likely to get any better, but after a long night of wiping the counter listening to everyone else's problems, it was a nice change of pace for him to go home and listen to his own inner demons.

As he disappeared into the night, the street lights began to turn themselves off. An inventive little feature that the local authority had decided would save power and therefore money, by switching off all the street illuminations across town after one a.m. The fact that crime had risen sharply in that time, didn't seem to change their minds. After all, it's always about the money.

The street lay dark, and empty. And silent.

Three stores down from Sisko's Bar, was an electronics store. In the window was the latest OLED televisions, much as the previous years' models, only with about four dollars of improvements for an inflated price of thousands. However, what was most interesting about these televisions, was that in the still and silent darkness, they began to flicker. At first, the image on the smallest screen, a mere thirty-two inches, began to flicker with the static of times long gone by. No crisp 4k pictures here. But then gradually, the other sets in the window began to switch on and show the same distorted imagery. Black and white lines vibrating violently like the scene as you would come to the end of a VHS tape in the eighties.

There was now an audible, but low hum in the air. Across the street, the lights in the customer area of the local *Starbucks* began to flicker on and off, and there was a low vibration. The air now seemed like it was charged with electricity, and up and down the street, more and more lights and appliances began to switch between on and off. The humming sound became more intense, and the glass in the windows of the stores began to vibrate more. The level of energy in the air was now extremely high, and the street lights began to turn back on, in sequence, as if a plane was coming in to land on a distant airport runway. As the first TV set exploded in the electronics store, so did the lights, one by one, in the *Starbucks*. The alarm panels blew off the walls in several stores, and then another TV exploded, it's components shattering the glass front of the shop window. The noise of the humming sound would have now been deafening had there been anyone around to hear it, and with another charge of energy, three more store fronts blew out, followed by the street lights, again in succession moving from the top of the street to the bottom.

As the last light blew out, a huge crack of light appeared in the sky, hundreds of feet above the tallest building, and dead central to the opposing sets of street lights. The split had a bright purple glow to it, as if someone was tearing open a piece of paper. The rip grew, and from within it, audible cries could be heard. Painful screams, and howling became louder and louder, and one individual scream was dominating the others, and seemed to get louder as the tear became wider.

Suddenly, something burst through the rip in the sky, the light disappeared, and all activity surrounding the energy and the lights were gone. The object hurtled down from above at a rate of knots, and as it approached the ground, it seemed to develop into a humanoid shape. As it did so, it veered to the left, almost as if it had been jolted awake, and speared itself through the front of the electrical store, seemingly folding the front of the shop inwards, such was the impact. No alarms sounded, they had all been blown by the immense power, but as the smoke cleared from the store front, the clear outline of a person was visible. Lying in the rubble of several TV sets and sound systems, was a woman. As she gasped at her first breath, she was immersed in a sense of terror. She was hurt, covered in injuries from the impact, and wearing no clothes. Panic began to set in, and she began screaming in terror, rubbing her hands over her face violently, as if trying to banish the sight from her own eyes. After a couple of minutes, she began to calm down slightly, and surveyed her surroundings. She recognised this place somehow. Not the store itself, but the street outside. A distant memory perhaps? She was unsure, but she definitely had a sense she had been here before. Pulling herself to her feet, she walked over the broken glass and plastic and climbed out of the store front. When she moved out into the open air, she felt the chill of the breeze on her uncovered skin, and seeing a clothing store, also with its windows blown out, she headed inside. When she emerged, she began to recall several more memories of this place. She stood in the middle of the street, still unoccupied by any persons. She was now clad in dark coloured jeans, combined with a red V-neck vest shirt, and a long dark trench coat. Her vibrant red hair seemed to contrast with the materials and colours perfectly. As she began to walk down the street, taking in as many sights as possible, the heels of her new black ankle boots echoed around the deserted locale.

A flash of imagery burst open in her mind, and she fell to the floor, placing a hand on her head to attempt to assuage the pain. She saw images of a train. An old steam train, and a woman. She recognised the woman but could not place her name. As she began to stand once more, another wave of imagery and she was knocked down a second time. The pain in her head was agonising. She saw pictures of purple ribbons being torn apart, heard screams of agony and terror, and felt a huge surge of energy within her body. As the imagery became more intense, her strength became more intense also, and as the imagery reached its climax, she let out a deafening scream, her arms flung out to the side of her body, and beams of bright purple light burst from her hands, tearing apart the front of the two buildings either side of her. Explosions rocked those buildings, and the force of the blasts hit the woman full on, but she did not move, her flaming hair cascading in the wind from the blasts. The beams of light were retracted, her arms dropped to her side, and she hit the ground on one knee. She stopped there for several moments, hands on the cold ground, crouched on the one knee, as her hair fell down around her face. As she gradually looked up, a smile began spreading across her face. She remembered who she was. A brief flash of purple light, and suddenly, her face was altered with a flash of red lipstick, a flick of eyeliner, and her hair seemed to deepen it's rich dark red hue. She knew why she was here again. Why she had fought so hard to get back to this place, and this time, nothing was going to stop her. She would hunt her daughter down and bring her back once and for all.

The flames began to die down from the initial explosions, and Jasmine sprung to her feet. She knew that she would be pursued by those of the council who had attempted to contain her before, but she would be ready for them. Her first task was to find somewhere to base herself, and then, find out which *time* she had found herself in. She knew where Ariella had been before, and when, so she realised that she may have to wait around for a while.

As Jasmine reached the end of the street, she paused. She did not want to draw attention to the fact she was here. As determined as she was, she knew that any clues to her whereabouts, would hinder the reasons she was here. She closed her eyes and moved her hands across her chest. When she opened her eyes once more, they were filled with a bright violet light, and sparks of purple lightning emerged from her fingertips. As she moved her hands across her body, the store fronts began to reassemble themselves, as if someone had pressed a rewind button. As she orchestrated the swathes of purple energy, the TV sets re-joined into single units, the light bulbs across the street began to reform, and as she lowered her hands once more, and the mauve glow vanished from her eyes, everything was exactly as it had been before she arrived.

"Now," she said to herself, turning on her heels. "Let's see what my daughter is up to."

9

"How is she?"

Ariella lowered herself into one of the large leather chairs surrounding a table which now sported a large containment unit, vacuum sealed, containing the mysterious dagger from the earlier assault. Daniella nodded her head.

"She's fine. The wound is healing fast."

"Impressive, that one," Ariella offered.

Daniella smiled.

"You could say that."

Deanna, Kristin and Kathryn entered from the kitchen with trays of snacks and drinks. None of them had eaten or drank much in the last few days, and the level of debriefing that was about to go down would require everyone to be alert.

"Jack, you, okay?" asked Kathryn, as she noticed that he was stood against one of the bookcases, his gaze fixed on the glass containment unit on the centre table.

"This is the knife that killed my fiancée."

The statement was as sharp as the blade and cut through the atmosphere with speed. Everyone fell silent, including Ariella.

"So, I want to know what you people are, and what the fuck is going on. And I wanna know now."

Jack joined Deanna and Kathryn on the biggest couch, and Kristin occupied the chair beside them. Max was upstairs looking after Grace, but he had already heard a significant portion of the details, and after a knife and gun fight like the events of earlier, in such close proximity to the events of the last few nights, he was exhausted.

"Ariella, I think you should start," suggested Kristin. "We need to know all about pain wraiths, what they can do, and why our activity seems to be ramping up."

She nodded and adjusted her new borrowed shirt which Grace had kindly offered her and stood at the front of the group. It had been a long time since she had felt like a teacher, but it was funny how lifetimes could come rushing back.

"Okay. Wraiths are designed to experience every level of pain millions of times over. Our very existence creates huge amounts of cosmic energy. Imagine your brain firing neurons when you're excited or having adrenaline rushes. Well, when you're in extreme pain, it fires more. That action creates energy. And in our realm, that energy is multiplied exponentially."

Daniella interrupted.

"So, you're effectively like a power plant?" Ariella nodded.

"Yes. The pain is experienced from birth, until each wraith matures, and they understand every possible aspect of emotional and ethereal based pain. After we mature, the energy is used to open a doorway to your world, where we are able to experience pain in a physical sense."

Deanna interrupted this time, a confused look clearly visible on her face.

"Sorry, can I just ask, why you exist to be in constant pain?"

Ariella stopped briefly, as she considered her answer.

"Once we have experienced all forms of both physical and mental forms of pain, we learn all we can and use that knowledge in our new life. We are free. Wraiths mature twice in life. Think of it as two puberty cycles. When we enter the second maturity phase, we are allowed to explore life as we see fit and use our knowledge of pain and suffering to make the perfect life on whichever world or in whichever dimension we choose."

"And screw with the people who are already here?"

Jack's words remained direct and speared towards the angry end of the emotional scale.

"My people do not care about the planets or species they encounter. They use them as experiments. Those who make the decisions for our race are called the Council. There are thirty-two of our oldest and strongest wraiths, and they rule our realm with an iron fist. Metaphorically speaking."

The conversation was drawing out more fear and confusion that it seemed to be giving clear words. Ariella was not entirely sure that they were following her, but she continued, nonetheless.

"I broke the rules. Once I had matured, I was shown just what I was capable of. I could manipulate certain aspects of reality. Only in small ways of course, we aren't Gods."

Kristin laughed out loud but received a series of judging looks for doing so.

"Sorry. Carry on."

"I was here to begin experiencing the physical pain. I inhabited the body of a young woman who was brutally raped and murdered in the Old West, I was a blacksmith's assistant and suffered death at the end of a blade with no warning, I watched my wife beaten and killed in front of me because I had engaged in an affair with a gangland villain. All different kinds of pain. But I was falling in love with this place. And every time I had to leave, I lost something. I wanted my freedom early."

Max and Grace gradually made their way down the stairs to join the conversation. Several people looked up at them, but Grace held her hands up to signal she was fine, and the two of them sat on the back of the larger couch.

"So, I decided to refuse entering another body, and to take my own form and begin my life here. This is the form you see now."

"And I'm guessing, you weren't left to your own devices?" asked Deanna.

Ariella shook her head, and Daniella thought she caught a glimpse of a tear in her eyes, but her thoughts kept reverting back to Duncan. She still had no idea where he was, or if he was even alive.

"I spent twenty years living in Victorian England, where I met a wonderful man, and we got married. I had spent so many hundreds of years experiencing nothing but pain, suddenly, the feeling of happiness was overwhelming. It became like a drug. After being married to Leonard for three years, we were blessed with a son, and two years later, a daughter."

The interest level had now peaked, and questions began flying at the resident wraith.

"How can you have children, if you're just taking human form?" asked Max.

"Well, when we take a human body, we are able to use its entire capabilities, including reproduction, so when we manifest using our own energy as a human, we replicate those abilities."

Jack held up his hands and shook his head side to side.

"Woah, woah, woah. Are you telling me that there are millions of pain wraith kids running all over the world?"

More questions began flying at Ariella, but she held up her hands to stop them.

"Please, please. One at a time. Jack, no there are not millions of little pain wraiths running around. The children are as human as you are. They possess no abilities whatsoever. We replicate human form, and so they are created in the same way. Pain wraith children, true wraith children, can only be born in ethereal form in our own realm."

As cutting as his previous words had been earlier in the conversation, Jack seemed a little disheartened by that. He had an image of a bunch of kids having tantrums, and then just creating the thing they were wanting out of thin air. A funny image, but it had given him some comfort.

"So, what happened?" asked Grace.

Ariella's mood changed, and her head seemed to bow. Clearly the recollections of the events were bringing back some of that pain.

"I saved a child's life. I used my powers, publicly, to help a five year old boy who had been hit by a runaway cart. Most people dismissed it as seeing things, but my husband didn't. Leonard confronted me when we got home, and I confessed to him my true nature. I told him what I was and how I had saved that boy's life."

Everyone was now on the edge of their seats. It was like watching a *Marvel* movie revealing the twists and turns from the previous movies.

"What did he say?" asked Kathryn.

That tear finally found its way down Ariella's cheek.

"I never found out."

"I'm confused," Kathryn started saying. "Surely he didn't

just leave?"

Ariella shook her head.

"I never found out, because the moment I revealed to Leonard who I really was, our house exploded. I was thrown through the front window and out onto the street, and my family burned alive inside the house."

The look of shock was universal. Every face in the room was expressing a small element of the pain that Ariella had felt that day.

"I'm so sorry," Jack offered. "What caused it?"

Ariella's face became the hardest they had seen yet, and a small flash of purple in her eyes suggested she was switching from pain to anger.

"Jasmine."

Kristin flinched at the name, seemingly triggering something in her brain. The name Jasmine had significance to her, but she couldn't remember why. During the fight earlier, Max had overheard the attackers asking Ariella where somebody was. He now understood the link.

"She's the one those men were hunting," he said.

Ariella nodded.

"Those weren't men, Max. They were wraiths sent by the council to apprehend Jasmine. They just occupied human bodies to carry out their work."

Jack held up his hands again.

"Okay, back up. Why would this Jasmine, kill your family?"

"Because she is a purist. She believes humans and other species are nothing but suits for us to occupy while we learn, and then discarded like a piece of trash. She saw that I was about to reveal our realm to humans, and she put a stop to it."

Grace's eyes were full of tears.

"Couldn't you just bring them back, like you saved the boy?" Ariella shook her head.

"The boy was near death. My family was gone. I have many wonderful abilities here in your realm, but resurrection is not one of them. Jasmine told me that I had broken the rules, and that I would be given one more chance to continue the traditional work of a wraith on Earth, and she thrust me into the body of a young accountant, looking for his first break in the advertising industry. You see, when we die in our physical form, we can choose which point in time we go to, in order to occupy our next life cycle."

Jack was more intrigued than bewildered, but still required clarification.

"So, you are borderline immortal, *and* you can travel through time?"

Ariella chuckled.

"No, Jack. We can't travel through time in the conventional sense. We choose a person from any point in time, in order to experience suffering at different levels of advancement. At the dawn of mankind, you can be killed with a spear, a thousand years in the future, you can be torn apart by an energy weapon. It's all about learning every kind of pain."

He sat back in his seat.

"Wow. Sucks to be you."

Ariella continued her long explanation, eager to get it over and done with.

"I was warned not to interfere with any aspect of my life in this body, or the people around me. But I had become so human myself, that I couldn't prevent it. My friend at work was about to lose his home and everything he held dear. All he had was a lotto ticket. So, I manipulated the draw, and his numbers came up. He became a huge success in business, had estates, cars, everything he had ever wanted."

Kristin swiped her phone into the unlocked position, and opened the notes app, typing 'remind me to ask her about my lotto ticket for next Friday.'

"But Jasmine found out?" asked Daniella.

"Yes. It was the second time she had seen me risk exposing our world, and she wanted to teach me a lesson. She had always told me that we can move forward through time, but not back when it came to choosing our hosts. So, she said, as punishment, I had to undo all that I had done. I had to 'correct' the universe. She forced me to hunt down and kill every single person that was alive who shouldn't have been and take out everyone who were deemed to be 'out of their timeline'."

Ariella paused again, as she began to recall the horrific things that she had done. The death, the blood, the anger. And it had all been as much of an experiment as all her other lives. Only she hadn't known it. She took a deep breath and continued.

"I became so obsessed with fixing things, I spent the next thousand years murdering my way through humanity. I caused so much death and pain, switching between

corporeal and ethereal forms, using my power to tear
people apart. Until I reached the end of the line. I
destroyed the final humans. All of them. Except one.
Mace he was called."

She smiled as she thought about Mace, and how he had
effectively reborn Ariella as a true spirit. The others,
however, were beginning to feel fear at the level of power
that was being described to them, seemingly by a being
who had ended the human race.

"He was the last human. He sacrificed himself to kill me.
As he piloted his ship into a sun, I felt myself being
ripped through time, and I finally realised that I had been
lied to. Jasmine had used the excuse of 'fixing things' as
another learning experiment for me to experience a
different kind of pain. When I woke up in this form, about
a week before I changed the lottery numbers, I realised
that I could move both forwards and backwards through
time. I immediately attempted to move back to my
family, but something was preventing me. I kept finding
myself at different points in time, but never where I
wanted to be. And this is where you guys come in."

The group was distinctly uncomfortable at suddenly being
roped into a tale that involved the end of humanity.
Vampires and ghosts were one thing, but destroying all of
mankind?

"Don't look so panicked," Ariella said through a forced

smile.

"Sorry, but you did just tell us you wiped out our species," replied Jack.

She held her hands up in acceptance of what he had said, but he wasn't quite sure if she was mocking his use of that gesture several times during this conversation. Regardless, he grabbed a beer from the tray of refreshments, and Ariella continued once more.

"Jasmine had been afraid that when I discovered my true abilities, her lenience towards me would have meant she was punished, when I inevitably revealed our realm to the humans. So, she took drastic action. She attempted to remove Leonard and our children *from time*."

The shocked look returned to everyone's faces, Daniella mid-way through chewing a sandwich.

"We have an immense supply of energy, we are after all made from it, but for the task at hand, Jasmine didn't have enough. So, she returned to our realm, and when she failed to garner any support, she murdered our own people to collect their energy. By the time she was done, five million wraiths were burning in my home."
This was a number that was hard to swallow. *Five million.* That many dead would be a disastrous number in any scenario. The Coronavirus pandemic of only a few years ago had not quite reached that number.

"She harnessed the energy, and when the Council failed to stop her, she directed all that energy and removed my family from ever having existed. No matter what I did, I would never be able to find them again. The only problem with this for Jasmine, was that in taking this course of action, the thing she had been trying to prevent was now closer than ever. The force of the power had cracked the doorway between our worlds, and concentrated beams of energy were now leaking into other realms. The lightning bolts you see, are physical representations of that energy, concentrated with the pain and suffering of the wraiths. It drives humans to the brink of madness."

Everything was now beginning to make sense to people. The stab wounds, referring to the thirty-two members of this Council that Ariella had described, the sudden surges in serial killers.

"I had been through so much in my time on Earth, that I decided I didn't want any other part of it, and I didn't want to be found. I turned my own energy onto myself and sent myself to a point in time where I was unfamiliar with the surroundings, the people, and most importantly, my own identity. I woke up in the body of a single marketing executive living in Wealdstone in 1998. I spent the next two years climbing the proverbial ladder to make a top wage. And then she showed up again."

Jack emptied his beer and reached for a second, wishing he had brought popcorn.

"This woman is relentless," he said.

Everyone else agreed, including Ariella.

"She forced me to replay my memories of who I really was, in her attempt to get me to return to our realm, but she didn't realise just how much of my past I would remember. We fought, and I managed to use the majority of my energy to banish her back to our realm. After that, I met Arthur. He'd been in the States for about six months, looking for work, and we hit it off. He used to tell me all about Newquay, where he was from in England, and it was during our honeymoon in 2000 that I learned I was pregnant. Annie. My little Miss Annie. I lived in bliss with my new family until my death in 2006. I pushed Annie out of the way of a drunk driver and took the hit myself. Then I woke up here, in the body of Sam Greenwood, and began to see all the activity here."

The story seemed to have come full circle, but Jack was incredibly focussed on the knife, still ever-present on the table before them.

"What does that have to do with all of this?" he requested.

"That is the blade of the first wraith ever to leave our realm. When he discovered how freely we could move here, he knew it could be used to a disadvantage, and so with some help, he forged this weapon. It subdues our abilities and restricts us to the form we currently occupy.

When attacked with the knife, it returns us directly to our realm, and we are unable to return."

For the next few hours, the group discussed the events of Wealdstone's recent history, and although there was hope regarding Duncan's whereabouts, those were dashed when Ariella revealed the pain wraiths had nothing to do with his disappearance. It wasn't until later, that Jack returned to the main conversation from earlier.

"So, this increased activity, you believe is a result of Jasmine coming back here, effectively breaking out of jail, correct?"

Ariella nodded. Jack continued.

"So, explain to me this one thing. Why, after all this time, or in your case, the entire existence of humanity, is this woman pursuing *you* in particular?"

It was at this point that Ariella realised she had missed out the most important point in her story. However, Daniella picked up on this, and seemed to see a common flicker in her eye. Something she had seen in Grace on numerous occasions.

"She's your mother, isn't she?"

Daniella's words were soft and delivered in a way like that of a mother speaking to her child. Ariella nodded.

Kristin's eyes now bulged as she remembered a brief conversation with a woman named Jasmine at a bar around a year and a half before, who was looking for her daughter. She felt she should volunteer this information but decided to keep quiet. Jack's tone changed, and he stood up to come face to face with Ariella.

"Did your mother cause those men to kill my fiancée?"

This was an answer that she just didn't have.

"I don't know. There are millions of wraiths inhabiting human bodies at any one time, it could be anyone. If the damage she has done to the passage between our worlds is that extreme, the Council may be hunting down all wraiths to return them back."

Jack placed his hand on top of the glass unit.

"And what is to stop me from running this blade right through your stomach right here, right now?"

The anger was on display for all to see, but Ariella remained calm.

"Because without me, Jack, you can't stop her. If she has truly grown so powerful that she can break out of her confinement, that blade may not be enough."

Jack backed away, seemingly accepting this explanation,

and the others knew she was right. They had only been in her company for a matter of hours, but they had never doubted her words were sincere. He walked out of the front door, and Kathryn followed to check on him. Deanna and Daniella stood up, looked at each other, and then back towards Ariella.

"So, what's the plan?" Deanna asked.

Ariella looked around, and each remaining member of the group were waiting for her words.

"Now… we need to find my mother."

10

"Hey! Wait up!"

Kathryn was now chasing after Jack as he tore down the driveway to the house.

"Please Kat, just leave me alone."

Jack was not slowing down, and although she considered herself to be athletic, Kathryn was struggling to keep up.

"Jack, we need you here!"

Jack stopped suddenly and span on his heels, coming face to face with a Kathryn, who was now desperately trying to arrest her movement.

"Why did I actually bother coming back here? I was happy where I was, and I finally had a life! I'd left all this bull shit behind and had almost forgotten what my father did. I came back because you asked me!"

Kathryn wasn't sure what to say. She didn't realise that they still had that strong a connection. She had primarily asked for his help because she knew he was a cop, and his training would be valuable.

"Um, thank you."

Her reply seemed to disarm Jack momentarily.

"Kat, something was drawing me back here. As happy as I was in San Francisco, every time I saw this place on the news, or had any mention of my dad, I felt like I was on this invisible leash, and every so often there would be a tug on it, and I'd stumble. But I'm not sure I can do this."

Kathryn reached forward and placed a hand on his shoulder. She had forgotten how much she admired him, and this was the first contact she'd had with Jack since they broke up years ago.

"Look, Jack. I can't make you stay here, but I'd be lying if I said that I didn't think you belonged here. Maybe you felt pulled back here because this is your home. Maybe you were just looking for an excuse."

Jack shook his head, and continued walking, slower this time, with Kathryn beside him.

"I don't know. I spent most of my life trying to forget about this place. Why would I wanna come back?"

Kathryn felt a twinge in her chest, but she quickly dismissed the feeling and put it down to Deanna's snacks having an adverse effect.

"Like I said. Maybe there's more for you here than you realised."

As the pair came to the bottom of the driveway and onto the main street, Jack noticed what appeared to be a person, slumped against the side of a car. As he squinted in the fading daylight, he could see a thin trail of blood trickling down the side of the person's neck. Kathryn followed his gaze, and immediately reached for her gun.

"Vampires."

Jack was startled at the sound of the name, even though he had just been at a very supernatural conversation just minutes before.

"Don't vampires turn their victims?" he asked.

"Yeah, usually."

Kathryn's eyes were now darting around searching for any movement. Confused, Jack probed for more answers.

"So, why is this guy clearly not getting up anytime soon?"

"All this heightened energy from this fracture between realms isn't just amping up the amount of activity in Wealdstone, it's altering behaviour, and increasing all forms of energy, not just paranormal."

Jack began to understand.

"So, they're basically acting closer to their baseline instincts? Food, and nothing more?"

Kathryn nodded.

"And that's great in terms of dwindling numbers overall, but not so good for the dozens of dead people."

The pair were now crouched next to the victim, eyes firmly closed, and skin white and cold to the touch. As Kathryn had suggested, this guy was long dead, and was in no way a threat to their safety. As much as Jack wanted to find out the man's identity and tell his family, he understood this wasn't your average homicide case, and he and Kathryn continued their search for the culprit.

"So how do you kill them?" he asked. "Wooden stake to the heart? Garlic breath? Silver bullets?"

Kathryn smiled slightly.

"You watch way too many movies, Jackson."

Jack cringed. Nobody had called him Jackson since he was a little kid. The only time he was referred to by his full name was to differentiate between him and his father.

"So? How do you kill them?"

Kathryn sighed.

"Yes, okay, fine. A stake to the heart does work, but it doesn't have to be wooden. It can literally be anything sharp of any material. Or you can cut off their head, or you know, if you happen to have explosives, you can blow them up."

Now it was Jack's turn to chuckle.

"Blow them up? How many vampires have you 'blown up'?"

Kathryn shrugged her shoulders as they rounded the corner onto the next street.

"I dunno, like, fifty?"

"Fifty!?"

"It was a big explosion."

Having literally no idea whether he was being joked with or not, Jack withheld his reply. Suddenly, Kathryn stopped and held up her hand for him to do the same.

"Wait. There."

Jack looked where Kathryn was now focussed. He could see an outline of a person, but what was really attracting his attention, was the glow of what he assumed were the eyes. So piercing, and the red contrasted with the green of the hedgerow the figure was moving along.

"Why isn't he hiding, or even running?" Jack asked.

"His brain is fucked. He doesn't know where to go or what he's doing. Normally you don't see them out before total darkness. The small amount of light left is weakening him."

The two of them began to move towards the vampire at a steady pace, as it continued to move away, but in a laboured manner. It did indeed appear to be weaker than normal. As they closed in, Jack saw Kathryn pull out what appeared to be cream coloured versions of the bullets that had taken down Sam Greenwood.

"What kind of ammo is that?" he asked.

Kathryn hesitated in response to the question and didn't provide an immediate answer. He asked again.

"What? Is it herbs, or powder, or what?"

Kathryn took a slow blink and let out a sigh.

"It's garlic."

Despite their situation, Jack couldn't help but gloat.

"Garlic? So, I've watched too many movies? So out of every method that I stated, and you ridiculed, you're using every single one?"

"Look, the important thing is that we take these bastards down…"

Jack interrupted gleefully.

"Oh no you don't, Kathryn. You guys are every bit as *Buffy the Vampire Slayer* that I thought you were!"

Kathryn stopped and turned to face him, slightly annoyed at the ridicule.

"Can we please concentrate?"

Jack held up his hand in apology and nodded.

"Sure."

However, when they turned back, the vampire was gone. Kathryn lowered her gun, and Jack did the same.

"See? Now look what you did."

Kathryn was now more agitated than Jack was prepared for.

"What did I do?" he protested.

"You literally got me to take my eye off the ball, and now we lost it."

"Hey, I didn't make you do anything! I thought you guys were trained for this kinda thing? I'm a cop, not *Blade*!"

Kathryn shook her head, holstered her weapon, and turned to head back towards the body, but stopped in her tracks. Jack caught on that she was no longer talking to him and turned to see the same image. Standing twenty feet from them, was a row of nine vampires, all stood in a line from one side of the street to the other, eyes piercing red.

"So, now what do we do?"

Jack was cautiously stepping back, and drew his gun once more, but he knew he didn't have the ammunition that Kathryn had, and even if he did, it was still nine against two.

"Now, we call for backup."

Kathryn reached into her pocket, pulled out her phone, and pulled up Kristin's number. She glanced down as she hit the call button and glanced up again just in time to see the vampire launching towards her, almost faster than she had blinked. The impact sent her careering through the air, her phone landing several feet away, and she fell back to the ground with a hard thump. Jack watched, helplessly, as a second vampire rushed him, and he too was thrown through the air, barrelling over the top of a nearby truck, the alarm blaring out, but his landing was much harsher, crashing into the windscreen of the car behind the truck. On the front lawn of the house where the phone had landed, Kristin's voice could be heard.

"Hello? Kat? You there? Is everything alright?"

Kathryn pulled herself to her feet, suspecting she had at least one broken rib, and her gun was nowhere to be seen. She made an attempt to look around for Jack, but before she had chance to turn her head, she was slammed into by a second and third vampire, sending her crashing through the front window of someone's house, landing on the carpet, and rolling into a table. The change in surroundings had added to her dazed and confused state. She looked up to see a vampire crouched in the bay of the window, tilting its head as it surveyed her.

"What? You waiting for a delivery? Get your own food, I'm not coming to you, bitch."

The creature smiled, its teeth slowly extending into long points, a quick flick of the tongue on the tip of one of them, and the creature leapt into the living room. Kathryn backed up on the floor, wincing at the pain in her ribs, and her back. She looked around in her peripheral vision for some kind of weapon, without taking her eyes off the creature before her. Her hand found a shoe behind her, but as her hand moved beyond it, she also felt a leg. She stopped and began to realise why there was a congregation of these creatures in this neighbourhood, and why it appeared to be so quiet.

Outside, Jack was being held in the air, by the throat, as the vampire that had rushed him, simply stared at him. It tilted its head with curiosity, as if he was trying to work out what Jack was. While he knew very little about vampires, he thought that this behaviour was definitely out of character. But this was nothing compared to the actions going on behind his attacker.

Several of the other vampires appeared to be turning on each other. Growling and swiping at each other, and one appearing to be eating another on the floor. At the sound of this carnage, his captor was distracted, and glanced behind him. Jack seized the opportunity. He felt that his gun was still in its holster. He reached down, grabbed it and pointed it squarely in the face of the creature. As it looked back towards him, he pulled the trigger, and the vampire's head exploded in an eruption of blood and brain matter, and Jack crashed back to the floor. This garnered the attention of the other, previously squabbling creatures, and Jack picked up his gun, and ran in the direction he had last seen Kathryn. Spotting the smashed window, he targeted the house as his focal point, and charged. He was pursued, though, and as he reached the window, and saw Kathryn, several bodies, and a vampire advancing on her, he raised his weapon, but was side swiped by another creature, and he face planted the house wall, and fell to the grass, barely conscious, and blood cascading from his nose.

Inside the house, Kathryn had reached the kitchen, the vampire now trying to decide whether or not to pounce, leaving a trail of drool behind, eyes more intensely red than Kathryn had ever seen before. Her arm bumped a chair, and she gripped the base of one of the legs, lifted the chair and slammed it to the floor. As it broke apart, she grabbed one of the sharpened chair legs, and as the vampire lunged at her, she held it high, allowing the creature to impale itself on the sharp end, and she used its momentum, to push it over her head with her legs, and heard it crash through the table behind her.

Outside of the house, she heard Jack's laboured moaning, and saw several shapes moving out there. Beyond them, she saw her gun lying in the street. Figuring Jack could take care of himself for a few minutes, she moved through the house, and past its former residents in various states of decay and walked out through the front door. As she moved across the tarmac and crept towards her gun, she attracted the attention of the original vampire, who was now no longer as weak as he had been before. Knowing it was now or never, Kathryn sprinted for her weapon, and just grabbed hold of it as she was punted across the front garden of another house. Jack stirred and came face to face with a creature, and purely out of panic, he screamed, and punched the vampire square in the face. Shocked at his own reaction, he scrambled to his feet and ran towards Kathryn. The vampire had been taken completely by surprise in an unexpected comedic scenario and struggled to get back to its feet. The remaining attackers were now all converging on Kathryn, as was Jack, who was now weapon less.

Kathryn was struggling to keep the original vampire off her, and was tussling on the grass, unable to get a proper grip on the handle of her gun. As Jack reached her and shoulder barged the creature from her body, her hand inadvertently squeezed the trigger, the bullet grazing Jack's neck, and flying through the eye of one of the other vampires behind him.

"You shot me!" screamed Jack, clutching his neck, which now stung from the combination of hot metal, and garlic.

"Can we focus?!" shouted Kathryn, as she scrambled back to her feet, and aimed her weapon at the nearest target.

She squeezed off three rounds, taking out the corresponding number of aggressors, before turning towards the original culprit. Between the defence of their own lives, and the in-fighting, he was now the only remaining obstacle.

"Why are you all here?" asked Kathryn, to the confusion of Jack, who was now urging her to pull the trigger.

"What are you doing?" he asked, perplexed.

"Getting information!" she replied, exasperated at being asked stupid questions.

"Just shoot it!" he exclaimed.

Kathryn asked again.

"Why are you all here? Out before dark, in such large numbers? What's going on?"

Contrary to expectations, the vampire responded, much to Jack's disbelief.

"We must stick together. She will not allow us to roam freely."

Kathryn's heart skipped a beat, and not in a good way.

"Jasmine?" she asked.

The creature nodded.

"She is too powerful for us. She has plans for this town, and we do not fit in. So, we hunt in packs, and stay out of her way."

Jack was now invested in the questioning.

"Where is she?"

The vampire laughed as he began to advance.

"Around."

"Where?!"

More giggling as he lowered his head and began to coil up, seemingly ready to strike.

"Closer than you think."

As he replied, the vampire launched into the air, and as Kathryn aimed her gun at his airborne body, he exploded in a shower of red and pink, coating both Kathryn and Jack from top to bottom in blood and guts. When they both opened their eyes again, they saw Kristin and Daniella standing opposite, both with shotguns raised, barrels smoking.

"You're welcome," Kristin said.

Wiping the entrails from her face, Kathryn replied.

"New guns?"

Daniella nodded.

"Double barrel enlarged rounds. Pretty effective as it

happens."

Jack and Kathryn looked at each other, and then back at their friends.

"Yep. Definitely effective."

11

__18 Months Earlier__

Sex was a completely different experience in corporeal form than it was in ethereal. The levels of pleasure seemed to be heightened to a much larger degree. Humans clearly had some value after all. At least, for a few minutes. They clearly weren't made for longevity.
As Jasmine climbed off the man, she had spent the last ten minutes exploring, she couldn't help but feel she might have been a little rough with him. The broken neck certainly gave that impression.

"You really are quite brittle," she said to the dead man in her bed. "Maybe next time I will find someone stronger."

She reached for her clothes, and as she got dressed, she heard what sounded like screaming outside. Walking over to the window, swinging her coat over her shoulders, she saw what appeared to be several well-built individuals standing in the street, eyes glowing red under the lights of the street lamps. Jasmine smiled to herself, and exited the apartment, leaving the corpse where it lay, and made her way down the stairs to the front of the building. As she strolled out onto the street, one of the creatures was feasting on a passer-by, and impressed at their boldness,

Jasmine began clapping her hands sarcastically. That certainly got their attention.

"Who are you, she devil?" asked one of the vampires, in a gruff, commanding voice.

"I would be someone who might find you very useful."

The feasting vampire dropped her victim to the ground and began advancing on Jasmine's position with the others.

"We don't work for you. We are free to do whatever we want."

Jasmine chuckled and glanced around at the now empty street.

"Yeah, you really seem to have conquered this town. I mean look at all the bodies, and... oh wait. There's just one."

Now angered, the gruff man moved more sharply towards her, and with a quick swish of her left hand, he was lifted from the floor by his throat, held there by some invisible grip. He grasped at his neck, but there was nothing there. The others stopped moving and watched.

"I wasn't asking you to be useful, I was telling you that you will be."

Jasmine released her grip and the lead vampire crashed back to Earth. The female vampire moved forward, her mouth still red with the blood of her victim.

"What is it you want?" she asked.

Jasmine moved over to the nearest bench, and stood on the seat, using the top of the bench instead to sit.

"I'm looking for someone. Or *something* to be more precise. And I haven't had much luck. So, what I want from you, is information."

The vampires began to laugh in chorus. Something which Jasmine was not amused by.

"We don't collect information, witch. We eat, and we rest. We are not some magical beings with crystal balls."

The chorus continued to laugh, but Jasmine simply looked down and sighed. She raised her hands once again, and as she pulled them apart quickly, the two nearest vampires were torn in half by invisible ropes, their guts and organs falling into a neat little pile in between the two halves of their bodies. As the lead man and the female hunkered down in fear, glancing at what remained of their brothers, Jasmine jumped down from the bench, weakened slightly at having used her power so aggressively. She still wasn't back up to her usual strength after using it to break free from her realm. However, she spoke calmly.

"I am not a witch, bloodsuckers. I am a pain wraith. That means I know all about how best to tear you apart, both figuratively, and literally."

She glanced at the pile of limbs that used to be two people, causing the others to do the same.

"What… what information do you need?"

The female vampire was now stuttering, the male still staring at the gruesome image before him.

"There is another like me. Well, there's millions of my species, but only one other I'm interested in. My daughter."

The vampires looked confused.

"You are looking for your daughter? Surely with powers such as yours, you don't need us?"

The male vampire had found his voice, but it was considerably more shaken than before.

"Normally, that would be true. But my daughter banished me to my own realm, and it took most of my strength to break free. Let's just say I can't seem to sniff her out. The last I saw of her, she was in this town. I want you to find her."

The female nodded.

"How will we find her?" she asked.

Jasmine thought for a moment, as if trying to remember a distant memory, before replying.

"Look up a woman named Caroline Harding. I want to know everything that happened to her after 1998. And when you find her, bring her to me. Alive."

Taking one last glance at their former brothers, as the pile of vampire debris began to turn to dust and melt away, the two nodded and walked away. As they turned the corner, Jasmine span back around, and headed towards the bar she liked. Alcohol was definitely something else she admired about Earth. It made her feel more powerful than she was, like she had gained her strength back. It was only temporary, but she would take it for now.
Despite the blatant attack on a member of the public, people began to move around the street fairly soon afterwards, but to avoid drawing attention, Jasmine gave a flick of the wrist behind her, and the human victim was evaporated into the air. As she approached the bar, she could see the neon lights above Sisko's shimmering, calling her in. But she didn't get that far.
Her movement stopped suddenly, and she found herself

held in place. People were moving around her, but they didn't seem to see her. She glanced around but saw nothing. And as quickly as the effect had taken hold, it was released. Confused, she turned on the spot, several times, but the only indication that anything had occurred, was a brief glint of purple in the sky above.

She moved parallel with the alleyway behind the TV store she had once incinerated, when a huge blast of the same purple energy hit her full force in the chest, and sent her flying down the alleyway, crashing through garbage bins, and rolling along the tarmac as she landed.

As she attempted to stand, she was unable to support her own weight, and her mind was full of flashing imagery. She had seen this kind of thing before, between life cycles before her maturity, but never this intense, and never whilst manifested in her own humanoid form. The pictures were filled with death, and blood, and fear. The intensive energy burst had seemingly contained memories. Memories of those that had gone before her. And then the imagery moved to a more familiar scene. Then another. And another. She was now witnessing the murders of each of the five million wraiths she had murdered in order to remove her daughter's family from existence.

She felt the pain, the anguish, and the guilt. Her head span, and she fell to the ground, screaming out, hands banging the side of her head. Amongst it all, in the background, she felt arms pull her up from the ground, and the vague feeling of being slammed into a brick wall. As the imagery reached its most intense point, her chest seemed to burst, and she let out a deafening roar of pain. Purple beams of light erupted from her arms and chest, and blew the offenders away from her, sending each one scattering into the darkness.

As Jasmine took a deep breath, the energy subsided, and she fell to the floor, severely weakened. She looked up to see her mysterious attackers moving back towards her, but she could barely stand. Then she saw the glint of the blade. She knew the knife well. This was very bad timing. Whatever had struck her had knocked her further back than she had been since she arrived here six months before. She was in no condition to fight. And yet, she had no choice.

"So, you finally found me?" she spoke through gasps of breath and forced a wry smile onto her face.

"You must return Jasmine. All must return."

The council members began to advance on her, the lead one grasping the elder blade tightly. Jasmine centred herself as best as she could and prepared for the attack.

"Not without my daughter."

The group leader spoke again.

"Your daughter is not here. You are too early."

Jasmine was slightly taken aback by this reveal, but she wasn't entirely surprised. It had taken her nearly twenty-one years to break free from her realm.

"Then I guess I'll have to wait then, won't I?"

She spoke with such confidence, and as the three individuals launched at her, she channelled that confidence into her defence. The lead attacker swung the blade towards her throat, but she ducked down and raised herself up behind him as he passed her, striking him in the back with her elbow, the crunching of bone audible, and echoing down the alley. As he fell to the floor, the second and third attempted an attack simultaneously, the second missing their target, but the third delivering a blow to knock Jasmine to the ground, where she hit her head, hard.

She felt her strength slowly building back up, but it wasn't enough to unleash her full power yet. As the lead member returned to their feet, the second and third assailant attempted to restrain Jasmine on the ground. She managed to headbutt one of them, and release their grip, and then swung her legs up to meet the neck of the third person, gripping tightly, and twisting their head to the side, sharply. The man collapsed to the floor, and moments later, a purple haze erupted from his body and vanished into the night.

"That's the second neck I've broken tonight," she muttered. "I really must be more careful."

As Jasmine jumped back to her feet, the blade slashed across her chest, cutting through the fabric of her shirt, but narrowly missing the skin. She knew that would finish her quest before it had truly begun. She looked up at the lead council member with a determined scowl.

"That is my favourite shirt."

She launched herself at the man, one hand securing the blade away from her, and the other around his throat. The only true benefit of the knife being present, was that it created a level playing field. Nobody could use their true power. Sensing the other member behind her, Jasmine dropped the hand holding the knife down, and swung it behind her, the sound of it penetrating the other attacker, was like music to her ears. She felt the thud of the body landing behind her, and then the sound of the wraith leaving the body. The lead council member broke free of her grip, and headbutted Jasmine in the jaw, sending her flying backwards. This was followed by a swift flying kick to the chest, and she fell back once more to the floor. Removing his mask, and spitting blood from his mouth, the lead council member raised the knife once more as he approached Jasmine, who was now slowly climbing to her feet, holding her ribs which now felt broken. Her eyes spotted something shining in the rubbish beside her, and as the man lunged towards her, she dipped beneath his arm, grabbed a piece of broken glass from the garbage, swung around, and plunged the shard into the ribcage of his human host. He collapsed to the ground, still maintaining his grip on the elder blade. Jasmine stood up and staggered towards him.

"I think I'll be taking that," she gestured.

"They will find you. They will find you all."

And with that, the man lifted the blade, and plunged it into his own chest. Jasmine was shocked and stepped back as the purple mist erupted from the mouth of the body, swirling around the blade, and both vanished into the sky.

"Fuck!" shouted Jasmine.

Her clothes were now torn, her body beaten, and her mind weakened. Her strength would return now the blade was gone, but it would not be a swift process. She staggered forwards once more to the entrance of the alley and remembered where she had been headed.

"Now I really need that drink."

Nobody seemed to take notice of her battered appearance as she walked through the doors of Sisko's and slumped down at the bar. It was almost as if this kind of thing happened all the time.

"What can I get you?"

Jasmine looked up to see a bartender standing before her, waiting eagerly for her response. His gaze down at her exposed bra did not go unnoticed. She forced a smile.

"What's the strongest thing you've got?"

She swore the guy flexed his muscles in response to that question, but when she failed to respond, his smile faded, and he replied to the question.

"That'll be the house whiskey."

Jasmine nodded, and held up two fingers, signalling a double measure was required. As she waited for her drink, she heard a group of women stumble into the bar, and as they sat in a booth opposite, she chuckled at their conversation. Haunted pirate ships, werewolves, she had heard it all before. She had even been there before. Not much came as a surprise to her. Except Ariella. Her own daughter had been quite the unexpected package. Being determined to break free of her duties and live her own life, risked exposure of their realm. She had already revealed it to one person, she couldn't risk it any further. She was almost proud of her. She reminded her of how she used to be, before her own mother had reminded her of her responsibilities. Jasmine sat at the bar for what felt like an eternity before the gaggle of women, having discussed the ups and downs of pirates, werewolves, vampires, and lesbian relationships, decided to leave. At this point, Jasmine had downed a total of six full bottles of something called Gentlemen Jack and was delighted with the result. She now felt more powerful than ever but wasn't prepared to try standing under her own power just yet.

One of the women approached the bar to pay the group's bill, and Jasmine looked her over, remembering part of the conversation she had overheard about the amount of pain they were all going through.

"You don't know the half of pain."

The woman was a little confused at the accusation. She looked at Jasmine, whose eyes were now focussed on her empty glass.

"I'm sorry?" she asked.

"Nothing. There is more pain in this world and the next than anyone can imagine."

The bartender refilled Jasmine's glass once again.

"Are you okay?" the woman asked her.

Jasmine laughed.

"I lost my daughter. She sent me away a long time ago."

The woman's eyes looked Jasmine over. She was clearly drunk, and from the looks of her, had been in a rough scrap. Her coat was torn, and her shirt was hanging open. The woman was concerned she had been assaulted. The woman's bra was clearly visible, and her inebriated state would make her a prime target for creeps.

"I'm so sorry to hear that. Do you need any help?"

Again, Jasmine laughed.

"I will be fine. I will find her. And then everything will be fine."

The bartender brought the woman the bill, and she handed over her credit card.

"If you're sure, this can be a rough neighbourhood at night."

The bartender returned the card, and the woman thanked him.

"I can take care of myself, but thank you…"

Jasmine waited for the woman to offer her name, but it took her a moment to realise.

"Oh! Sorry, Kristin. My name is Kristin."

"Pleased to meet you, Kristin."

Jasmine offered her hand and Kristin shook it.

"My name is Jasmine."

As Kristin walked away, she shot another concerned look over her shoulder towards Jasmine, who simply smiled and raised her glass, before downing it once more. The bartender approached Jasmine again, but without a bottle this time.

"Coming up on last call, Miss."

Jasmine looked up at his face, which had become stern from not getting anywhere with this beautiful woman all night. Even a free drink or two hadn't gotten him any closer to a companion for the night.

"I'll take a bottle to go, please."

He pulled one from the shelf, slammed it on the counter, and took her money, fished from the pocket of her conquest earlier in the evening. As she finally made the move to leave her stool, her legs buckled slightly, but she managed to stay upright. As she exited the bar, the cool night air seemed to wake her up slightly. She would never get used to the feeling of being tired. So much time was wasted when humans were sleeping. Wobbling along the pavement towards her apartment, she remembered that she had left a dead man in her bed, and chuckled at herself for being so forgetful, when she was interrupted by the appearance of the two vampires near her front door.

"Ah hey! It's you guys!" she shouted, swaying from the effects of the whiskey, much to their confusion. "So, what did you find out?" she asked as she raised the bottle of Gentlemen Jack to her lips.

"She's dead."

Jasmine spat the whiskey over the female vampire, who bared her teeth in response.

"I'm sorry?" Jasmine required clarification.

"She died in 2006. She saved her daughter from a drunk driver, and she died from the impact."

Jasmine's mood lightened a little, and she handed the now half empty bottle across to the male vampire, as some sort of reward.

"A daughter you say?"

The male nodded, before the female continued with their information.

"Annie Watson. She's dead too. Or at least, probably. She disappeared in 2018. She bought a shop down on Hanson Street and vanished one night while she was working late. Nobody ever found out what happened to her."

Jasmine sat on the ground, the cold floor sending a shiver through her simulated nervous system. She pondered the facts being presented to her. *Disappeared.* That was not the same as being dead. A daughter would certainly give Jasmine an edge if Ariella did show up. She would just have to find her first.

"Anything else?" she asked.

The vampires both looked at each other, before the female spoke.

"There is one other thing," she volunteered.

Jasmine raised her eyebrows to signal she was ready for this new piece of evidence.

"She was the second person to disappear from that store."

The male continued.

"The owner, some guy named Fredericks, he vanished from there seven years before. Never found his body either."

Jasmine appeared delighted with this news, and leapt to her feet, her strength seemingly having returned.

"Well, it would appear that I have a store to visit!" she exclaimed.

She strolled past the two vampires and began heading back the way she had just walked. The female called out after her.

"Hey! What are we supposed to do now?"

Jasmine didn't look back, simply raised her arms above her head, and shouted back one word.

"Die!"

And with the same flick of the wrist as before, both vampires were ripped apart, their torsos and insides falling to the ground, gradually beginning to turn to dust as Jasmine lowered her arms, smiled, and headed for Herman's Curiosities.

"This could be fun."

12

"Thank you for your custom, Sir."

As the man left the store, Scarlett slumped down on the counter, head in hands, and her eyes rolled back from boredom.

"Oh, come on, Scarlett, it's not that bad."

Scarlett looked up from her hands with a look that showed she definitely disagreed with her colleague.

"Amy, I'm selling screws for a living. Screws. Where is the adventure in that?"

Amy chuckled, and patted Scarlett on the shoulder as she walked by.

"Cup of coffee?" she asked.

Scarlett nodded in the affirmative, and the sound of the kettle beginning to boil seemed to buoy her spirits up.

"Sweet, sweet caffeinated glory."

Life had certainly not been as exciting as she had hoped

lately. When she met Deanna, she had figured that her experiences would become more and more exciting. But when they joined the others, her role became incredibly diminished. Helping track down Duncan at the shopping district was the first involvement she'd had in months, and since then, she had been at work, doing her usual boring job selling hardware and screws, waiting for the next call. Considering the team kept saying how short staffed they were, they were in no rush to throw her into the action. Amy strolled over and placed a mug of coffee next to her. She breathed in the steam, and her soul seemed to rejuvenate a little.

"Surely you can't feel bad after that," asked Amy. "That's my speciality. Black Hole coffee."

"Black Hole?" asked Scarlett.

"Five spoons of coffee, half a spoon of sugar, no milk. Black Hole. Designed to raise the dead."

Scarlett cautiously took her first sip, and the strength of the liquid had her eyebrows raised, and her eyes squinting.

"Fuck me! I feel like my very being was just swallowed by a…"

"…Black Hole?"

Scarlett laughed.

"Exactly."

Amy hunched down next to her friend, as another man came into the store and started to flick through the mail order catalogue.

"So, when are you gonna tell me what's up?" she asked.

"You've been pulling more shifts lately than I expected you to, now you're part of your little gang of *Winchesters*."

Scarlett raised her hand to her lips and attempted to quieten Amy down.

"Hey, keep quiet! I only told you that so you wouldn't think it was weird when I shot off with short notice!"

Amy giggled.

"Relax, I know it's all a secret. Even though nearly everyone in this town has seen something in the last year or so. You can't really hide werewolves behind a 'gas explosion' excuse from everyone."

Scarlett thought back to that news coverage and smiled.

"Yeah, I can't believe we actually got away with that

one."

"So why are you still here? Shouldn't you be ghost busting with the others?"

Scarlett nodded.

"Yeah. I should. But I don't think they trust me."

"Didn't you get shot like five times?" asked Amy.

She nodded in response.

"Yeah, but I only survived because I had some magic necklace thing. Everyone else had training or experience or an immortal soul."

"Deanna?" Amy asked. "Still?"

"Hey, I'm not pining after her, I'm just a little jealous of her abilities, that's all."

Amy wasn't buying it.

"Yeah right, and *Orange Is The New Black* was all about straight women, learning how to straighten up and fly right."

Another scolding look came her way, before they were interrupted by the man who had now left the catalogue stand.

"Excuse me, I can't find this in your book, but I need this screw."

The man placed a worn, rusty screw on the counter, with no tip or visible screw head. The two women looked at each other before Amy volunteered to take the lead.

"Do you actually know what type of screw this was before it rotted away, Sir?"

"Don't you? You're supposed to know what you're selling!" replied the man.

Scarlett chuckled and signalled to Amy that she was going to pop outside for a break. As she walked out of the store, she heard the man refer to the mystery screw as 'something that holds wood together' and laughed to herself at the true ignorance of the general public. Staff were not permitted to vape or smoke in front of the store, so Scarlett wandered further down the road. As she moved past the fruit and vegetable store, her phone vibrated in her pocket. Fumbling to find it, she looked at the screen, smiled and swiped to answer.

"Hi Kristin, what's up?"

"Hey Scarlett, I need to borrow you for a couple hours. Are you free?"

"That depends, what is it this time? Sweeping the mansion, or just ferrying somebody to the grocery store?"

"Hey, no need to be rude about it. I need someone to talk to, and Kathryn is a bit preoccupied with this new guy she's hanging around with."

Scarlett was a little surprised by this. Nobody confided in her normally. They'd rather talk to Max than her, just because he can weld and strengthen metal.

"I mean, sure. I'll try and get off work and head right up."

"Thanks, I'll meet you at the house, I'll be about an hour or so."

Scarlett hung up the phone, feeling a new sense of purpose. She turned around and headed back towards the store. The air felt heavier than it had earlier, and the clouds seemed thicker than before, but concentrated above her.

"Looks like rain," she mumbled to herself.

Ahead of her, she could just make out the shape of the customer still stood at the counter, and a rather exasperated looking Amy staring into space. Scarlett smiled to herself. They went through this dance every day. Somebody would come into the store and either not bother looking in the catalogue or say that they had seen something online they wanted to buy but had not bothered to write down the product code, or actually purchase the item online to save time.

Customer service really was an intense field. Scarlett had spent most of her life in retail and was desperate to get out. Maybe if she could be a confidante to Kristin, then she could finally become a fully-fledged member of the team. And spend more time with Deanna. Scarlett stopped walking, as she felt a twinge of pain in her temple. As it went away, she felt like eyes were on her, but upon looking around, she saw nobody behind her, and the nearest people were a couple in the distance waiting for a bus, and they were looking the other way.
As she moved forward a couple of steps, she felt another twinge in her head, and this time it was much more intense.

"What the hell?" she asked herself.

Above her, the clouds thickened even more, and flashes of purple began appearing in them, blinking silently. Scarlett looked up and saw them, and she immediately began to panic.

"Oh shit."

She took off towards the store at speed, knowing exactly what was coming. Another sharp pain knocked her off balance, but she kept her footing and although slowed, continued running toward the store. But it was too late. A thick bolt of purple lightning shot down from the clouds above and struck her in the shoulder, sending her spinning off to the side, and clattering to the ground, around ten feet from where she had been previously. The clouds parted within seconds, and as Scarlett's jacket continued to smoulder from the impact, she sat up.

Her head was swimming with random imagery, flashing through her mind. She saw people being stabbed, having their throats slit, hanging bodies, purple ribbon like creatures being torn apart. The pain was causing her head to implode. She scrambled to her feet, gripping the nearest wall for strength and balance. In the distance, the couple who were waiting for the bus, seemed to notice something was not right, but made no attempt to approach her. Scarlett's chest was visibly pounding in reaction to her rapidly increasing heartbeat, but she continued forward, knowing she had to try her very best to control what was going on. She was determined not to fall victim to this intense energy the way the others had. Her eyes came across the door to the store, and she managed to focus enough to enter the store, but the images would not relent.

"Hey, Scarlett, do we have screws that work in wood, metal and tiles, but all in one screw?"

Amy had now lost the will to live, but Scarlett couldn't

respond. Her face was twitching, and her expressions kept changing from twisted, to horrified, and then a look of anger as she moved towards the counter.

"Are you okay?" Amy asked, but again got no response.

Scarlett clattered into the display stand of screwdrivers and pliers, and the whole thing crashed to the floor, taking her down with it. Amy sprinted from behind the counter, shoving the man out of the way.

"Scarlett!" she shouted, desperate to hear a response, but none came.

She gripped the top of the display and began to lift it. The unit was a heavy one, but she managed to lift it enough to see underneath it. She could see a foot, and movement beyond that suggesting Scarlett was still conscious.

"Hey, asshole, you going to help me or not?" Amy shouted at the man, who until this point had just stood there looking on.

But the man did not respond, and it wasn't until she looked more closely, that she could see his clothes were smouldering, and his eyes were flicking around wildly. Glancing to her left, she saw the main window to the store had been shattered. A noise she must have missed when Scarlett has brought down the display stand. The man's eyes suddenly flashed purple, and his face became deadly serious, and he fixed his gaze on Amy.

"Hey, are you okay?" she asked, backing up slightly.

The man began advancing towards her, his eyes now glowing with a purple haze. Amy's feet backed onto a small pile of screwdrivers, and she stumbled. Her gaze was fixed on this seemingly possessed man, a pained expression developing, but the eyes remaining purple. Suddenly, a huge crashing sound came from behind her, as the display unit rose up from the floor, and tools clattered everywhere. Scarlett stood tall amongst the wreckage, and Amy was quickly relieved.

"Scarlett!" she shouted in joy.

But the emotion was short lived. Because staring back at her, was another set of purple eyes. As Scarlett thrust the slotted screwdriver she was clutching into Amy's stomach, her friend looked back at her with disbelief, and pain. Her shirt began to darken with blood, and as Scarlett pulled the screwdriver out and plunged it back in, the man behind her thrust a pad saw into her back. From outside the store, the two people who were waiting for the bus watched on in horror as Scarlett and the customer took turns in stabbing their tools into Amy's body over and over. They were frozen in place. When the assault came to an end, both of the murderers turned towards them, and they finally broke their stance, and ran screaming down the street. In her head, Scarlett briefly managed to force her consciousness back to the surface, enough to see Amy's brutally mangled body lying before her and saw the customer standing opposite. A new wave of fear spread through her, just long enough for her to raise her screwdriver and plunge it into the man's heart of her own free will. Screaming with every motion, she continued stabbing until the man collapsed alongside Amy to the floor. She dropped the instrument to the floor, her hand now dripping and thick with her friend's blood. But the despair of that crime only lasted a moment, as with another flash of imagery, Scarlett was gone, and the violent memories contained in the energy from the realm of the pain wraiths, once again took over, and Scarlett's possessed form headed out of the store, and towards the mansion.

13

Jack sat in the chair, staring at the blade in the jar, still present on the table in the reading corner. Ariella was sat opposite him, working away on a laptop, researching any possible examples of incidents or activity which could be linked to Jasmine. There appeared to be more than she first realised. So far, she had discovered sixty-three incidents which appeared to be related to either her directly, or potential pain wraith involvement. Occasionally, she would look over at Jack, but his gaze didn't leave the jar very often. She felt bad that she couldn't answer his question about who his fiancée really was. She suspected that it was a simple case of mistaken identity, and it had been another wraith who just got caught in the crossfire. But she doubted that explanation would comfort him.

Jack, however, was not feeling sadness any longer at the death of Kimberley. He was staring at the blade to try and force himself to feel the need for vengeance that he had felt when he came back to Wealdstone. And the reason for that was because other feelings were re-emerging and making him feel very uncomfortable. Kathryn had not come back downstairs following her multiple showers to wash away the vampire essence which had remained following the attack, and Jack felt for the moment that it was probably better if they kept their distance. Grace and Max were attending Highfield Manor, after reports that the resident spectors had utilised the increased energy to the point that they were beginning to leave the confines of the house and affect other homes on the block. Deanna was still out looking for any trace of Desmond and Duncan, and Daniella was shackled in the basement pool, as the full moon was due that night, and she had neglected to take her injections. And with Desmond gone, she had no way of making more. He had never revealed how those serums had been made, but now he was gone, and precautions had to be taken.

The front door clicked open, and both Jack and Ariella looked up to see Kristin walk into the mansion. She clearly wasn't expecting to see them but engaged them anyway. She started with Jack, as she wasn't sure she could look at Ariella without confessing what she thought she knew.

"Hey Jack, how's it going?" she asked.

"Yeah, I'm still here, so I guess it's going good."

His reply was very laboured, and seemed a little awkward, which Kristin didn't quite understand. A little nagging doubt crept into her mind, given the history between him and her wife, but she shoved that to the back of her mind, because Ariella spoke to her, and the uneasiness of what she knew came rushing back to the surface.

"How are things with you Kathryn?" asked Ariella.

Answering almost too quickly, and quite loudly, Kristin replied like a teen caught off guard by her parents.

"Yeah good! Really good!"

Jack looked at Ariella, and she returned the 'I'm not sure why' look.

"Are you sure?" Ariella pressed. "You seem a little… on edge."

Jack nodded in agreement.

"No, I'm fine. I was just expecting to see Scarlett, that's all."

"I think she's working tonight," Jack suggested.

"Yeah, no I know, I called her, but she's meant to be here so we can, you know, catch up, on any leads."

The cop side of Jack now began to take over. He had been trained to smell a liar, and right now, Kristin reeked of it.

"Okay, what are you hiding?"

The question was direct and to the point. And Kristin didn't have a response ready.

"I'm not… nothing… it's just…"

Ariella stood and walked over to her, placing a hand on her shoulder, and looked into her eyes.

"Do you know something, Kristin?" she asked in a very softly spoken voice.

It wasn't fair, Kristin thought. How could she refuse to answer someone speaking to her so nicely, and full of emotion. She suspected this was some sort of pain wraith interrogation technique.

"I think I might, yeah."

Ariella led her down to the couch, where she sat down beside her, moving the laptop across. Kristin caught a glimpse of a headline from 2016 regarding the John Martin serial killings. The event that started the path to her and Kathryn's marriage. Weird to think fondly of a serial killer. It was only since then that they discovered Martin had likely been one of the first victims of the purple lightning strikes.

"Now tell me what you know."

Ariella's voice had become sharper, to keep the attention of the person she was talking to. A teaching trick she had picked up in the eighteenth century. Kristin took a deep breath and began.

"I think we… well I, may have met your mother already."

Jack immediately broke his staring contest with the jar, and Ariella too, appeared shocked. She calmed herself and took a deep breath herself, before pushing for the details.

"Please, explain to me when and where you think you met her."

Kristin nodded and began.

"Around a year and a half ago, when me and Kat had returned from our honeymoon and the encounter with the *Sapphire Serpent*, we were in Sisko's with the others, and having drinks and a meal. When we were leaving, I went to pay the check and sat at the bar was a woman, who looked like she had been in a bit of a scrap. She started telling me about how I knew nothing of pain, and how much she had suffered. Frankly I figured she was just drunk, but then she told me that she had to find her daughter."

Ariella and Jack were now fully invested in this tale. Ariella spoke first.

"Think very hard please Kristin. Did she say anything else?"

Kristin closed her eyes. She didn't want to say the next part, because she knew how stupid she was about to look for not revealing this information sooner. She nodded.

"Okay, so what did she say?"

"She asked for my name, and then said that hers… was Jasmine."

That last sentence landed like an anvil on a cartoon coyote. Jack sprung up from his seat and began pacing furiously, and Ariella's eyes began to flash with purple, and there was clearly anger within her.

"You didn't feel it important to mention this yesterday? I mean what gave it away that this might be useful. The fact that she said she was looking for her daughter, or the fact she said her fucking name was Jasmine?!"

The air began to rush around the house as Ariella's eyes switched to solid purple. As Kristin glanced down at her hands, she saw tiny sparks of lightning flickering between her fingers.

"I'm sorry! I wasn't thinking, and I wasn't even sure I was remembering right at first! It had been a seriously fucked up few days, and it wasn't exactly a detail that lodged in my mind!"

Ariella spoke much more aggressively.

"So, you're telling me that she was here a year and a half ago, you knew, and yet you chose not to tell us, even if you weren't quite sure? Kristin that could've been very important."

More lightning flickering. Kristin went on the defensive.

"Look, little miss sparkly fingers! If you and your horde of undead power plant goddesses hadn't messed with our fucking realm, then we wouldn't even be in this situation in the first place!"

Ariella's cool evaporated quickly. She thrust her left arm forwards, and a bolt of purple lightning shot forwards, striking Kristin in the centre of her chest, and she flew backwards into the front door, splintering the wood, and dropping to the ground.

"ENOUGH!"

Kathryn came walking down the stairs, hair still wet from the cleansing. She had been observing for the past few minutes and didn't like what she had seen.

"You keep your super powers for the people that really need taking down, or so help me God, I'll open that jar and slit your throat myself!"

~ 173 ~

Jack stood back, eyes wide with surprise from such a strong statement, but also kind of impressed. Kathryn turned towards her now limping wife and continued.

"And you, what were you thinking hiding something like that? You didn't even tell me! How am I meant to trust you when you keep something like that from me?"

Nobody dared to provide responses to any of the questioning, such was the look of Kathryn's face and the tone of her voice. Ariella eventually made the first move.

"I'm sorry Kristin. I shouldn't have acted out that way. That's not me. Actually, that's my mother."

Kristin held her hand up in acceptance.

"I'm sorry I didn't tell you sooner. I should have realised it was important, even if it seemed insignificant at the time."

Kathryn calmed slightly but couldn't help focussing her attention on Jack. This did not go unnoticed by her wife. Kristin however, decided to remain quiet, once again.

"Can I just point out one thing?" Jack asked, stepping between Kathryn and her wife.

"And what is that?" replied Ariella.

"We aren't asking the most important question from all this."

"And what is that?" asked Kristin.

Jack sat down on the chair, and once again began staring at the blade in the jar. He leaned forward and gave his reply.

"What has Jasmine been doing in Wealdstone for the past eighteen months?"

14

The screams echoed around the house. They were intensifying with every hour. Soon, they would break glass, such were the vibrations within them. Desmond had tried to block them out, but he couldn't help it, knowing that he was responsible for inflicting this harrowing punishment on Duncan. He was one hundred percent certain that he was doing the right thing. He just wasn't enjoying the waiting around, or the noise it was creating. Moments later, Herman Fredericks stepped out of the room.

"How is he?" asked Desmond.

Herman shook his head in the negative sense.

"He is losing the battle, Desmond. I'm not sure his werewolf side is strong enough to counteract the effects of the treatment."

Desmond nodded.

"I understood it was risky, but I was almost certain this time would be different."

The door clicked open again, and Annie Weston walked

through it. The screaming had now stopped.

"He's resting now, but it isn't looking good. The amount of garlic coursing through his bloodstream is killing him slowly from the inside."

Desmond slumped down into a chair and placed his head in his hands. Herman walked up to his side, and placed a reassuring hand on his shoulder, before walking through the neighbouring doorway, and back into his book store. It had now been four days since Desmond and Duncan had crossed the threshold at the site of Herman's old store in Wealdstone, and for three of those days, his friend had been in constant agony.

"I did say that this treatment was experimental, Desmond."

He nodded in agreement.

"I know. But I was really hoping this time would be different. I've seen it used on vampires before, and some of them almost made it. I figured someone with his strength would be able to pull through it."

Annie sat beside him.

"I know. But have you ever considered the fact that maybe he has had enough of fighting?"

"What do you mean?"

"From what you've told me, Duncan has been battling himself for the last few years, switching between a human and a relentless killing machine. That takes its toll on a person. I imagine. I mean I can't say for sure, because this is the first hybrid I've ever seen, but you get the idea."

Duncan chuckled, and some of the concern lifted from his mind.

"I know the feeling. I've been living this life now for the last three hundred years, give or take. And it's never ending. There is always something trying to take over a town, or some kind of portal to a ghost dimension opening up somewhere. I don't remember the last time I had a vacation. Now I know how my mother felt when I found her again."

The flames in the lamps began to flicker, from the breeze coming through from the hallway. It was a stark reminder that Desmond was no longer in the comfort of the twenty-first century. Talking to Annie made him feel at home. But he wasn't. He had learned to navigate between the time periods, but each time, the gap between the years was widening. He assumed it was becoming unstable, and this was his last chance to help Duncan. Annie tried to reassure him.

"How long have you been coming here, Desmond?" she

asked.

"In your years, or mine?"

Annie chuckled.

"In mine, obviously."

He thought for a second.

"Twelve years."

"And in all that time, have you ever felt that what you were doing wasn't worth it?"

Of course, he hadn't. The reason he had started crossing the void in the first place was so he could help bring more and more information back to Annie to try and advance the development of weapons against the supernatural forces, much earlier. He knew they were on the back foot in the future, and he was trying to tip the balance in their favour.

"No. Never."

Annie smiled.

"Exactly. We will help your friend as much as we can. If he is as strong as you say he is, then he will make it through."

Desmond uncharacteristically, leaned in for a hug, to which Annie obliged. She had grown quite fond of him the more she got to know him and was saddened each time he returned to the future. She missed her home, but after all these years in the past, she had developed her own life, and couldn't see herself leaving it.

"So, what do you say we take a look at the other prize you brought me huh?" asked Annie.

Desmond's face became much more serious, and he nodded as he stood. They walked down the corridor, past the door leading to the shop, and into another room. In front of them was an extremely thick piece of glass, beyond which was a sealed room. Annie and Desmond looked through the glass window to the subject within.

"What's a girl gotta do to get some food around here?"

In the middle of the room, sat on the floor with her legs crossed, was Jasmine.

"I'm not sure how much longer this room will contain her. My incantations aren't exactly *Doctor Strange* levels," said Annie.

Desmond did not break his stare from the woman gazing into his eyes.

"I know. I'm not sure witchcraft can hold her, but for now

it's all we have. I need to know what she is, and what she is capable of."

Jasmine chuckled behind the glass.

"You know, you could always just ask me."

"And would you tell me the truth?" Desmond asked.

Again, Jasmine laughed.

"Maybe. That depends on whether you would tell me what I want to know."

"Try me."

Jasmine stood up, brushed herself down and approached the glass. As she did so, the edges of the glass pane began to glow red, the incantations doing their job, pushing Jasmine back slightly. She surveyed the effects before continuing.

"What do you know about Caroline Harding?"

Annie's heart dropped into her stomach. An effect which must have been visible on her face, because Jasmine leapt onto it.

"Ooh, that stirred something. You know something don't you gorgeous?"

Desmond turned to Annie and asked the inevitable question.

"What is it, Annie? Who is this, Caroline?"

Annie took a deep breath and blinked away a tear.

"She is my mother."

15

"Do you remember the days when we used to be ghost hunters?"

Max was asking rhetorically, because he didn't remember that either. Since he became involved with the team, hauntings were seemingly taking a back seat. He had spent many nights in Kathryn's museum with various spirits, but when they were 'out in the field' as it were, all the attention went to the vampires, and the werewolves, and that one random appearance of a yeti during the summer in 2021.

"No Max. Because I've never been a ghost hunter."

Deanna had spent most of the night trying to tune out the constant need for conversation coming from her partner. Max seemed to have a need to be involved in anything. It was almost as if he worried that if he wasn't part of whatever was going on, that he would fade away.

"Seriously? In the thousands of years, you've been alive, you've never once hunted spirits?"

Deanna stopped him in his tracks.

"First of all, I am hundreds of years old, not thousands. Let's make that very clear. Secondly, I was around when TV was invented, so I've seen *Most Haunted, Ghost Hunters, Ghost Adventures, Paranormal Lockdown*, and pretty much every paranormal investigation programme ever made. But no, I have never personally gone out of my way to do it myself. I spent too much time trying to find a way to die."

Max had definitely hit a nerve and given the fact that there were noises coming from upstairs, he backed off. Deanna signalled for him to go ahead, and he nodded before moving up the staircase slowly. When it came to dealing with aggressive hauntings, the brief was simple. Salt, crucifix, holy water and a bible. But more often than not, only one of those items was needed.

A loud bang came from down the hallway. They had spent two hours in Highfield Manor, supposedly one of the most haunted buildings in the US, and not yet bumped into a single spirit. It appeared the suggestion the spirits had all moved out was true. However, something was still here. And it was becoming more aggressive.

BANG!

Deanna jumped as the door directly ahead of them slammed shut.

"Fuck me!" she shouted.

Max turned to give her a disapproving look.

"What?! That shit was loud!"

"Please chill out. It's a door, not a wild beast that's gonna tear you to shreds."

"Since when did you become the fearless leader?" Deanna asked, surprised at how calm Max had remained.

"I dunno, thought I'd try it out, and then if it goes well, you could maybe big me up to Grace a little bit."

Deanna smiled.

"Must be about three, four months now?"

Max span around, caught off guard.

"How did you…"

"Everybody knows. You two are the least discreet couple in the world."

Max seemed to accept that, but before he could form another comment, every door along the corridor slammed shut in sequence, starting at the end and moving swiftly towards them, accompanied by a harsh breeze.

"Uh, Max?" Deanna started backing up, panic setting in.

"Yeah, maybe time to go!"

The two of them span around, but the oncoming presence caught up with them, and they were both thrown down the staircase, tumbling all the way down to the ground floor, crashing over each other until they landed at the bottom in a heap. Max let out a loud cry of pain, as Deanna tried to move off him. She winced as she realised, she had sprained her ankle, and as she swept her hair away from her face, she noticed a cut on her forehead.

"Max, you, okay?"

Max pulled himself into an upright position and leaned against the wall.

"I think so, but my back feels like I've been used as a punching bag by Anthony Joshua."

Deanna stood up, resting on the banister.

"Well, whatever it was, it's gone now. Blew straight past us."

Max nodded in agreement.

"I'm not sure how much more of this I can take. If this energy build up is going to come to a head, I just wish it would hurry up so I can go back to a more relaxing way of life."

"I thought you liked being at the centre of everything?" asked Deanna.

"Yeah, well maybe this job is ageing me. I feel like I've been fed through a cement mixer on an almost daily basis."

The two of them hobbled out onto the street, where they were met by the sound of sirens nearby.

"Wonder what that's all about?" Max enquired.

Deanna shrugged her shoulders.

"Beats me, but whatever it is, we've done our bit for the night. Let's get back to the mansion."

Max was in total agreement and in no mood to argue, and they both staggered down towards the car. As Deanna opened the door, she spotted someone moving towards them. As she squinted, she recognised the face.

"Scarlett? Is that you?" she asked into the darkness.

No reply.

"Max does that look like Scarlett?" she asked.

Max who had now made his way around to the passenger side, looked towards the figure moving erratically towards them. As she stepped into the glow of the street light, Max could indeed make out Scarlett's face. But it wasn't as it should have been.

"Scarlett are you okay?" he asked, moving away from the car and towards her.

Deanna looked concerned, uneasy at the lack of response from her friend. The sirens intensified in the background. As Max moved closer to Scarlett, Deanna saw what she had hoped she would never see. Scarlett's eyes flashed purple.

"MAX!"

Her shout of his name caused Max to turn his back on Scarlett.

"GET AWAY FROM HER!"

Max's expression remained confused, but it was all the time that was required. As Deanna watched on, a blade erupted from Max's chest, and as his eyes bulged, Scarlett's face appeared next to his shoulder. She tore the blade back out of his back, and he dropped to the floor. Deanna sprinted towards them, as Scarlett raised the blade again. It was only now that Deanna could make out that Scarlett's clothing was drenched in blood. She scrambled for her gun as Scarlett plunged the blade into Max's torso again, and again, the sickening sound of squelching as blood began to fill the wounds, becoming deafening to her. She pulled the weapon and aimed it at Scarlett.

"Please Scarlett! Stop it!"

Her cries fell on deaf ears. The woman she knew was gone. She continued to inflict the violence on her former friend, unmoved, and uninterrupted.

"Scarlett don't make me do this!"

Deanna blinked away tears and closed her eyes for a moment. She took a deep breath and fired. The first bullet hit Scarlett in the shoulder, knocking her backwards, but she began to get up again, still clutching the knife. Deanna fired again, and as before, she got back up. Deanna now ran as she fired, screaming with each pull of the trigger, unloading another six bullets into Scarlett, and as she reached the horrific scene that had unfolded before her eyes, Scarlett continued to twitch. Deanna stood over her body, aimed the gun at her head, and closed her eyes again.

"I'm sorry."

The final shot was the decisive one. Scarlett remained motionless. Deanna fell to the floor between two of her friends. Despite the immense level of aggression unloaded onto him, Max was still breathing. Deanna turned to him, and held his face in her hands, dropping her gun to the floor. He was attempting to speak.

"T..T..Tell...Grace…"

"Don't talk Max, save your strength, it's gonna be okay!"

"Tell her… I was a badass."

Max smiled, and then as he let out his last breath, his eyes rolled back, and his chest stopped moving. Deanna sat motionless, cradling his body, in a pool of blood. She rocked back and forth, the tears falling down onto Max's chest. Her friends were gone.

16

Annie sat on the floor in disbelief at what she had heard. In her recent life she had learned about many different aspects and facets of supernatural creatures, and spiritual activities. She had even studied advanced levels of text containing witchcraft and spells, but she had never for one moment considered she was the product of such a creature. And yet, here she was, face to face with her maternal grandmother. A creature of untold power, who they had apprehended attempting to kill Duncan in his sleep.

It had been nearly a week since Jasmine had crossed the crack through to Victorian England. As soon as she had discovered such a conduit existed, and at the end of that conduit, she may have leverage against her daughter, she had wasted no time. When she arrived, she had become disorientated. Travelling to a different point in time when choosing a new host was one thing, but to experience it first-hand had created a numbing effect on both her and her abilities. More specifically, her ability to control her power. When she had arrived, she lashed out, directing powerful blows at dozens of people in the street, and causing such carnage, that Desmond and Annie were forced to subdue her. That had been no mean feat either. Whilst Annie was becoming quite skilled at utilising these newfound powers of witchcraft, she was far from accomplished, and it had taken much of her own strength, and Desmond's firepower to get her to a point where they could approach her. Herman had needed to release Duncan for the extra strength required to place her into custody. An option they no longer had due to his treatment. And yet Annie was still considering letting her out to see if what she said was true.

"We can go back together, granddaughter. Your mother is waiting. We can be one happy family."

"Don't you think we might need a little more proof?"

Desmond had not moved during this four or five hour conversation and was far from convinced. The power this creature had demonstrated led to him wondering how they would cope if she managed to get out of her room. It did not bear thinking about.

"You're frightened of me, aren't you?"

Jasmine spoke directly to Annie now, ignoring Desmond's presence completely. Her eyes flashed violet as she spoke.

"Why should I not be? For all I know, I could possess the same powers you do, but so deeply hidden they might erupt at any point and cause the same kind of chaos you did when you arrived! How am I supposed to accept that?"

Desmond was proud of her reaction. Ever since he had first come here, he had admired Annie's convictions. She was the purest person he had ever met. Driven only by good, and the determination to learn. He had learnt a lot from her too. Much more than he could have imagined. She had helped him to combine the elements of his ammunition to take back to the future with him, and in turn he had researched the potential cure for Duncan with her and Herman. He was a little surprised she hadn't asked to go back to the future with him now she knew it was still possible.

"You do not have any powers, child," Jasmine replied. "Human children even though born from a wraith, do not have our abilities. We reproduce human form, and everything that comes with it. There have been hundreds of millions of pain wraith children on Earth and not one of them has ever displayed any signs of our abilities."

Desmond approached the glass and placed a reassuring hand on Annie's shoulder.

"You claim to have come in search of your granddaughter, correct?"

Jasmine nodded, a wry smile creeping onto her lips.

"You claim to have been imprisoned by your daughter

against your will, correct?"

Again, Jasmine nodded, although the smile had quickly faded again.

"Then let me ask you this. Can you guarantee that you are not here to kidnap your supposed granddaughter, and take her back to the future as leverage? And that you will bring no harm to me or any of my friends?"

Annie eagerly awaited the response, but behind the glass, she could feel the air becoming thicker, denser, almost like you could feel anger resonating off the window. Jasmine was no longer prepared to sit there and accept this questioning.

"I am here to take my granddaughter home. Frankly, I don't care what you think, you small minded creature. And that beast you have contained next door is of no concern to me. If I wanted to, I could have broken free of these shackles days ago, slaughtered you all, and taken what I wanted. But I didn't. And do you know why?"

Annie had slightly backed off, as the feeling became more intense, and Jasmine's voice became sterner. She turned to look at Desmond, and his body had clearly tensed up. He was anticipating a fight.

"Do enlighten me."

"Because I have no intentions of harming anyone here."

Duncan could now also feel the power in the air. He suspected that Jasmine was now growing in strength and very soon, the incantations used by Annie would no longer hold her. He reached in his pocket, and Annie noticed him tap numbers into his smartphone. She was confused. He knew that there would be no way of calling anyone. Cellular phone technology would not exist here for a very long time. He slid his phone back into his pocket and gave a return explanation to Jasmine, of a theory that was such an obvious one, Annie realised how distracted she must have been by Jasmine's stories, not to ask it herself.

"Or is it actually the case that you don't know *how* to get back?"

Jasmine's anger was now no longer contained within, and her face was tensing up. Her breathing was becoming deeper and more frequent. Annie stood up and accused her directly.

"That's why you've been feeding me all of these lies! To distract me and convince me to let you out! All this crap about my mother. You wanted me to take you back!"

Purple sparkles began emitting from Jasmine's fingertips, as Annie continued.

"You heard us discussing how the crack that allows us to move back and forth is becoming unstable, and you need a guide to get back there!"

"Don't push your luck, sweetheart."

Jasmine was now beginning to tremble with anger. Desmond's eyes flicked between the sight before him and the doorway, seemingly waiting for something.

"Why not? Let's have the truth you sparkly fingered bitch! What do you want with me?!"

With a deafening roar, Jasmine let out all of her energy, and anger, and fired a hand toward the glass, a huge purple energy beam erupting from her palm, and shattering the glass into millions of pieces, scattering everywhere, and showering Desmond and Annie as they flew back onto the ground. Jasmine lowered her hand, and stepped forwards through the glass, teeth gritted and still furious. She bent down and grabbed Desmond by the shoulder, picking him up, and throwing him through the now destroyed window into the room she had spent the last week in. He hit the wall and dropped like a ton of bricks to the floor. As he struggled to get back to his feet from the initial impact, Jasmine closed her eyes and moved her hands around, and before Annie's very eyes, the fragments of glass lifted from the ground, and began reassembling in the air. Within seconds, the window was reformed, and Desmond was trapped behind the glass. He ran forward and pounded on the window, but he could not break it. His ammunition would be no good either, as the glass was three inches thick, and therefore bulletproof. Herman flew down the steps as fast as he could at the sound of the noise, but as he rounded the corner, Jasmine gestured again with her hands, and Herman gripped his throat, grasping at an invisible threat. With a swift jerk of the wrist, his head snapped to one side, and the sound of his neck breaking, filled the air. Jasmine released her grip, and his body fell to the floor, his dead eyes still open and looking at Annie. She held a hand to her mouth, the speed and shock of everything happening before her, had got Annie mesmerised like a deer in headlights. She scrambled to her feet and began running down the corridor away from the horrific scene, but as she passed the door to the other room, she too felt herself lift from the ground and she span in the air to face Jasmine, who was now marching towards her.

"And now, you're going to show me how to cross back into Wealdstone, or I'm going to kill a lot more people."

Annie's arms were pulled tight behind her back.

"Is that clear?" Jasmine asked.

"I won't help you!" Annie screamed through the pain, as the pull on her arms tightened, and she felt her shoulders beginning to strain.

"I'll break every bone in your body if I have to, now tell me what I want to know."

Annie's legs were forced behind her, leaving her in excruciating pain. Her joints were under immense stress and the slightest movement would cause her bones to break. But she remained resilient.

"Never!"

Jasmine sighed, and with another flick of the wrist, Annie's left shoulder crunched, and the bone snapped. Annie let out an incredible scream of pain, gasping for breath.

"And now?" Jasmine asked.

Annie took a deep breath, trying to slow her heart rate.

"Fuck… you."

Jasmine flicked her wrist again, this time snapping the right shoulder. The screams of pain were so incredibly loud, they drowned out the sound of Desmond trying to break the glass in the room behind them.

"You can't take much more of this, granddaughter. Tell me how I get back, or I'll break some more limbs."

Finally, Annie relented. She couldn't take any more of

this pain. Besides, she wouldn't be much good in a fight if she couldn't use her arms and legs. Even though the pain was severe, she was trying to formulate a plan.

"Okay! I will show you, please just make it stop!"

Jasmine released her grip, and waved her hands, and by the time Annie landed back on solid ground, her arms had been popped back into place. Jasmine approached her, looming seemingly taller than before.

"Tell me."

Annie sat up and propped herself up against the wall. She took several deep breaths and began to speak.

"You have to go to where you came in, on Market Street, opposite the bank. There is an alleyway there. Exactly central to the wall at the far end, there is a section of the bricks that is discoloured, like they've been burnt. Walk through that part of the wall, and you'll find yourself in a brightly lit room. Turn to the left and walk forwards, and you'll find yourself back in Wealdstone."

Jasmine raised her eyebrows.

"That's it? Go back the way you came? That's the big secret?"

Annie shook her head.

"The secret was not to go right. If you go right, you won't end up anywhere. This crossing has been weakening for years. There were many doorways, now there is just the one. If you go right, you'll fall out of existence."

The wry smile returned to Jasmine's face.

"Thank you dear."

She stooped to pick up Annie, as the door behind her burst from its hinges, and flew into the wall opposite. Jasmine span around to see Duncan charging towards her. She moved to swipe him away, but his speed was impressive, and he vaulted into her, and the pair smashed through the door behind Annie, and out onto the street behind the shop. Annie ran back towards Desmond, but as she turned to see Duncan and Jasmine wrestling, she noticed a red blinking light on his belt buckle. She returned to Desmond, and uttered an incantation, with her hands pressed against the glass. When she finished, the glass seemed to resemble water, and Desmond was able to step through.

"What did you do on your phone?"

Desmond pulled out his weapon.

"I put a mild shock collar into his belt buckle. There's enough energy coming from that woman to amplify any signal. In effect, she let out the beast. I just hope he's strong enough."

Outside, terrified onlookers watched as Duncan's shirtless body was slammed through the window of a shop, glass flying everywhere, the sound of Jasmine's marching heels echoing on the cobbles beneath them. A loud roar from inside the shop, and Duncan launched himself out and into the air. Before he could land, a blast of purple energy side swiped him through an iron lamp post, the metal snapping from the impact, and the lantern crashing to the ground, a small contained explosion as the gas supply erupted.

"You're stronger than you look, werewolf," Jasmine commented.

Duncan regained his footing.

"Thanks. So are you. What's your diet?"

"Energy. Yours?"

Duncan smiled.

"Garlic."

Again, he vaulted into the air, his new found strength flowing through his veins. Before he had been powerful, but this was something else. It was like his inner core had been tapped, and he felt bulletproof. However, Jasmine's speed was formidable too. He couldn't quite get near her before she would swipe him away. Four loud pops echoed around the street as people continued to run, and she felt strong impacts in her back. As she turned, she saw Desmond pointing a gun at her, the barrel still smoking, and Annie stood next to him, holding what looked like a crossbow.

"Who are you now, *Robin Hood*?"

Annie placed her finger over the trigger.

"I prefer to think of myself as *Hawkeye*."

As she pulled the trigger, a silver arrow pierced the air, rotating as it went. Jasmine's face was decidedly unimpressed, and she moved her hand to dismiss the projectile. But it's flight plan remained unchanged. Her face panicked, and as the arrow pierced her chest, she flew backwards. Upon entry, the arrow head blew open, and water erupted into Jasmine's body. She began to burn on the inside, and her back also began to tingle from the impact of the bullets. She was not a demon, or a ghost, but holy water was clearly having an effect. Duncan, Desmond and Annie watched on as she flailed about trying to regain her strength. As they approached, and Desmond prepared to fire again, she ripped the arrow from her chest and threw the body of it back towards Duncan, the broken tip piercing his left thigh. Grimacing with the pain, he dropped to one leg, and

Jasmine directed an intense beam of energy at the building next to them, which erupted in a fireball, sending all three of them flying through the air, the flames and smoke encompassing everything in a fifty foot radius. People ran screaming, as the upstairs floor of the building collapsed into the wreckage. Duncan hobbled clear of the smoke and debris and looked around. Desmond was lying unconscious in the middle of the street in front of him. Annie was nowhere to be seen. And Jasmine was gone.

17

Jack held Kathryn's hand tightly as they gazed down at the scene before them. He felt her squeeze back as the tears continued to flow from all those in the room. Grace was simply sat on the floor staring at Max, white as a ghost, the blood now seeping through the sheet Deanna had placed over the body. Daniella was sat next to her, attempting to comfort her, but Grace had gone mute. Still. No visible expression on her face of any description. Even with all the violence, death and activity in Wealdstone over the last year and a half, it had never seriously threatened any of the team to the point of death. Not since the incident in Alaska with Daniella, Grace and Duncan, had there been a genuine fear that one of them would die. And here they were, staring at not one, but two of their friends lying dead before them.

Jack however, had been here before. And recently. He knew what they were going through. He had of course witnessed his fiancée brutally murdered before him with no way of preventing it. He looked over at Deanna, her eyes swollen from the crying. But he didn't see the grief. He saw eyes filled with vengeance. He had seen that look dozens of times before in the eyes of the families of those taken from them during his time on the force. He released Kathryn's hand and headed over to her.

"Deanna, can we talk?" he asked.

She nodded and followed him out into the hallway.

"Look, I know this is painful and none of us were expecting this to happen, but I don't want you running off into the night like some sort of vigilante to find revenge."

Deanna looked at him with her puffy eyes, and very calmly gave her reply.

"And how exactly would I get revenge, Jack? Hmm? Max was killed by one of his closest friends. She was possessed by some pain wraith memory shit. Am I supposed to go out with a weather vane and attract as much lightning as possible, and try and stab it to death with the special knife?"

Jack wasn't prepared for the response, but the anger itself was expected. Deanna didn't know what to do. She didn't know who to blame, and he feared that unless she expressed it, she would implode. And that had happened with this group before, and they had reiterated on several occasions they did not want a repeat of the Duncan situation.

"What we need to do is find a way to stop these strikes, and my guess is that it starts and ends with this Jasmine. We find her, and deal with her."

Deanna chuckled sarcastically.

"And exactly how are we supposed to do that?"

Jack was still harbouring slightly hostile feelings towards Ariella and had wanted to go full cop on her with the knife, and interrogate her, but he knew she wasn't the one to blame. His track of thought was interrupted by the sound of glass and furniture being smashed and screaming coming from back inside the next room. He suspected Deanna was not the only one venting her emotions now. A wine bottle narrowly missed Jack and Deanna as they re-entered the room, sending a shower of Yellow Tail Shiraz all over the wall. Grace was now tearing through whatever she could find, and as the nearest table found itself buried in the corner bar, he felt he should speak up.

"Okay! We know why this happened. We know the lightning strikes have been getting more frequent. We need to stop it. So that means we need to find Jasmine. We deal with her, and then we see what happens."

Daniella walked over to join him.

"Jack's right. There will be time for us to mourn later. The key now is to make sure that this doesn't happen again. Max wouldn't have wanted us to stop, and neither would Scarlett."

Grace began to calm down, her breathing becoming more regulated, and the veins in her temple starting to subside.

"I loved him," she said softly between sharp intakes of air.

Deanna moved to comfort her. She was still reeling from the death of Scarlett, perhaps more so than she was for Max, as she had known Scarlett the longest. She had felt a spark there, but now the spark had been extinguished.

"He loved you too, Grace. He might have been more restrained than he would've liked, but he was the heart of this team. And you know what else?"

Grace shook her head.

"What?"

Deanna smiled, looked over at Max, and then back at Grace.

"He was badass."

They both laughed, and Deanna knew somewhere, Max was watching and laughing along with them.

"Now we need to go and find this Jasmine. Can you do that?"

Grace nodded, and followed Deanna upstairs, taking one

last look at Max and Scarlett's bodies as Daniella pulled the sheets over their heads. Jack felt his phone ringing in his pocket and pulled it free to see he was being called by Kristin.

"Hey, what's up?"

"JACK! We…. Centre…. Town is…. Lightning… people…"

The signal was breaking up, but in the background between words, it sounded like absolute carnage.

"Kristin? I can't hear you, say that again?"

The sound of her wife's name caught Kathryn's attention, and she walked towards Jack, followed by Daniella.

"There's explosions… purple… strikes all over… collapsed… you now!"

"Where are you?" he asked. "We… fire… cinema…" The line went dead.

"Kristin? KRISTIN!"

It was no use, there was now nobody on the other end of the phone.

"Where are they?" Kathryn asked, voice wobbling with

fear.

"I think they're near the old cinema, but the signal kept cutting in and out. It sounded like absolute madness in the background, and I think I caught the words explosion and purple lightning. I think we need to go."

The three of them sprinted up the stairs, and quickly explained to a bewildered Grace and Deanna.

"Wait, look!"

Daniella was pointing out of the main lounge window, which had a view down across the town. The entire group looked on as multiple lightning bolts struck at various points in the town. And it was continuous, a new one striking every few seconds. Every four or five strikes was accompanied by an explosion. The town was under attack.

"Think of how many people that must be affecting," Grace said.

"I'd say that gateway between realms is pretty much imploding. We have to find Ariella and track down Jasmine. Now."

Jack led the group towards the front door, and as they approached, the huge wooden slabs swung open with force, the doorknobs embedding themselves in the walls on either side. Everyone drew their weapons and aimed them squarely at the entrance. But they were not prepared for who would walk through it. As the group lowered their weapons, and stared at the entrance to the huge mansion, Duncan and Desmond walked through. Duncan had seemingly become more defined and was walking with confidence. Desmond on the other hand looked like he had started to age, a feat which they knew to be impossible.

"What the actual fuck?" was the first question out of Grace's mouth.

"Good to see you too kiddo," came Duncan's reply.

Daniella ran over to him, and Duncan expecting a loving embrace, held his arms open, but instead was met with a swift punch to the face, square and hard, and the impact on his jaw sent him clattering into the coat stand.

"Where the fuck have you been?!"

Daniella was bursting with anger. Her face had turned crimson, and her inner strength was beginning to rise to the surface even without the use of the full moon. Desmond ran across to intervene, before more damage could be done.

"Please, Dani, wait!"

Daniella swung for him, but he ducked and held up his

hands in defence.

"You took off a week and a half ago, no word, no note, and you expect us to welcome you back with open arms?"

"Dani, please just listen!"

Desmond's pleas were being ignored, and Daniella moved past him to storm out the front door, when Duncan spoke up instead.

"Dani I'm cured!"

She stopped dead in her tracks, and turned back to face her husband, who was now stood up and moving towards her, occasionally glancing back at his daughter.

"What?" was her only reply.

"Desmond took me to see... a friend. They managed to remove my vampire side. And apparently, merge my human and wolf sides. I'm free now."

Grace was trying to work all of this out in her head, as was Daniella, when Deanna interrupted and spoke directly to her own son.

"Desmond, what did you do to him?"

Desmond looked back behind him at the carnage

unfolding within the town, and despite the urgency, still felt the need to explain himself.

"I've been crossing a crack between times for months, trying to work with a friend on advancing our tools for fighting all of this stuff. She helped me devise an experimental treatment for Duncan in the hopes his werewolf genes would brace his body against the removal of the vampire genes."

Deanna recalled something he had mentioned to Scarlett when they had first met back up with each other.

"The curiosities store?"

He nodded.

"But they bulldozed that place years ago."

"Actually, we didn't. We camouflaged it."

Daniella now turned her attention to Desmond.

"What do you mean, you camouflaged it? How do you camouflage a building site?"

"Look I'm happy to show all of you later, but right now, town is being torn apart by dozens of pain wraiths and my friend has been kidnapped by one of them."

Jack looked at him, like someone had shoved two-hundred and forty volts up his backside.

"Jasmine?" he asked.

Desmond immediately walked over to him.

"What do you know of this Jasmine?"

"More than you were expecting obviously."

"Is she here?" Duncan asked from across the room.

"We don't know," replied Jack.

"But her daughter is."

This caught their attention even more.

"Her daughter? Then she was telling the truth. And now she has Annie. We need to find them. Now."

Desmond bolted for the door, and Jack ran after him.

"Woah, hey wait a second! Look all we know is she's incredibly strong, and powerful and... did you say Annie?"

Desmond nodded.

"Ariella's daughter was called Annie, right?" asked Grace.

"Yeah," replied Daniella. "Desmond, where did you go to find this friend of yours?"

He paused momentarily, before confirming.

"Victorian England. Every time I went back, more time had passed there, than here. I don't know why, but the conduit is becoming more unstable. I think the increase in energy from the fractures is pouring into it, and it's tearing it apart. I've been going there from here for seven months, but over there it's been twelve years."

Jack span on his heels and twisted the lid off the containment jar behind them on the table. He pulled the blade from inside and slid it into his belt. Turning around, he walked forward and re-joined the others.

"Then we had better move. Something tells me we don't have long before these wraiths tear the place apart. We need to find Kristin and Ariella."

Duncan nodded and he, Daniella and Grace headed through the door. Desmond put his hand out and stopped Jack from going anywhere.

"Now just wait one minute, who the hell are you?"

Kathryn pushed his arm away from Jack.

"He's Jack Marsters Jr, and apparently, he's a damn sight more reliable than you are. So, get out of his way. Now."

Taken aback by this unusual show of dominance, Desmond stood aside, and smiling ear to ear, Jack followed her through the door, accompanied by Deanna. Desmond remained on the spot for a moment, trying to take it all in.

"I think we *all* have some catching up to do."

18

Ariella wiped the blood from her forehead as she hauled herself to her feet. She had forgotten how fragile human skin was during battle, and often wondered why the wraiths hadn't shown more interest in a species like the Deltarians. She had quite fancied having skin layered with diamond. Nevertheless, she had chosen human, and now she was tasked with helping to save the race she once helped destroy.

The energy strikes were now so rapid and intense, that the sky was in a permanent state of purple flux. People were screaming and running everywhere, buildings were exploding, crazed versions of humans were running amok through the streets, murdering passers-by or tearing their own hair out. The scene was carnage, and Kristin had spent most of the last hour picking herself up off the floor, same as Ariella. But the conversions of the people of Wealdstone were not the only challenge the pair were having to deal with.

As Ariella tackled another crazed individual to the ground, and turned its weapon onto itself, five targeted bolts struck the stone of the pavement, sending a wave of energy along the neighbouring buildings, blowing out every window in sequence, and shattering glass throughout the area. As the bolts fazed into humanoid shapes, Ariella noticed they were all wearing a similar outfit, and standing together in a unified stance. Kristin launched her latest attacker through the windscreen of the nearest vehicle, before looking up to see the arrival of yet more members of the pain wraith council.

"These guys never quit, do they?" she asked rhetorically.

"They won't quit until they have Jasmine, and they don't care who or what they take down along the way."

Ariella prepared herself for attack, but was sideswiped by another crazed person, who proceeded to repeatedly punch her in the face. In response, the council turned their attention to Kristin, and began advancing toward her. Dozens of possessed people targeted the council members, but they were swiped away in brutal fashion, several effortlessly torn apart by the unrestricted force of these entities. Without the presence of the elder dagger, they were no longer limited to what they could do. Kristin ran towards Ariella to help her, but she didn't need it. Before she could reach her, a beam of purple energy blasted through the torso of her attacker, and she launched the body into the sky, before jumping back to her feet. At the demonstration of her powers, two of the council members veered towards her, and directed their own energy beams towards Ariella. She had just enough time to block the beam, and redirected it away from her, but impacting it into another building. The front of the structure exploded with immense force, and the building collapsed onto several people who had been attempting to run to safety.

Ariella felt a distinct tinge of pain and guilt at what her action had caused, and this momentarily distracted her enough for the council to land a blow on her. She was sent spinning through the air, unable to stabilise her flight and she penetrated a fourth storey window in a nearby hotel, bouncing across the bed and flying through the wall into the bathroom, where she stopped, the back of her head slamming against the tiled wall. Back down on street level, the other council members were firing blasts of energy in all directions. This wasn't an attack, it was an attempt at sterilisation. They incinerated people from all directions, possessed or not, and as a news chopper came into view, one of them aimed a beam of energy directly at the cabin, sending the copter into free fall, crashing into the Texaco garage and blowing the fuel pumps and the attached convenience store sky high. Flames rained down from above, and chunks of fiery debris landed on cars and trucks causing mini explosions everywhere. The landscape before Kristin resembled that of a high scale disaster movie, and yet the destruction continued.
A beam of energy was sent hurtling towards Kristin, and she narrowly avoided it by leaping into the street, only to be hit by a fleeing car, and knocked out of the way once more. As she hit the ground, she felt her ribs shatter inside her chest, and began coughing violently. She wiped her mouth. Blood. She attempted to stand but couldn't

summon enough strength through the pain.

As the council members continued to sterilise the area, Kristin felt one of them grab her head. As she began to move, her body still fairly limp, it felt as if she was in the grip of a fairground claw machine, and she was the cuddly toy dangling from the blades. She spun around and came face to face with one of the intruders.

"Where is she?" they asked in a harsh voice, the eyes displaying the same purple flashes she had seen in Ariella when her temper had been roused.

"I don't know," replied Kristin through exasperated breath.

The wraith punched her in the gut, sending shockwaves of agony through her chest. She let out an intense scream as another building behind her erupted into flames.

"WHERE IS JASMINE?!"

The offending council member was blown backwards, and his grip released, allowing Kristin to drop to the floor in a heap. Grimacing through the increasing pain, she glanced up to see Ariella walking out from the entrance to the hotel, arms raised, firing balls of purple energy at each of the members. Three of the five hits were deflected, one of them striking the building above Kristin, and as the wall above her collapsed, she raised her arms for protection, knowing it would do no good.

But the hit never came. She felt something grab her ankle, and she was pulled with a high degree of force and dragged just beyond the collapsing rubble. As she lowered her arms, she was met by the smiling face of her wife.

"Looked like you could use a hand."

"And here's me thinking you were still showering vampire guts out of your hair and missing all the fun."

Kathryn presented her hand for Kristin to grab, but there was no strength in her grip.

"What's wrong?" asked Kathryn.

Kristin winced again and released her feeble grip.

"I think my ribs are broken. I took a pretty bad hit."

Kathryn lay her wife back down.

"Okay, then I'll stay with you. Let's see if we can get some of these sparkly fingered bastards back to where they came from!"

Kathryn handed Kristin a gun, and the two of them hunkered down behind the rubble for protection and watched in awe as Ariella continued to fire energy beams at the attacking council members. However, three of them directed a combined beam at her, and she was once again blasted through the air, this time smashing through the wall of Sisko's bar. Kathryn fired several shots towards the attackers, but only one bullet hit, dropping one of them to the ground. It was clearly causing them discomfort, even if it wasn't effective in stopping them. The member in question, turned and attempted to fire a beam towards them, but the energy fell short, fizzling out before it reached their position.

Confused at the effect the holy water had on him, the wraith remained in position. This proved a mistake, as while Kristin and Kathryn watched in awe, Duncan charged down the street, at full speed, smashing the possessed people out of his way with single swipes, and he leapt into the air with a defined roar, and brought himself down onto the wraith with immense strength, which on impact, shattered the road around him.
He continued to pummel the wraith into the ground with a Hulk-like rage, until it's face resembled a flattened steak. As he backed away, even he was astonished at the strength he now found himself exhibiting. Whatever the treatment had done to his vampire side, it had seemingly strengthened his animalistic side without the need of the moon to help bring it to the surface.

In the distance, he could see the others racing down the road, Daniella leading, holding the modified shotgun they had developed, and she smiled at Duncan, and he smiled back. For the first time in a long time, he felt free. But Daniella's smile faded quickly.

"Duncan! Watch out!"

Her call came too late, and Duncan was blasted in the back by another energy beam, and he was sent spiralling across the street, through the window of Sisko's where he fell in a heap next to Ariella's battered figure.

"So, you're the good wraith?" he asked, attempting to catch his breath back.

Ariella smiled.

"Apparently, yeah."

"That's good. Because I don't like your mother very much."

Ariella's smile faded quickly.

"You've seen Jasmine?" she asked, panic clearly audible in her voice.

Duncan nodded.

"She's here. And she's got your daughter."

Ariella fell back to the ground, her mind racing. Annie was alive. And Jasmine had her. The rage began to build within her, as it had done at the mansion, but this time on a significantly higher level. Jasmine had hunted down her daughter to use as leverage. Duncan felt the air get much heavier and started to slide away from Ariella. He watched in awe as her body seemed to rise up from the ground with no effort, and her eyes began to glow with a violet rage.

The four remaining council members felt the reaction too, and all advanced on the bar. Desmond ran towards them with Deanna, both firing multiple shots, but each being deflected by bursts of light. Another bolt of purple lightning struck the ground between the two of them and they were both blown off their feet. Grace leapt over Desmond's fallen frame and sprinted towards the bar, but she too was blasted backwards. Inside the bar, a glow had begun to appear around Ariella, and Duncan was now shielding his eyes from the light. It was as if she was charging up, like an energy weapon. But she didn't have the chance to fire it. The four council members stopped metres from the bar, and gestured their arms towards it, and with a single intense blast, combined their energy beam into one concentrated burst, blasting at Sisko's. As Duncan's eyes widened, the bar exploded in an immense fireball, the entire building erupting from within. The shockwave blew the two buildings out on either side, the roof collapsing, fire shooting into the sky, and all the members of the team and indeed the council, were thrown a clear sixty feet in all directions.

As the bricks and mortar and glass began to rain down onto the street, and the smoke began to clear, Kathryn noticed that there was nothing left of Sisko's. The bar had been reduced to rubble along with the surrounding buildings. There was no sign of movement. Daniella struggled to get herself to her feet and ran over to help Grace to hers. The two of them looked around but could not see any sign of Duncan.

"Duncan!" Daniella shouted through coughing fits induced by the smoke and the ash. "DUNCAN!"

Grace ran over to the rubble and began to dig through it, but there was simply too much of it. She sliced her hands on broken pieces of glass but continued to dig through the bricks with determination. Behind them, Jack crawled out from under the truck he had been blown into, blood trickling from his nose. He surveyed the scene and could just make out Grace and Daniella digging through the wreckage, and in the distance could see Kathryn and Kristin hiding behind a similar mound. He felt the back of his jeans. The blade was still there. He would need it and would need to act swiftly as the dust settled. He would not have an advantage for long. Deanna awoke inside the electrical store, amongst a sea of broken TVs and stereo systems. She could see Desmond walking through the shattered facade of Starbucks opposite and dragged herself upwards and staggered forwards. Desmond nodded at her, and she did the same, and the two of them surveyed the situation.

"You, okay?" Desmond asked his mother.

"Yeah. Although I'm pretty sure I've got liquid crystal in my shirt," Deanna joked back.

"Where's Duncan?"

Deanna looked around, and when she saw Daniella and Grace frantically throwing bricks aside, she feared the worst.

"Oh no."

Desmond followed her gaze, looked back at her in acknowledgement, and the two of them ran to help. As Jack advanced on the now stirring bodies of the council members, their moans suggested they were feeling the effects of the blast, which reassured Jack that the blade was having the desired effect, but he was also aware that in such close proximity to the bar, it would also be limiting Ariella's chances of survival. He had to act fast. He reached down and grabbed the back of the shirt of the first member. He pulled the blade from his belt and ran it across the throat of the wraith from ear to ear. A garbled cry erupted from its throat, before Jack released the body, and it dissolved into purple smoke, flying back up into the purple haze above. He moved onto the second, and then the third, repeating the action, much to the shock of the watching Kathryn and Kristin. There had been no slowing in his stride, and no hesitation in his actions. However, after Jack plunged the blade into the mutilated remains of the member Duncan had beaten to a pulp, just for good measure, he paused near the final attacker. They span quickly, and struck out at Jack, but he dodged the swing, and directed the butt of the blade between the eyes, sending them back to the ground. Jack grabbed the scruff of his collar and placed the edge of the blade against his neck.

"What are you doing here?" Jack asked, fairly calmly, considering the situation.

The council member refused to answer.

"Are you just here for Jasmine? Or is there more to it?"

Again, no response. Jack hit him in the face again with the butt of the knife, before again dragging him forward and placing the blade on his throat once more.

"You've destroyed half of this town, and potentially killed several of my friends. Why are you attacking us?! We are not part of her plans!"

The council member began to laugh. Jack persisted.

"You killed my fiancée. What was she? Was she one of

you? Answer me!"

The wraith rolled his eyes and continued sniggering but decided on a response.

"She doesn't care about you. You humans are nothing compared to us. We aim to return all wraiths to our realm, and if we have to wipe out your puny species to do it, then so be it."

The wraith continued to laugh at Jack, and he felt the anger rising within him. He raised the blade into the sky and plunged it into the wraith's chest. His eyes rolled back into his head, and his form dissolved in Jack's hand, the resulting smoke moving off into the sky, as the strikes of lightning began to ease up. He slumped down onto the ground, letting the knife drop from his hand. Kathryn had helped Kristin to her feet, and supporting her weight, they staggered forwards, and Kathryn slid her wife into a nearby truck. She closed the door and walked over to Jack.

"What the fuck was that?" she asked.

Jack looked up at her.

"What was what?" he replied.

"You murdered those wraiths in cold blood, no hesitation, methodically one by one. That's not you."

Jack grabbed the knife, stood up and holstered the blade once more.

"I don't need you to tell me who I am and who I'm not. They needed putting down, so I did it."

Kathryn had become unnerved by what she was seeing in someone she thought she knew. But she had to admit to herself, that she had not seen Jack in a long time, and there was a chance he was no longer the person she knew. Circumstances had certainly affected that.

"What did he say to you?" she asked, attempting to alter the course of the conversation.

"We're in their way."

Jack walked past Kathryn, pushing her aside and walking past the truck, Kristin watching as he did so. Kathryn called after him.

"JACK! What about helping find Ariella and Duncan?"

He turned and pulled the knife out.

"If I don't get this away from her, she's got no chance."

He put the blade away and continued walking back towards the mansion. Kathryn turned towards the pile of destruction where Sisko's had once stood and saw her friends scrambling without delay. She ran over to them and started pulling the bricks apart.

"Any sign of movement?" she asked Grace.

"Nothing yet. But Dad is strong. If anyone can live through all this, it's him."

Kathryn nodded. Daniella on the other hand was not so convinced. All of this was drastically out of her comfort zone. Even someone with her hidden abilities was not equipped to deal with beings firing pure energy from their bodies, and now they may have lost their two best weapons in Ariella and Duncan. A single tear rolled down her cheek. She had only just gotten Duncan back, and still didn't know what Desmond had done to him. She was terrified she wouldn't get to find out what her husband had now become. She thought back to how many times in the past she had hurt him. The betrayal of their marriage, hiding what she had become, and still he had stood by her. Even now, there were secrets she had not shared with him. She needed him to be alive. She had to tell him everything. Was she being selfish? Possibly. But either way, she couldn't rest until he was found.

Beneath them, the ground began to rumble, and all five of them stopped digging, and looked at each other. The vibrations intensified.

"What the hell is that?" asked Deanna.

Desmond looked around and began to see a purple glow emanating from the gaps between the bricks.

"EVERYBODY OUT OF HERE! NOW!" he screamed.

Without hesitation, all five of them leapt down the pile of rubble and ran for the truck where Kristin was waiting. As they reached it, the rubble was blasted upwards into the sky, and a shaft of purple light emerged from within. Seconds later, it was gone. Daniella and Grace looked on, waiting, and as the rubble began to rain down from the sky, landing around them, Grace saw a hand emerge from the blast area. Then another one. Not wanting to wait, and not willing to see if she had lost yet another loved one, she bolted from behind the truck, dodging the raining bricks as she ran. She reached the bottom of the rubble, just as Ariella began to emerge from within it. She scrambled up to meet her, and helped her out, gently laying her on top of the bricks.

"My Dad?" Grace asked impatiently.

Ariella simply shook her head and pointed into the hole. Grace leapt down into it, Daniella shouting for her to wait as she approached, but it was too late. Grace dropped down through the cavity Ariella had created and slid between the bricks and mortar. As she landed on what felt like solid ground, she saw the limp body of her father lying on what used to be a section of the bar, the emblem of Sisko's visible on the splintered wood.

"Dad!"

Grace scrambled forward, grazing her head on a low hanging piece of metal, water dripping around her from the severed plumbing. Duncan moved slightly at the sound of his daughter's voice, and his eyes flickered.

"Grace?" he murmured through broken vocal tones.

"Yeah, it's me. Can you move?"

Duncan managed to widen his eyes and looked down to find his leg was impaled by debris.

"My leg," he said whilst pointing with his bloodied arm.

Grace followed his direction and saw the injury. It was bad. The metal pipe embedded in his thigh was at least two inches thick. Even for someone of his strength, removing that could lead to him bleeding out.

"Grace?"

Daniella's voice came from behind her, and she was relieved at the arrival of her mother. She indicated the situation, and Daniella's face dropped. Duncan's however came to life when he saw his wife had joined them.

"Hey moonshine, fancy seeing you here."

Daniella could not help but chuckle at the nickname he had given her after he found out she was a werewolf.

"With the force you tore down that street with, I'm a bit disappointed you haven't smashed your way out of here," she joked back.

Duncan chuckled. This was the first time his family had been together for a long time. But he could feel that something was not right. His strength was leaving him, and whatever the treatment had done, was now beginning to fade away. His other hand felt damp, and as he lifted it and looked down, he could see that he had a second wound. His side was thick with blood, and there was a large shaft of splintered wood embedded in his side. The rubble groaned around them, the suggestion was the building had not yet finished collapsing.

"We have to get him out of here!" Grace pleaded with her mother.

Daniella felt Duncan's hand grip her wrist and he looked her directly in the eyes. He lifted his other hand and drew Daniella's gaze towards it. She knew from his look and the state of the wound what the outcome had to be. She sat back and held Duncan's hand. Grace did not go along with the suggestions their body language was making.

"What are you doing? We need to get him out of here! Mom, help me!"

Grace's face was now streaming with tears, as she realised that there was nothing they could do. Daniella began crying tears of her own, and Duncan gripped his wife's hand.

"I need you both to go now," he said as calmly as he could, wincing through the pain. "This place is going to collapse any minute, and I'm not letting it take my girls down with it."

"NO!" shouted Grace. "I've lost Max, I'm NOT losing you too!"

She tried to lift the rubble around Duncan's legs, but despite her increased strength, more just kept piling on top as fast as she was clearing it. Duncan turned to Daniella.

"I'm glad I got to see you one last time, moonshine. Take care of our daughter."

Daniella leaned in and kissed her husband's lips as his final breath escaped from his lungs. As she felt his chest sink, and his hand fell from hers, she planted her face on his forehead and sobbed. Grace stopped lifting bricks and moved to join her mother. When she realised her father was gone, she too began to sob uncontrollably, but the grinding of the obliterated structure around them reminded them that they needed to leave. Grace was holding tight to her father's arm, but Daniella was tugging on hers. They needed to go.

"No! We can't just leave him here!"

Grace resisted her mother and refused to leave. Behind them, Desmond climbed into the shaft.

"Dani? Grace?" he called.

When he came face to face with the sight before him, his heart plummeted. Everything he had worked so hard to bring to this family, was gone. He saw Daniella trying to move Grace away, and as he took one last look at Duncan's body, he helped drag her away. Grace was kicking and screaming, and as they moved into the daylight, the cavern below them collapsed. They felt the rubble shift as the hole was filled in, and they fell down the mound, landing hard on the tarmac of the road.

"You left him there! He's dead and you left him there!" Grace was hysterical, and she jumped to her feet and picked up a piece of metal piping and launched into a vicious attack on a nearby car, smashing the windows, the lights, the mirrors, and hammering at the bodywork, all the while crying and screaming. Kathryn, Kristin, Ariella, Deanna and Desmond watched on, as they realised, they had lost yet another member of their family. Daniella approached Grace, as her strength began to weaken, and as her daughter span to face her, she aimed the pipe at her mother, but Daniella blocked the aim, knocked the pipe away, and the two embraced each other, both crying into each other's shoulders. Through the tears, Daniella stared at the rubble, her heart breaking. Now she would never be able to tell her husband the truth. The secrets she had kept hidden. She would never be able to tell him that Grace was not his daughter.

19

The screams were deafening to Annie, each one torturous to her ears, and despite her lack of direct contact with what was happening outside, she could almost feel the pain seeping through the room. Slumped in the corner, Jasmine was sat, head buried into her hands, purple sparkles emanating from her finger tips, like static electricity. Crossing the void between the two time periods had seemingly had a negative effect on her, in her already slightly weakened state from the injuries sustained before they left. Annie had not been able to make sense of what Jasmine had told her back in the shop, but seeing her power demonstrated in front of her very eyes, it was difficult to argue what a dangerous creature this was. And Herman. Poor Herman had suffered the most. She had known him for nearly her entire life, and now he was gone. Murdered in cold blood simply for being in the wrong place at the wrong time. Whatever the outcome of this situation, she would make Jasmine pay for that.

As Annie continued to contemplate the events in the past more in her mind, Jasmine began attempting to fire her energy forth, but it fizzled out at each attempt just inches from her fingers. She kept running her hand over the wounds in her body from the impacted bullets. Annie had studied the supernatural for a long time, and clearly this creature, these pain wraiths, were not a religious based entity, and it confused her how Jasmine could have been affected so much from the likes of holy water. But it clearly had done so. The detonated arrow head had done the most damage. And then her focus began to shift slightly.

As Annie watched, Jasmine appeared to pick a piece of metal from her shoulder, and visibly wince at its touch. As she tossed the fragment to the ground, her skin seemed to burn slightly, but with its removal, the range of her directed energy beams, had increased another foot or so in distance. Now it was beginning to make sense. The pain wraith was not affected by the holy water at all, it was the casing of the ammunition. The silver. Similarly, to the werewolf, the pain wraith obviously did not react well to silver. The arrow had a head composed of silver, as did the bullet casings, and the tips of the blades they used in their knives. They had discovered a weakness. Not enough to stop one, otherwise Annie would have been able to escape by now, but certainly something to give her an advantage.

"Fucking primitive weaponry."

Jasmine spoke through gritted teeth as she pulled another fragment of silver from her skin. The wounds had begun to heal around the impacted areas, but she was desperately trying to remove the metal before the wounds healed fully.

"Feeling a little under the weather, are we?" teased Annie, risking a reaction.

Jasmine was not amused.

"Quiet, granddaughter, or I'll blast you through that wall."

Annie pushed further.

"I don't think so. I'm six feet away, so I'm out of your range. Grandmother."

Jasmine bared her teeth towards Annie, but again, her attempt to fire energy fell short, and she continued tending to her wounds.

"If you are so powerful, and I don't doubt this for a minute, having seen what you did to my home, why do you need me to convince your daughter to go with you?"

Jasmine launched a large chunk of bullet casing across the room, before responding.

"Ariella is what you would call extremely stubborn. Just like her mother, I suppose. She does not have a choice. She's broken the rules too many times and the risk of exposure of our world is too great. But she won't go willingly. That's where you come in."

Annie was not impressed and wasn't buying the story for

a second.

"You could have sat in the middle of a street, and simply blasted her into oblivion. You want to hurt her, don't you?"

The smile which spread across Jasmine's face was strong and spread quickly. A flash of flame glinted in across her perfectly white teeth as another explosion rocked the outside of the building.

"Well, I'd be lying if I didn't say I had a bone to pick with her."

Annie attempted to wriggle free from her invisible restraints but failed yet again. Jasmine seemed to notice but took no further action.

"Why are we holed up in a building? Wealdstone has grown a lot since I was last here, but it's still a fairly small town. Ariella could be down in the street below, right now. So why are we here?"

Jasmine leapt to her feet, but had not yet regained all of her strength, and stumbled forward. As she did so, the invisible grip on Annie's hands released, and as Jasmine dropped to one knee, she flew towards the door. As she turned the door knob, Jasmine let out an annoyed grunt, and Annie felt herself being pulled back, although not quite as in dramatic fashion as she had been thrown around previously. She could feel herself pushing back. She reached the door again, and managed to swing it open, but Jasmine threw all of her strength into restraining her granddaughter.

"NO!" she screamed, and Annie was yanked across the room, slamming through the chair she had been restrained on, and hitting the ground, rolling against the wall. Her head was a little off kilter as she sat up, and she saw that Jasmine had also been affected by the display of her power.

"You will stay where you are, or I'll kill you now," she mumbled through strained breathing.

Groggy, Annie leaned against the bare brick of the wall.

"You're planning to kill me anyway. What do I have to gain from not trying to escape?"

Jasmine took another deep breath, seemingly beginning to regenerate once more.

"What if I told you, that I could give you the powers your mother has? What if you and me could really be part of a family?"

Annie was caught off guard by that response, as up until now, there had been no family discussion in a positive manner, and she had constantly felt threatened and in danger of being killed. Now she was unsure of how to respond.

"What? What do you mean? Turn me into... one of you?"

Jasmine nodded. She swept her bedraggled hair from her face and stood up once more, but cautiously this time.

"Your mother has had her chance. But you, Annie, you still have a future. Not among these petty humans, but as more. Much more."

Annie's head was swimming with the possibilities, but also with a large degree of disbelief and resistance. She was by no means convinced that the offer was genuine, or that she was not still in danger, but she wanted to learn more. Knowledge was her greatest power, and it always had been. Ever since her mother had taken her to Herman's Curiosities all those years ago. Even after her death, her father Arthur, had continued the weekly tradition. Books were her wonderland, and now as an adult, she had used the knowledge contained in those musty pages to help so many people. And so, she pushed for other information.

"You intend to kill Ariella, and transfer her powers to me?"

Jasmine emitted a wry smile, as she gazed out the window at the sight of hundreds of police being hacked down by the crazed townspeople of Wealdstone.

"Not exactly."

She turned to face her granddaughter, and raised her hands, the sparkles now developing into mini bolts of the purple lightning.

"I tapped into an incredible energy source once before to achieve a necessary task. The council of thirty-two did not see the logic of this, but they did not stop me either. Now they seem to have grown a backbone. I used up my remaining energy to attempt to break free of my restraints when Ariella banished me back to our realm, but the council did not send me back to my prison. They made a request of me."

Annie did not like where this was going.

"They tasked me with rounding up all pain wraiths in your realm, by whatever means necessary, and return them. If I was successful, they would grant me my freedom, and Ariella's powers. I intend to remove her powers, transfer them to you, and then when she is in human form, kill her. I want her to feel as helpless as she made me feel, shackled and powerless for over twenty years. You see Annie, I didn't escape. They let me out."

Annie's fears had been confirmed. Jasmine was not interested in being a family, she was interested in destroying it. And she doubted she would hold her end of the bargain.

"What would be stopping me if I decided to turn my new powers on you?" she asked.

Jasmine's smile faded immediately.

"If you betrayed me, I would kill you. Simple as that."

"And if I refuse to accept the powers?"

Jasmine strolled over to her granddaughter confidently, clearly feeling stronger.

"There is no way where this ends with me not destroying you, little one, unless you do as you're told. You can have whatever you want, any desire in the universe, and I can train you in how to use this power. All you have to do, is do as I say. If you don't, then you and your mother will be heading straight for oblivion. Along with those council members who weren't exactly convinced with the plan of releasing me, you'd find that I can be very difficult to reason with. A small group attacked me when I arrived here. It did not go well for them."

Annie looked out of the window.

"And the people out there? The humans? What will become of them?"

Jasmine turned and strolled back to the window.

"I have no more interest in this petty species. They've been more trouble than they were worth. Once we return to our realm, and there are no more wraiths left on Earth, the distortions will cease, and the gateway will be closed. Then we can find other realms to explore."

Rather sceptically, Annie already knew the answer to her next question, but asked it anyway.

"So, you won't hurt them?"

No response.

"Jasmine?" Annie asked again.

Still looking out the window at all the carnage below, Jasmine watched as in the distance, she saw a huge explosion, flames and dust visible over the roofs of the other buildings.

"No, of course not. You have my word."

She watched as the roof of that building disappeared from view.

"Oh, that's a shame. I really liked that bar."

Jasmine smiled and walked away from the window.

20

2 years ago

"Her suffering is not of concern to us, she is a war criminal!"

"But she remains too powerful for us to contain for much longer, brother. We must strengthen our restraints to their maximum. The stolen power of five million of our family does not simply dissipate."

Titus agreed. Even in their natural ribbon energy form, a nod was clearly visible. Jasmine was far too powerful to be left without intervention. However, she was not their only concern. Too many wraiths were now on Earth, and the more that explored their world and culture, the more risk there would be of their realm being discovered. That could no longer be an acceptable risk.

"Galen, it is your decision. We must face the reality that we may have to destroy her."

Galen glowed more brightly as he became more frustrated. It was not in the council's nature to destroy their own kind. This is why Jasmine's actions in the first place had caused such devastation. But he could no longer ignore the facts. Jasmine's screams echoed around their world constantly. Whilst there was no construct of time in the Realm of Screams, they had seemingly been continuing for an eternity. The council had been keeping Jasmine in constant agony for almost two decades of human time, and they had needed additional help and power to keep her there. She was an anomaly. Somehow the absorption of those lost had given her stronger abilities beyond their comprehension.

However, their concerns would be debated no longer. A wave of energy blew through the entire realm, and screams of other wraiths could be heard, random strikes of lightning coursing through hundreds of entities. Jasmine had finally broken free.

"We must stop her from breaching our realm!"

Titus and Galen twisted their way through the developing destruction, passing through other wraiths in a new form of agony as Jasmine's efforts to break through the gateway intensified. Ahead of them, was the chamber of the council. An enclosed part of their home where the leaders of their species resided and made the ever increasingly difficult decisions on their actions. Most recently, it was discussed that Jasmine could in fact be useful, but this is a risk that some of the members such as Galen and Titus were not willing to accept. As they moved beyond the chamber, they saw the other council members, floating in a seemingly unconscious state.

Jasmine had clearly been through here.

The agonising screams ahead of them led them in the correct direction, and ahead of them, they could see Jasmine, still occupying her human form, attempting to blast her way through the gateway. Cracks appeared all around the realm and bursts of energy diverted the creatures away.

"She is attempting to reach the humans again. We must stop her!" Titus protested.

"Then we will need the elder blade. It is the only way to ensure she returns to her holdings."

As they flew back into the chamber, in the centre of the enclosure, was the only physical item able to be present in this place. A blade, constructed by the first wraith to leave the realm, eons ago, as a method for returning wayward entities back to their realm. In the presence of a wraith, it weakened their powers to almost undetectable levels, allowing them to be subdued, and if the blade was used on them, would separate their ethereal form from the physical and return them home. As Titus took possession of the blade, he felt his powers begin to wane, and being in close proximity, so did Galen.

"We must get the blade as close to her as possible," suggested Titus.

As they returned to Jasmine's location, her powerful hammer blows began to slow and become less intense. She sensed their presence and turned to face them. It was taking an immense amount of her power simply to retain her physical form. This was not commonplace here. She was rebelling against the rules at every turn. She staggered forwards toward them, and managed to fire off one blast of energy, knocking Galen out of his sweeping stride, and he too became a floating ball of energy. However, Titus was faster. He was one of the more proficient members of the council, and as Jasmine made her attack, he swirled around her like an ink in water, and slid the blade between her shoulders, the resulting scream the most deafening in all the realm. As she exploded into a ball of purple and violet smoke, her physical form was gone, and her ethereal form was dragged at speed back into the holding cells within the council chambers.

It was several hours of normal time before the council was recovered and reassembled in the chamber. Titus and Galen had returned the weapon and joined them, completing the full thirty-two members. The leader of the council, Navar, addressed the members with a stern and commanding voice.

"Members of the Council of Thirty-Two. What we have witnessed here has been a deeply concerning encounter. Jasmine provides a threat we were never prepared for. The things she has done were never foreseen, even by our elders. There is growing concern, that something must be done."

The chamber erupted into agreeable cheers, most notably from Galen. He had narrowly avoided destruction when Jasmine attacked the five million. He had a personal interest in this. Navar continued.

"However, a greater threat has emerged in the realm of the humans. Jasmine's daughter, Ariella has begun developing further than we anticipated, also. She has demonstrated incredible strength and powerful abilities, firstly to be able to resist the train designed to ensnare our criminal population and return them here, but also to defeat her mother and send her back here against her will. It is becoming clear that she is even more powerful than Jasmine. And she too must now be stopped."

The murmuring around the chamber became violently loud and disorganised. There were cries from some of the other energy forms that they should be allowed to evolve further. Others were demanding the return of all wraiths to their own realm, and for those who strayed to be punished. Navar demanded silence.

"When Jasmine slayed five million of our brothers and sisters, she splintered the gateway between our worlds. Every time a wraith has crossed this gateway, the cracks have become more and more frequent. However, the power demonstrated by Ariella has created nothing short of a splintering effect. Every piece of travel weakens the gateway, and concentrated bursts of our experiences, and pain are striking their world and creating chaos. I believe the only way to stop this, is to bring them all back, and seal the gateway. Permanently."

The chamber once again erupted in both protest and support. Navar simply watched on as fighting began amongst the other members. There was clearly a divide here, and he intended to find out who was with and who was against him. His power was absolute, and he knew what needed to be done. A powerful blast of lightning ran through each member of the council, silencing them once more.

"I propose we release Jasmine."

Silence, for the first time. Nobody spoke, nobody murmured a word. Navar was unsure whether they were afraid of his reprimands, supportive, or simply in shock at his announcement. He continued, nonetheless.

"She is the only one powerful enough to destroy Ariella, and she knows where she was last located. If we continue to restrain her here, either we will be forced to attempt to destroy her, or she will destroy us. We failed in our duties once before and it cost us the lives of the five million. We must not fail again."

Galen broke the silence.

"If we release this murderer, we will have doomed us all anyway! She will never agree to our terms!"

Titus joined his brother in voicing his concerns.

"Navar, we must reconsider. If we send her through the gateway to the humans, she will use whatever force she deems fit, and it will be the end of both of our realms! There must be another option!"

"SILENCE!" Navar bellowed. "The decision has been made. Jasmine will be released, she will find her daughter, and she will destroy her. We will send out smaller groups to return the other wraiths from their world in the meantime. The chamber is dismissed."

And with those final words, the wraiths moved their way out of the chamber, and returned to their work. Titus and Galen joined each other, before being met by two others.

"This is suicide for both us and for the humans," stated Galen.

"Then it is agreed. When she is through the gateway and out of the sights of Navar, we will pursue her."

Titus' response was met by approval from the others.

"Then we will require the elder blade," Galen reminded his brothers.

"Leave that to me."

~ 251 ~

Titus returned to the chamber, and the others dispersed. The fate of both their realm, and the humans, was now in their hands.

21

There were seven cockroaches scrambling over each other in the corner of the office, all fighting to get the scraps of sandwich that had fallen to the ground. Grace looked at them and saw the same chaos as that which had been happening outside. She never expected them to be holed up in a building, hiding from the carnage that their friends and acquaintances were now causing out there. Her chest was aching heavily. In the last thirty-six hours, she had lost the man she loved, and her father to this madness. She should feel nothing but rage, but since the events at Sisko's, and her initial outburst, she had felt numb. Disbelief, perhaps that any of this was actually happening, and it was in fact an illusion. She often thought perhaps she had died in Alaska at the hands of the vampire clan, and this had all been some kind of nightmare afterlife. As she watched the cockroaches devour the crust of the sandwich, she heard the shouting coming from the next office along.

As Desmond was launched through the cubicle dividers, Deanna attempted to step between him and Daniella, but she was pushed aside, and Daniella continued to lay into Desmond.

"You took him away from me, then suddenly you show up

again, and now he's dead! What did you do to him?!"

Daniella swept computers and desks aside like they were toys, and as Desmond stood up once more, she swung a fist squarely at his jaw, sending him crashing through the table next to him.

"Daniella please!" he shouted from the floor. "I was trying to help him! To help you!"

"You didn't help us, you destroyed us! Ever since you came into my life twenty years ago, you've done nothing but corrupt this family!"

Deanna was confused at something in that statement and interjected.

"Woah hold on, you two knew each other twenty years ago?" she asked.

Desmond looked toward Daniella, a pleading look in his eyes, but there was only fire in Daniella's. She turned to face Deanna.

"He turned up in Wealdstone in 2003. Claimed he was a new resident, looking to buy property in the area. I was having a bit of a rocky patch with Duncan, not the first and certainly not to be the last. He used me to find out everything he could about the local area. We went out for coffee on my lunch breaks, he took me to dinner. Then

one afternoon, he told me how much I reminded him of
his wife, that he had lost some time ago. I felt sorry for
him, and we kissed. I was twenty years old, I didn't know
what I was doing. The next thing I know, I'm waking up
in his bed the next morning, and he's gone. Turns out all
he wanted was to pretend I was his wife, and then go. I
was an emotional booty call."

Deanna looked at Desmond, horrified at her son. He
remained on the floor, saying nothing. Deanna
approached him.

"Is this true?" she asked.

Desmond did not respond.

"I asked you a question Desmond! Did you use her to
make yourself feel better? Did you know that she had a
boyfriend? Did you even care?"

Desmond leapt to his feet.

"Of course, I cared! I had spent hundreds of years trying
to end this stupid curse that had been placed on both of us
and gotten nowhere. No texts anywhere had any spells or
incantations to remove it. I found myself in Wealdstone,
lonely and thinking back to when I was the happiest. And
then I met Daniella. Everything she did and said
reminded me of Amelia. I just wanted to know what it felt
like to be loved again. When I woke up, and I realised

what I had done, I left. I didn't see her again until five years ago, when I discovered she had been turned by a werewolf."

Deanna turned back towards Daniella.

"Did Duncan know? Did you ever tell him?"

Daniella shook her head, as tears began to roll down her cheeks.

"I was going to tell him everything before what happened in Alaska. But since then, it's been non-stop. And now he's gone, he will never know."

Desmond took a step forward.

"You can't tell her. She needs to not have this weighing her down right now. It's not the time."

"She deserves to know! How can I keep this from her now? Duncan is dead!"

"Let her grieve! That man *was* her father. He raised her, he loved her. Let her hang on to that! Please!"

Deanna looked toward the doorway, and saw that Grace was standing there. She assumed she had heard everything.

"Grace, honey," Deanna started to say, but she was cut off.

"He is my father? You lied to me? And Dad?"

Daniella ran towards her daughter, but Grace held up her hands and stepped back.

"Dad didn't deserve you! You're nothing but a plague on this family. It should have been you under all that rubble!"

And with that, Grace stormed out of the building, despite the chaos still occurring outside. Deanna moved to follow her, but Ariella indicated she would follow. Desmond was now sat in a chair by the window, contemplating the fallout of what had just happened. He began muttering to himself.

"I've spent years trying to repair the damage we caused, Dani. I researched every known text in regard to a cure for the vampire condition. I thought if I could cure him of the thirst and the rage, then I would have at least given you the complete family. And it worked. The intensive garlic treatments worked. Had the situation been different, you'd have been able to… what is it they say in fairy tales? Live happily ever after."

Daniella walked towards him, rage and grief still bubbling beneath the surface.

"You took advantage of me for your own personal gains. I know I should have resisted, but you had an agenda, I didn't. I loved my husband more than you can ever know. I may have caused him pain, and I may have made mistakes, but it was all compounded by you and what you did. I will *never* forgive you for this."

She reached into her jacket pocket, and pulled out a small case, and as she opened it, she pulled out four glass vials of solution.

"And as for this?"

She threw them all against the wall, shattering into tiny shards across the office space.

"I don't want your serum anymore. I don't want anything from you. Stay the fuck away from me and my daughter."

As Desmond watched the liquid slowly dripping down the walls, Daniella left the office, stopping by Deanna, only to confirm her intentions.

"I'm going to look for Jack."

Deanna was shaken by these events. With everything going on in Wealdstone at the minute, this seemed fairly insignificant, but the team splitting into different directions could prove disastrous. And she could not help but blame Desmond for this too.

"You tried it your way and look what it got you."

As Desmond looked up at his mother, she turned away from him and she too left the office, leaving him alone, staring out of the windows. He began to cry, for what felt like the first time in centuries. It had in fact been so long, that the sensation felt alien to him. He watched through the glass, as the people he had come to regard as friends and colleagues, walked away from the building. Across the street, Kathryn and Kristin joined them from the grocery store, carrying as much food as they could muster, and they all moved up the street.

"What have I done?" he asked himself.

"I'd say you've pretty much destroyed your entire little family. If you're actually asking for an opinion."

The voice startled him, and he span around to be confronted by a familiar, and unwelcome sight.

"What's the matter Desmond? You don't seem very happy to see me."

"What do you want?" he asked through gritted teeth.

Jasmine strolled across the office floor and stopped inches away from his face. She smiled intently as she looked into his eyes. Then, without warning, she grabbed him by the throat, and as he gasped for air, she spoke into his ear, whispering the words.

"What do I want? Why you of course."

22

Ariella was now sat on a bench at a bus stop, staring into the sky. Having been rebuffed by Grace, she had decided to leave her to cool down. Despite the immediate danger, she knew she would be able to take care of herself. As she watched the flames die down in one of the burning police cars in the street, she felt the bench move slightly as Deanna sat beside her.

"Tough day huh?" asked Ariella.

Deanna chuckled slightly.

"Yeah, you could say that. You know, I've lived for so long, I thought I'd seen everything. I really don't know anything do I?"

Ariella was the one to chuckle this time.

"Deanna, I've lived far longer and through far more lives than you have, and even I don't understand what is going on right now. Things just don't add up. Why would my mother break free and risk the very exposure she was trying to prevent? Why would the council members be trying to get all the wraiths back. Jack's fiancée was killed for a reason, but I just can't put my finger on why."

Deanna nodded.

"It had occurred to me why in such a small town, she hadn't made her presence known yet. If she is as powerful as you say, then why is she in hiding?"

Ariella had wondered about that herself. Either some outside force is affecting her, or she had a long term plan. And it was the second one that worried her the most.

"Can I ask you something?" Deanna asked.

Ariella nodded, gesturing for her to continue.

"Do you remember all of the lives you've had as a wraith?"

Ariella's face became reflective at the question, and she immediately began to replay moments from her various forms in her mind.

"I remember every single one. And everything I've done during each life. Some I adore, and others I would rather be able to forget."

"I've been alive since the thirteen-hundreds, and the only things I seem to be able to focus on are the negative emotions. I remember the hurt of losing loved ones, the pain of being forced to continue through life with no purpose. The only positive I can focus on was when I found Desmond again. And now, I don't even know him."

Ariella placed a comforting hand on Deanna's leg. She too had shared her existence with pain, and loss and suffering, after all it was in her nature and her design. But the reflections between life cycles always helped her to remember the positive attributes too. She figured this might help Deanna to see the positive side to humanity.

"When we leave one physical form for another, there is a brief period between the transition, where each wraith goes to their spiritual home, and we can reflect on our teachings so far, relive the memories of some of our past lives. It only lasts for a few minutes, but to us, it is like time is suspended. We create a space where we feel safe, and for that brief moment, we are content."

Deanna was invested in this idea. She had often reflected on her past, but not having the benefit of seeing it visually, the memories sometimes became distorted.

"What is your space like?" she asked.

Ariella smiled as she remembered the contemplation zone she had created in her mind.

"For me, it is a vast stone library. I once visited this place as a child in the eighteen-hundreds. I walk into the building from a storm outside. I take the same path each time, past the single librarian, who is herself as old as time. Then I find myself walking past these flickering torches on the walls, and huge ornate windows, the rain pouring down the glass, and the lightning raging outside. I move towards the darkest corner of the library, and there's a tall, leather backed chair there, with a small lantern on the ground. I reach for a volume from the shelf behind the chair and sit down. And as I open each book, I relive the memories of my past, places I've been, or even places other wraiths have been. On a spiritual level, we are all connected. And then I close the book, choose my new host, and leave the library."

This was fascinating to Deanna, and it presented such an evocative image, that she was now a little jealous of this ability.

"That sounds amazing," she offered.

Ariella did not seem to share that feeling, or at least, not entirely.

"There is a tinge of sadness that comes with each of these lives. Whenever a wraith enters a new host, the person who was there before, the consciousness of the person, is gradually faded away. The wraith absorbs the memories and the energy of the person, but then their consciousness dissolves into nothingness."

Until now, Deanna had been completely unaware of any

details surrounding how a wraith moved from host to host. This new detail presented a certain horrific aspect.

"So, the person you inhabit, dies?" Ariella nodded.

"Effectively, yes. Each time I have been placed into a new body, I am aware of what is happening to this person. The process is peaceful for them, they are in no pain. But the immediate guilt is in itself a form of pain for us. Whenever I have been fortunate enough to have a family, or a loved one, while I have loved and protected them as my own, I always feel guilt at the fact I have denied the real owner of that form the opportunity to do the same. But it is the nature of our existence."

Deanna was unsure how to respond to that. It seemed barbaric to simply remove a person's soul from their body. But it was seemingly not a choice the wraiths could make for themselves.

"Are you placed into random bodies at will by your council?" she asked.

"No. We have a say in where we go. The thoughts we have immediately prior to our death affect where and who we end up occupying next. For example, when I was a young blacksmith once, hundreds of years ago now, I was unaware that my death was imminent, and at the time, I was thinking that it would be amazing in a hundred years' time to see what kind of weapons were being forged.

When I returned to a physical form, I was now occupying another master of the forge, but nearly a century later."

"I have to admit, while it sounds incredibly callous to remove someone from their bodies without their consent, the appeal is certainly there. To move through time, living different lives and learning throughout all of it."

Ariella felt that she had a different level of rapport with Deanna. She was the only one who came close to have living the amount of time she had. Even Desmond seemed unapproachable, now more than ever. But with Deanna, she seemed to understand more. It had been a long time since she had been able to confide so completely in a person.

"You may be interested to know that we have also met before."

That captured Deanna's attention more than anything else that had been said up until that point.

"Excuse me?" she replied in awe.

Ariella laughed.

"When we enter a new form, we remember our past lives, but not necessarily in the order in which we inhabited them. For example, when I woke in Sam Greenwood's body, the last memory I had was of being inside the body of a woman named Caroline, saving my daughter from being hit by a drunk driver. However, as my memories gradually returned and sorted themselves out, I realised I had been to a couple of places since, and each time I returned to my library world, I would see them all. We have all met before."

The legend was expanding, and Deanna was all ears.

"You've met *all* of us before? When? How?"

Ariella held up her hand for patience.

"Before I was Caroline, I was actually further forward in time. I was in a host called Julia. She was a waitress at a diner, here in Wealdstone. I actually served you and Scarlett food when you first came here."

Deanna was in a state of shock. She remembered the diner, and the conversation between her and Scarlett, but had no idea that anything else was out of the ordinary.

"That was you?" she asked, in more shock now than before.

"Yeah. After you two left, and I locked up, I walked to my car and was attacked by a group of vampires. I fought them off but died from the blood loss anyway. That was when I encountered Daniella, Grace and Duncan. I found myself in the body of a man named Garrett. He was very interesting. Garrett was a werewolf. The feeling of being so free and strong, and living in amongst the Alaskan wilderness was one of my strongest memories. After Daniella's family left following the ordeal with the vampire clan, I retreated into the forest, only to be attacked by the remaining members of that vampire clan later that week. That's when I became Caroline. And had Annie."

The tone descended into sadness as Ariella remembered her daughter's face. Every time she would go into that curiosity shop, her face would light up and you could actually see the cogs of her imagination whirring away.

"I'm sorry you lost her," Deanna offered, and this time she was the one placing a reassuring hand on Ariella's leg.

Amongst all of this conversation and series of revelations, the streets had become quieter. Everyone was now either dead, or fleeing, and the police had been overrun. Wealdstone was now fast becoming a ghost town.

"I've never given up hope of finding her. A trait I've picked up from you humans. I've seen it many times before. I was a soldier in the first world war, I've been an architect designing houses to give my family a better life, I've even been a pirate, Captain! And in all those randomly different scenarios, I've seen one thing. Endurance. The human race always endures, and that is a quality I strive to have in myself. Something I saw in Max when we first met. I was his professor, tutoring him after school. I was murdered by thieves trying to take one of my rare specimens of spider. On that occasion I was in the form for such a short time, only a matter of days, that the consciousness of Arlington, that was his name, remained in the body after death. It was quite amusing to watch as I drifted between lives how he managed to exact his revenge from beyond the grave."

"So, you really have been in all our lives before," Deanna acknowledged.

"I could go through them all, but one thing has remained pretty much constant throughout. Wealdstone. I seem to be drawn back here more than anywhere. I suspect the gateway to my realm is located here. That's why I keep being drawn back, and that's why the concentrated bolts of pain and energy are only striking here."

Suddenly a thought occurred to Deanna.

"If the activity has been increasing, and the cracks into your realm have been increasing, what are the chances we can leave the town? If this gateway is here, chances are it's cutting us off. Nobody knows what is happening here. There's been no news reports since Duncan's rampage, no army presence. It's like we don't exist."

Ariella had not noticed these things, but with everything

going on, they had barely had a chance to breathe. But it did seem to make sense.

"Perhaps we should find out."

The two of them ran across the street to an abandoned car and headed for the nearest point in the town limits. As the car increased speed, Deanna made a fair comment.

"Maybe you should slow down as we get there. We don't want a *Simpsons Movie* scenario where we smash into a dome wall. I'd like to see this thing through."

"Fair point. We should be there in a minute."

The whole drive only took ten minutes, but the anxiety levels were rising within them both. Deanna began to panic more as they got closer to the town limits. She began thinking thoughts like, what if they really couldn't leave town? How would they call for help? She didn't have to wait long for her answer. As the car approached the sign which read '*Now leaving Wealdstone*', Ariella brought the car to a halt.

"Would you mind getting out, Deanna?" she asked politely.

Slightly confused, but obliging, she exited the vehicle, as did Ariella. Moving to the side of the road, she watched as Ariella let go the parking brake, and walked to the back of the car and began pushing. The car continued forward under its own momentum, and Ariella moved to the side of the road to join Deanna. As they watched on, the car hit what appeared to be a purple forcefield of energy, and as it passed through it, the car began to disintegrate before their very eyes. When it finally came to rest on the other side, there was nothing remaining but four burning tyres, which collapsed, billowing thick black smoke into the air.

"Well, that's a definitive answer to that question," Ariella remarked.

Deanna nodded, and the panic really set in.

"We're trapped here."

23

The mansion was quite a mess. It was clear that several people had attempted to hide out inside but had failed. As Jack walked up the driveway, he himself covered in blood, having fought his way through the town, he could see bodies strewn along the edge of the road, blood staining the tarmac. He felt the knife handle digging into his waist and felt the heaviness of what he had just done. He had never been so calculated and cold blooded in any action as he had done just now. Something had stirred within him that he didn't like. As he approached the doors to the house, he could see one of them had been broken open. Drawing his gun, he saw he only had one bullet left, but he was poised to strike all the same. His joints ached and his muscles were strained, but he was ready. As he moved into the main entrance, he could see blood on the floor, but no bodies.

"Hello?" he called out.

There was no answer, and it appeared that whatever scuffles had taken place by those possessed and those who had been fleeing the crisis, had taken place mostly outside. Nevertheless, he made a quick sweep of the building, and when he found nobody, he holstered his weapon, and walked upstairs to one of the old bedrooms, taking the glass containment unit with him that had remained untouched on the coffee table.

As he entered this room in particular, he felt a wave of energy move over him. Almost nostalgic in nature. He had never been in this room before, and yet it somehow seemed familiar. As he sat himself down in one of the wing-back chairs, he noticed a small green music box on the end table beside him. Compelled to open it, the music began to play, and from inside the lid, a small piece of paper fell to the floor.

Bending down to pick up the paper, Jack was almost overwhelmed with a sadness. He wasn't sure where it had come from, and he couldn't seem to stop it. As he opened the paper and read the words within, the sadness seemed to grow more intense.

'Anthony, or Timothy? Ask Jonathan which name is best for his son.'

As he finished reading the note, the music stopped, and as quickly as the emotion had entered his body, it left. Jack folded up the note and placed it back into the music box, closing it and returning it to the table. Out of the corner of his eye, he thought he saw a figure moving on the balcony. However, as he looked in that direction, there was no presence visible. He did, however, get the distinct impression that he was not alone. Jack placed the knife back into the containment unit, closed the lid, and set it down behind the chair. He'd had enough. Everything that was happening here was turning him into something he could no longer recognise. He was becoming more violent, more critical, and much more aggressive than he was used to. He now wondered if it was this kind of behaviour that led to his father doing what he did that fateful night. Again, he had the feeling he was not alone. He glanced around the room but saw nothing. And then came the voice.

"I too know what it means to be consumed by sadness."

Jack looked up to see the figure of a woman sat in the chair opposite, now holding the music box. She was wearing a white flowing dress and had a definite glow surrounding her. Her eyes were so piercing, Jack couldn't break his gaze, but did manage to find his voice.

"Who are you?" he asked softly, not wanting to scare the woman away.

"My name is Abigail. It is nice to meet you, Jackson."

To say Jack was taken aback by this would be the understatement of the century. The woman was not entirely solid, the back of the chair barely visible through her form.

"How do you know my name?" he asked, keeping his voice quiet and soft.

"I've lived here for a very long time. I like to watch you come and go. I know how you're hurting."

Jack felt somewhat compelled to continue the conversation, despite the fact that he could now make out on the wall above the doorway, a portrait of the woman he was now conversing with. That sealed the deal. He was talking to a dead woman.

"When did you die?" he asked.

Immediately, he felt the question was insensitive, but he got a straight answer from Abigail.

"Fifteen years ago. In this very room."

Abigail looked towards the balcony, and Jack followed her gaze. He now understood why it appeared he had seen movement out there. She had leapt to her death from that location.

"I see you here, Jackson, and I see you changing. You're allowing your past to cloud your future, and it is going to destroy you if you are not careful."

The spirit spoke with such conviction, and yet spoke in a way in which Jack could not ignore.

"I worry that I am becoming my father. He committed terrible acts in this town, and now I face significant threats, and I'm wondering if I am doomed to do something similar."

Abigail stood, and seemingly floated across the floor as she moved toward the balcony doors.

"You are not your father, Jackson. You know what you are doing, and you know that you don't want to be doing it. Don't make the same mistake I did and give up on yourself."

Jack swore he could make out tears falling down Abigail's ghostly cheeks. She clutched the music box tightly.

"I don't know if I can stop it," he replied.

Abigail chuckled.

"You have people around you to help you. Don't turn your back on them."

As she finished the sentence, she walked through the doors as if they weren't there, and as Jack watched, she leaned forward, and disappeared over the edge of the balcony. Jack sat bolt upright in his chair, as his eyes opened wide. He looked around the room, but he was alone. At his side, on the table was the green music box, as it had been when he arrived.

"Was that really a dream?" he asked himself out loud.

He glanced up above the doorway, and sure enough was the portrait of Abigail. Unsure if this was a dream or not, Jack was now feeling more like himself again, and annoyed with himself that he left the rest of the team alone to deal with the situation. A noise from the corridor startled him, but as he went to stand up, Kathryn entered the room.

"Hey, you, okay?" she asked.

Jack, still perplexed at his experience in this room, nodded and took a deep breath.

"Is everyone else, okay?" he asked, but the look on Kathryn's face told him that they weren't.

"We lost Duncan," she replied.

An immediate ping of guilt struck him in the gut. He had left at the height of what could have been a rescue mission. He had been consumed with rage and sadness and had left his friends to fend for themselves.

"I'm... I'm so sorry. I should've stayed, and maybe..."

Kathryn cut him off.

"It wasn't your fault. He had too many injuries. Even if we had managed to get him out of the rubble, he wouldn't have survived."

"Yeah, but at least Grace and her mother would have had a body to bury."

"Jack, you had to get that blade away or we'd have lost Ariella too. Let's not forget that."

Jack had to accept that she was right, about that fact at least. The blade was too valuable to discard, but too dangerous to keep near their strongest weapon. Kathryn moved to sit in the chair opposite, where moments before in either reality or a peculiar dream state, he had spoken to Abigail.

"Jack listen, I know things have been difficult for you. And to be honest, they've been difficult for me too. I didn't realise when I actually saw you that I would..."

"... still have feelings for me?" he finished.

Kathryn nodded.

"When I saw you on the lawn of that house, I was relieved to see you, but then as we came back here, I realised it was a more *comfortable* feeling. A feeling I hadn't had for a long time."

Jack understood what she meant. He had loved Kimberley very much, but he didn't even know who she was. Had he fallen for the woman, or the entity that resided within her?

"I'm not sure your wife would appreciate you talking like this."

Kathryn's facial expression changed into one of annoyance as she stood up from the chair and launched an accusatory tirade of abuse towards him.

"It's not my fault that you actually answered my emails! It's not my fault that we have history together, and it's not my fault that Kristin seems to feel less and less for me the longer all this fucking bullshit goes on! Sometimes, I don't even know if she loves me anymore!"

Jack stood from his chair and placed both of his hands gently on her shoulders.

"Your wife loves you very much, Kat. If she didn't then she wouldn't have married, you. This whole situation has everyone under a lot of strain right now. Losing our friends doesn't help either. You just have to reassess what is really important to you, and then you'll know your way forward."

Kathryn nodded. She had never seen this side of Jack before, and in all honesty, he was a surprised to hear the words as much as she was. However, he had spoken to Abigail, her words seemed to have had an effect.

"You're right. She has done so much for me. She altered my life completely, and through all of the shit we've waded, she's still here. A little broken, but still here."

The pair chuckled, and all their cares seemed to fade away, just for a moment. Kathryn looked at Jack with a new admiration. She had forgotten how comforting just having his presence there could be. It had been a long time since she had felt at ease in any sort of way. Even before the whole pain wraith situation, her and Kristin had constantly been arguing or fighting about something or other. And just in this moment, she felt the opposite.

She leaned forwards and placed a kiss on Jack's lips. He stepped back, his reaction of slight shock. But then as the moment passed, he stepped forwards and returned the kiss. The two of them wrapped their arms around each other and as the passion intensified between them, Kathryn directed Jack towards the chair he had just been sat in. As he sat, she straddled him and continued kissing him. Jack moved his arms up underneath Kathryn's shirt, and slid it upwards, discarding it onto the floor. Kathryn responded by removing his shirt and reaching down undoing his belt buckle. Jack reached up to slide the straps on Kathryn's bra down as she reached behind to undo the clasp. But after sharing another intense kiss, Kathryn pulled away.

"What am I doing? I'm so sorry, I shouldn't have done that."

Realising that they were on the cusp of no return, Jack too was tinged with regret.

"No, no, it's fine. I kind of got caught up in the moment."

Kathryn moved back to stand and leant down to retrieve her shirt and her bra from the floor. Jack too collected his top and stood looking into her eyes.

"I guess we missed our moment, didn't we?" he asked, a wry smile forming on his face.

Kathryn smiled and nodded.

"Yeah. Me and Kris have our problems, but I really do love her."

"I know. And she loves you. I think this is one of those things that we pretend didn't happen."

"Thank you, Jack. Maybe in another life."

The two of them gazed at one another for a minute, and they moved in before sharing another long kiss, but this time it felt more of a parting embrace. As they moved away from each other, they smiled. Kathryn walked towards the doorway, and as she reached it she looked back at Jack, just for a moment, and then disappeared down the corridor. Jack walked over to the balcony doors, opened them and stood outside in the fresh air. He took deep breaths and felt the breeze through his hair. He looked across the view of the town, and there were still small fires, and plumes of smoke. He heard gravel crunching underfoot, and as he looked down, he saw Desmond walking up the driveway. He nodded in his direction, and Desmond smiled back, entering the front door.

Jack was now more confused than ever. He seemed to be at peace with his emotions regarding his father, but now there was the re-emergence of his feelings for Kathryn. This was not going to be an easy battle, either in the town, or in his own mind. He exited the room and walked down the corridor until he came to the staircase. Kathryn was propping Kristin's legs up onto a cushion and lay her back on one of the sofas. She looked like she had taken a fair bit of damage. Desmond walked past them all and headed straight down to the basement. Kathryn's eyes caught Jack's as he started descending the stairs, but he looked the other way. As he reached the bottom of the staircase, Grace walked through the front door, and she too looked as though she had been in an emotional battle. Of course, now Jack knew why.

"Hey, how are you doing?" he asked her.

"I've been better," came her reply.

"I'm sorry about your Dad."

Grace looked down at the floor, before looking back up after composing herself.

"It's okay. I'm going to find this bitch Jasmine, I'm going to run that blade through her guts, and then I'm leaving."

As Grace stormed into the kitchen, Jack could not help but think that this happy little team, was gradually coming to an end.

24

Wealdstone had been decimated. There was no other way of describing the situation that had unfolded. It was as if some great force had swept down from the cosmos, and scooped all the life from the place, leaving behind nothing but rubble, debris, and bodies. The police force and emergency services had been completely overwhelmed and now whoever was left, were on their own.

In every street, bodies were strewn around, blood now drying on the roads and pavements, fires still burning in buildings throughout the entire confines of the city. The population of Wealdstone, had begun to flee before the intense barrage of energy strikes, scared by the seemingly impossible events unfolding. Some had seen what can only be described as werewolves, other vampires, and some had claimed that previous owners of their homes had thrown them onto the street, claiming they had 'come back' to claim their property.

Deanna and Ariella had determined that the town itself was now cut off due to the intense nature of the energy now spewing from above. Several residents had tried to cross the barrier at various points after exiting their homes but had been burnt to a crisp for their efforts. However, it was not just humans who remained. Several council members continued to march through the town, searching for any sign of Jasmine and Ariella. Besides them, there were still dozens of vampires lurking in the shadows, now utilising the cover of the fallen buildings to move to places they otherwise would not have access to.

The humans may have fled, but now this was the chance of the vampires to take the town as their own. On the south side of town, looting had inevitably played out. As people fled for their lives, others had broken and smashed their way through jewellery stores, electrical outlets, and in many cases, private homes of the residents. Some who had refused to leave had fought back and been slaughtered for their troubles. But there was another point of interest in the south of Wealdstone. Something that had been building and building in strength as more and more energy poured from above. Just opposite what was now a pile of rubble sporting a shattered *Starbucks* logo, was a large construction fence, with all the usual safety signs warning people not to enter, and there was a danger of death. The warnings were not for show, for despite what was behind them not being a construction site, it was indeed a perilous voyage for those who decided to cross the threshold and didn't know what they were doing. A long time previously, a shop used to stand on this plot, and within it was a powerful corridor to the past. Not only to the past, but half way around the world. Nobody could figure out what it was, so it was all hushed up by those who knew about it, and the building was demolished. But within the confines of the fences, what had been within the building, could not be destroyed. For years, construction workers, teenagers, random passers-by who got too nosy, had all been enveloped in the temporal stream from within. However, the energy spewing out from the realm of the pain wraiths had been amplifying it beyond measure. Each time someone would cross the void, more time would pass than before.

Desmond had been the one to experience it first. If it was December the first now, by the time he appeared in the past, it was December the sixteenth there. And the gap was getting wider. The past was being pushed further away and, in the process, it was beginning to influence the town. Buildings were showing signs of cracking, there were sinkholes appearing all over the area, and before too much longer, this scientific miracle, would implode. The question was, could the pain wraith gateway be sealed before that happened, and take all its energy back with it? As Annie looked on at what used to be her favourite place in the world, she couldn't help but feel the pull to return. But she knew she couldn't go back. It would undoubtedly have been nearly a year in their time since she left and leaving behind an experimental place of witchcraft and monsters, and the body of the owner, would surely have put her on Victorian England's most wanted.

She placed her hand on the surrounding fence and could almost feel the energy pulsing from within. It had taken quite a lot of her own strength to break free from Jasmine's invisible restraints, but she was clearly using her power elsewhere. She didn't fully understand it yet, but she was weakened when she concentrated her power. Perhaps she had overstretched her abilities too often, or perhaps all the energy she was said to have stolen, was now dissipating, and she could not cope with the withdrawal.

Whatever the reasons, Annie knew she had to find help. She did not know where Desmond or Duncan were, or if her mother was indeed still alive. But this was the place she would come to learn, and maybe she still could. She pushed open one of the site doors, inevitably left unlocked by Desmond as he had chased after them, walked through onto the rubble, and closed the door behind her. Her hand covered her mouth as she looked in shock at the crater and piles of bricks that used to be Herman's Curiosities. As Annie began to walk around the site, she felt a wave of nausea, and staggered backwards, tripping over what felt like a book, and landing on her back.

Annie sat up, cautiously, where she could see the air moving in waves, almost like hot air coming from an engine. Her foot twitched and she kicked the object she had tripped over. Looking at it, she saw that it was indeed a book. Leaning forwards to pick it up, she couldn't help but smile. The cover had an elephant engraved on it. As she turned the front cover, she recognised the book from when she was a child. She had purchased the exact same one all those years ago. But Herman never stocked more than one of the same thing. How could this book be here if she had taken it away. In her confused state, she let the rear of the book slip from her hands, and she noticed a piece of paper fall from the back. She lowered the book to the floor and reached for the paper.

'Annie. My sweet Annie. I don't know where you went, but I wanted you to know that I hope you're with your mother. You've inspired me to be more like you. Always seeking out new adventures and exploring new possibilities. I hope that it brings you joy to know that wherever you are, I am living my life just as you told me. I'm returning this book to the store where we first found it, the place you loved the most, in the hopes that your spirit will one day find it, and you will know how very much I loved you. Forever yours, Dad.'

Annie's tears stained the page as she read those final words. Her father had always been a spiritual man, which is one of the reasons he never thought much about adventures. But while she didn't know where he was, or what had happened to him, she had something of his. A smile spread across her face as she thought about that. Her thoughts were interrupted, however, by movement on the other side of the fence. As she picked herself up, and slid the paper into her pocket, the door opened and standing there, clutching his side, and holding what looked like a necklace of some sort, was Duncan.

25

"We have to get you some help!"

Annie was now pleading with Duncan to listen, and she could not help but watch as the wounds in his leg and his abdomen appeared to be retracting.

"I just need a minute," he replied, taking heavy breaths, still clutching the unusual piece of jewellery.

Something clicked in the back of Annie's mind, that she had seen something like this before. Desmond had come to visit her, with details of the holy water ammunition idea, and they had been involved in a series of supernatural events in London, which had involved witchcraft and an amulet. There were reportedly three of them. They had found and destroyed one, Herman had come across a second, which had also been destroyed, but Desmond had leads on the third. After communicating information that he had a suspected location, he never revealed any further information about it.

"Is this what I think it is?" she asked Duncan directly.

He nodded.

"I borrowed it from Desmond when he wasn't looking. Figured after his experiments, I might need it."

"The amulet of immortality."

Annie was now in awe of the shimmering yellow stone at its heart, which appeared to continue to glow as it healed Duncan and his wounds.

"Everybody thinks I'm dead. It was a pretty bad explosion. I was pinned under the rubble, and I couldn't move. I bled out. I thought I was actually dead."

Duncan stopped moving and seemed to hold his breath as he stared ahead at nothing, and contemplated what his family must have gone through, or even if they were still alive.

"We have to find out what's happened to everyone else."

Duncan leapt back to his feet, now with a spring in his step, and tucked the amulet into his pocket. He took a few steps forward, before pausing and thinking over his decision. He gazed down at his wounds, which were now healed, and pulled the amulet from his pocket once more.

"Here., I think you should take it."

He handed the piece to Annie, who was a little confused.

"Why would I need it?" she asked, innocently, but fearing she would not like the answer.

"Because Jasmine wants you, and you're not as tough as I am."

Annie smirked.

"And which one of us was dead?"

Duncan laughed at the comeback and held his hands up in defeat. He winced, a small amount of pain still residing in his muscles, but other than that, he was now ready to fight once more.

"We need to get to the house," he suggested.

"What house?" Annie asked in reply.

"Our base of operations. Sort of like a hideout. Some of us live there, but it's mostly where we hide our technology, weapons, do our investigating. It's where everything happens."

Annie sure liked the sound of that. It beat hanging out in the back of a book store in Victorian England where there was no technology, and everything was done in secret.

"Let's go!"

She placed the necklace into her own pocket, alongside the note from her father, and Duncan led them back through the door in the fence, closing it and locking it behind them. As they made their way down the street, Duncan spotted a car, engine still running.

"That's handy. Never could hot-wire a car."

They climbed inside and closed the doors. Ahead of them, they saw what appeared to be a pile of burning bodies. As Duncan approached them, he slowed the car to take a look.

"What is it?" asked Annie.

"Vampires. They must've ventured too far out into the sunlight and burned to death."

Annie watched the pyre gradually extinguish itself as they moved past and out of the main part of town. She looked at the desolate buildings, and the bodies of the people who had just been too slow to escape. She felt sick in the pit of her stomach. Spending years learning and reading about it is one thing. Seeing the aftermath of it is quite another. She had only had to deal with minor issues in the past, but nothing on this scale. As Duncan approached the street where the mansion was based, he stopped the car.

"What are you stopping for?" asked Annie. "Isn't this it?"

Duncan looked around with a stealthy eye. He could see nothing out of the ordinary, but he was taking no chances. Glancing through the trees, he saw Deanna and Kathryn standing on the driveway, chatting. Duncan breathed a sigh of relief.

"Who are they?"

"Friends."

The two of them climbed out of the car and headed up the driveway. About half way up, Kathryn spotted him, and her face went white as a sheet, and her mouth dropped open. Noticing that her attention was diverted, Deanna turned to see what was so shocking, and she too became lost for words. After all, a dead man was now walking up their driveway. As Kathryn tried to formulate words, Duncan smiled, and Annie held the amulet high in the air. Deanna had seen it before, and knowing what it meant, she rushed to Duncan, Kathryn not far behind her, and they both embraced him in a hug.

"I don't believe it!" shouted Deanna.

"I do, but I still feel like I'm seeing things," replied Kathryn.

"How is everyone?" Duncan asked.

"A little overwhelmed with everything that has happened.

Grace and Daniella aren't speaking, with each other, or with Desmond. I think there's a few things you all need to talk about."

Duncan did not like the tone being suggested.

"You can't tell me that Kat?" he asked.

Kathryn shook her head.

"Family business."

She said the last two words with a tinge of sadness. She knew what the truth was, and he didn't. He had been through a death experience, but so had his family, and it had changed everything. She did not want to be around when it all blew up in there.

"Very well. Where is Desmond?" he asked.

At his very sentence, Desmond began walking towards his car, having just left the house.

"Desmond!" Duncan called.

Desmond stopped and hesitated for a moment, his face a look of shock and uncertainty. His eyes then moved across to Annie, and the look of shock deepened. Annie couldn't quite work it out, but there was something different about him. However, without signalling a reply,

Desmond continued to climb into his car, and as he tore down the driveway towards them, it was all they could do to get out of the way.

"What the fuck was that all about?" demanded Deanna.

Duncan watched as the car disappeared around a corner.

"I don't know, but that did not look like Desmond."

Kathryn interrupted the thought process.

"Let's get you back up to the house. You could do with a fresh set of clothes, and Ariella is just sitting in the woods… contemplating."

Duncan nodded, before completely forgetting he had company.

"OH! I completely forgot, I'm so sorry. This is Annie Weston. She's a friend from… work."

Annie smiled and held out a hand to shake, but the others just looked at each other and then looked back at her.

"What is it?" asked Duncan.

"Well… we've met your mother," replied Deanna.

Annie's heart nearly leapt out of her mouth.

"My… mother?"

Kathryn nodded.

"Ariella. She told us about you, and how she died saving you. It's a long story. We should get up to the house and she can explain everything."

Staggered and completely off centre, Annie followed the rest of the group up toward the main house. As they approached the porch, Duncan stopped and held his arm out.

"What is it?" asked Annie.

"Do you hear that?" he asked.

The others shook their heads, but gradually the sound began to meet their ears too. Almost like a distant scream.

"Hold on, I hear it now," replied Deanna. "Who is that?"

As the sound became louder, it was evident the source was getting closer and at a high speed. As Ariella emerged from the woods, a look of terror was cast over her face, her hands waving wildly.

"Get out of there!" she shouted.

"What is she doing?" Kathryn asked.

Duncan didn't have time to answer that question, because as he looked back towards the house, his eyes bulged, and there was an enormous flash from inside the house. In a seemingly frozen moment in time, he saw the onset of flames rushing toward him. The house exploded in a gargantuan fireball. The distinctive windows, and doors all blew out one by one as the fireball tore through the house. Glass fell from the sky like raindrops, shimmering in the sun. The walls blew out sending golden brick fragments metres away from the house. Duncan, Kathryn, Annie and Deanna were hit full force by a shockwave and debris, sending them flying through the trees landing in various points of the woodland nearby. Ariella held her hands forward, diverting the energy and pieces of wreckage away from her, almost shrouded in a violet ball of protective energy. The mansion, however, continued to explode.

The chimney crumbled as the roof began to collapse into the flames, the marble balconies, slipping from their perch, falling and crashing onto the ground, shattering into dozens of huge pieces. As the front of the building fell under its own weight, the remains of the inside of the house were exposed to the outside, and as the flames continued to rip through the back of the building, the structural supports in the basement failed, and the spectacular sight of an entire house sinking into the ground was visible. It was almost like watching a house of cards collapse from a great height. As the movement slowly ceased, and the groaning quietened, the flames too began to recede. The smoke slowly began to clear, and as Deanna managed to climb to her feet, some two hundred yards away, she found herself frozen in place.

The mansion was gone.

26

The absence of any police or ambulance sirens heading in their direction was now more deafening than the sounds themselves. The dust particles continued to fall from the sky, shimmering in the afternoon sunlight. Ariella, however, was now not looking at the pile of rubble before her. Her attention was focussed on the battered young woman standing, leaning on the nearest tree. She knew that Jasmine was behind this attack. She had felt her presence, hence her attempt to race towards the house to warn her newfound friends.

But her mind was only focussing on Annie. How she had grown, and how many years Ariella had missed, all because of one drunk driver. She had been in a family before, of course, back in Victorian England, but she had never expected to see one of her children again, and yet stood in the aftermath of destruction, there she was. Around her, however, cries of pain began to emerge from the self- imposed silence, and as her mind came back to the present, Ariella began to scan the fallout. Deanna was lumbering forwards, her face blackened by smoke and dust, and sticking out from her left side, was a large stake of splintered wood. The blood continued to darken her shirt, but she continued forward until she reached Annie, and began to check on the young woman, as her true mother watched on.

"Oh my God, Deanna, your side!" Annie exclaimed.

Deanna reached down and smiled slightly to herself. She grabbed the end of the wood, and tore it out of her body, like ripping off a band- aid. The blood began to pulse as she screamed in pain, but as quickly as it had started, the flow began to subside. She looked back at a horrified Annie and smiled again.

"Don't worry kid, I'll be fine, just give it a few minutes."

The pair looked at the sight before them and could do nothing but look on. As Kathryn and Duncan made their way over to Ariella, who was still transfixed on the scene playing out before her, nursing their own wounds, she decided to take charge.

"Ariella, what the fuck was that?" she demanded, grabbing her shoulders and shaking her vigorously.

"Jasmine."

The one word reply did nothing to quench Kathryn's thirst for details, and she continued to pressure her for more.

"How? That was Desmond! That explosion was our fail-safe device to protect the mansion from outsiders. Only Desmond and I knew about that. He set that off deliberately! Why?"

Ariella's gaze had returned to her daughter, who had now noticed her presence, and the two shared a seemingly endless stare, before Kathryn shouted her back to concentration.

"HEY!"

Ariella looked terrified. At the events, at her lack of readiness to see Annie, at her failure to see what was coming sooner, and it caused Kathryn to back down slightly.

"It wasn't Desmond. It was Jasmine. She's taken him."

Duncan looked to the ground. He had known something wasn't right when he saw Desmond's face. Ariella continued.

"And if she has taken possession of his body, then she knows everything he knows. *Everything.*"

The group were interrupted by the sound of a faint cry for help coming from the rubble.

"*Help!*"

Kathryn snapped her head around. She had been so focussed on finding answers, she had forgotten that her wife was trapped somewhere in that building, perhaps lying dead. The realisation hit her hard and she lost her calm demeanour and went into full on panic mode. How could she forget there were people in there? Kristin, Jack, Grace, Daniella. They were all still in there.

She sprinted for the rubble as the cry came once again and joined Deanna digging through wreckage for the second time in a matter of hours to save members of the team. Duncan placed a hand on Ariella's shoulder.

"Go to her. She needs you."

"I don't know what to say to her. She doesn't know what I am. She doesn't know what I've done. How can I just walk up to her and tell her I'm her mother?"

Duncan began to move away to help the others.

"We need all the help we can get right now, and she knows it. You might not be able to restart your relationship right away, but we need the two of you focussed. We have people in here."

He began tearing through the bricks, and glass with no difficulty at all, launching rubble meters into the air, his wolf-like strength really showing itself. Ariella felt that she had been 'out of the action' too much. Weakened by the presence of the elder blade, in the woods when the bombs were being triggered because she couldn't formulate a plan, and now she had potentially lost four of her colleagues. No longer. This was where she would draw that line in the sand and go on the offensive.

Annie now fed up with waiting for her mother to respond, had joined the others, giving a cursory look over her shoulder. Ariella though, was now focussed on the task at hand. Compartmentalising the different aspects of the job before her, she took large strides forward, and small sparks of purple electricity began to form on her fingertips.

Swipes of her hands, removed huge lumps of rock from the site, launching them into the air like asteroids flying in reverse, lost in the depths of space. The others digging towards the cries of pain, began to fall back, for fear they would be struck by these huge boulders. More angry swipes of her hands and thrusts into the sky, and the building began to lift piece by piece into the sky. As what used to be the large central staircase joined much of the other wreckage in being flown to the cosmos, the cry they had heard became crystal clear.

As Kathryn and Deanna closed in, they saw a hand reaching up, and grasped it with all the strength they could muster. As they pulled the hand, the rest of the body began to emerge, and a battered and bloody Kristin was lifted beyond the rocky depths of the house. Kathryn seriously had to restrain herself from gripping her wife in a loving embrace but could not prevent a few tears from slipping out. At the sight of this, Kristin, through the pain, smiled.

"You didn't think you'd gotten rid of me, did you?"

Kathryn laughed, wiping the tears from her face.

"You are the real indestructible member of this team, never mind Deanna!" she joked.

Kristin smiled back, but then her face fell, and her eyes rolled back as she fell unconscious. Kathryn's face returned to panic and fear, and despite the injuries her wife had, began to shake her violently.

"Kris! Come back! Wake up!"

Kristin snapped her head back up, scowling at her wife for such careless behaviour.

"Jesus can't a girl sleep!" she said.

Kathryn's heart was now visibly beating in her chest, her shirt moving with the rhythm. She lifted Kristin and carried her down the pile of debris, leaving the others to continue the search. As the kitchen doors were removed, Ariella stopped her efforts immediately. Annie noticed this and made her first contact with her mother since she was five years old.

"What is it?" she asked, not sure what else to say.

Only momentarily distracted by who had asked the question, Ariella replied.

"The containment jar. It's smashed."

Annie looked down at the fragments of broken glass.

"What does that mean?" she asked.

Deanna had noticed the change in behaviour and joined the mother and daughter.

"The jar is smashed, but my powers aren't being limited."

Annie did not understand, but Deanna did. She answered the question that Annie's expression was asking.

"Jasmine has the elder blade."

Ariella looked at her and nodded. But Annie's attention was distracted by something else in the vicinity of the broken glass.

"Oh no."

She pointed her arm towards the left of the cavity, and the others followed with their eyes until they fell on a discarded shoe, just peeking out from under the rocks and piles of books. Ariella gestured for the two of them to move back and she directed her powers at the stone and as each piece lifted, it revealed more of the gruesome reality that they had feared. When she stopped removing the rubble, lying before them, eyes wide open, but no life in his body, was Jack.

His face was bloodied and beaten from the explosion, his knee clearly dislocated, and his clothes darkened from his wounds. His eyes were wide with fear, but despite the miracles which seemingly kept Kristin alive, and brought Duncan back from the clutches of death, Jack was long gone, and beyond saving. Ariella broke down. This was the first time she had let the emotion wash over her and take a hold. Beyond the anger and the determination to take action, this had caught her completely off guard. Annie placed a hand on her arm, and Ariella placed her own hand on top of it.

"You knew him well?" she asked.

"He wanted to know who killed his fiancée. He blamed me and my people, and he wanted answers. I promised to help him find them. He never really trusted me, but I felt like I owed him. And now he will never know."

She broke down again, and the uncharacteristic show of sadness caught the attention of Kathryn and Deanna, who had managed to drag Grace from the rubble at the other end of the house. As Kathryn laid eyes on Jack's body, she too began to weep. Kristin lay in the background and watched helplessly as her wife shed tears for someone, she had been very close to. She'd had her concerns over his presence at first, but she could not help but feel her wife's pain at this moment. Grace also began to feel tears moving down her blackened skin. Until she saw Duncan. Her mind went into flux and couldn't focus on anything other than the image before her.

"Dad?" she asked, in a high pitched voice.

Duncan span around and felt a wave of relief wash over him. He ran over and embraced his daughter, who still felt like she was being hugged by a ghost. Before she could formulate any words, Duncan held up the amulet, having found it on the ground following the explosion.

"Thought I might have needed this. Guess I was right."

The two continued to hug while the others wept over Jack. And yet nobody seemed to realise that somewhere under the rubble, was Daniella.

"Where's your mother?" Duncan asked.

Grace simply looked down at the carnage before them and held a hand to her face. Through her fingers, she muffled a response.

"I think she was in the basement."

Duncan sprang back into action and began launching rocks and wood and steel fragments into the air. As Ariella gently lifted Jack's body out of the hole and onto the grass, the others put aside their grief for the time being and began to help continue the search. Duncan shouted back towards Ariella.

"HEY! Get over here! Daniella was in the basement!"

Ariella took one last look at Jack, waved her hand over his eyes to close them, and walked over to the others, joining Duncan in launching the obstacles into the sky. Twenty minutes went by, and still they had not found Grace's mother. Just as it looked hopeless, they came across the steel reinforced door to the basement and stopped. Duncan knew this door well. It had been installed to keep him within its boundaries. The necessary containment of a violent and ferocious beast. A killing machine. He could not do anything to fix those actions, but he was determined to find his wife.

As Ariella lifted the door, however, the sight before them was one designed to mock their very efforts. Grace turned away and began to be violently sick, such was the devastation before them. Revealed beneath the door, was indeed Daniella. Her body had been impaled on a metal spike which seemed to have been fashioned from the silver used to create their ammunition. Her arms had been cut from her torso, but remained in chains, the same of her legs. Had this been a medieval setting, you would have assumed she had been hung drawn and quartered. However, her head whilst wrapped in chain, was still attached, and impaled on the same metal rod of silver as her body, was a note, folded in half. On the top was written two words.

"For Ariella."

27

As Desmond crashed through the door, his hands gripped the sides of his head, digging into his temples, like there was an internal wrestling match going on inside his mind. He span on the spot three times, before collapsing to the floor, pounding the floorboards with his fists, screaming in anger.

"Get out… get out… GET OUT YOU FUCKING BITCH!"

He picked up the chair in which Annie was previously an occupant and launched it across the room, smashing into dozens of wooden fragments. What followed was an incredible display of what to an outsider would appear to be a split personality on full display.

"Get out of my head!"

"This is where I live now, Desmond."

"No! What you did, you killed my friends!"

"We killed them, Desmond. Your knowledge caused their demise. Now they will learn. They are nothing. They will all fall."

"No, you made me do it! It… it wasn't me."

"Oh, but it was. I'm sorry Desmond, but it's time for you to go."

"NO! You will NOT take control of me! I will stop you!"

An evil cackle emerged from Desmond's own throat, continuing the madness unfolding in this solitary room.

"It's not your choice, Desmond. My daughter will know. You've now outlived your usefulness."

"Daniella… what you made me do to her… I… that wasn't me."

"She was weak. All that power, and all that ability, and for what? None of them are a match for me. It's clear to me now that the exposure of my realm has already taken hold of this pathetic little town. So, the only option now, is to wipe it off the map."

"You can't do that! What about your daughter?"

"She ceased being my daughter the day she sent me back in chains! And as for my so-called granddaughter… no flesh and blood creation is worthy of our care and devotion. She is no granddaughter of mine!"

"You would kill your own family?"

"I have no family, Desmond."

Desmond felt his hand reach into his coat pocket and slowly draw the elder blade from the fabric, and he held it in front of his face, watching the metal glint in the light.

"You took this, even though it takes away your powers. Why?"

"I've had an untapped source of energy within me for decades, Desmond. But your weaponry in the past disrupted the balance. The silver and garlic elements had an unexpected effect on me. Since then, I have been unable to concentrate my power in long bursts. I suspect that is how my granddaughter was able to escape. I was too focussed on controlling you. So, it's time to level the playing field. If I cannot demonstrate my powers, then neither will Ariella."

"What are you planning to do?"

There was no response from Jasmine inside his head. Without his consent, he found his mind thinking up the images of the time rift on the former location of Herman's Curiosities.

"No, you can't!"

An internal laugh rattled around his mind.

"Take some credit, Desmond. If it wasn't for you, I wouldn't even know of this phenomenon. It has the perfect concentration of energy for me to complete my mission."

"But how will you do it? We don't know enough of how this thing works! All we know is that it is becoming more and more unstable, the more energy that spills through from your realm!"

"You've got it all wrong, Desmond. It's the gateway to the realm of screams that is being affected by the energy of the time rift. With the right push, it should implode, and take this pathetic little town with it."

"Please don't do this!"

Desmond knelt on the floor, and held his hands together, praying to an invisible force.

"I'm afraid it's too late for you Desmond. This is where you check out."

Desmond suddenly found a glimmer of light in the darkness and had a small chuckle to himself.

"And how do you plan to facilitate that? May I remind you, I am immortal? That's one of the reasons you took over my body, wasn't it?"

Another internal giggle took away his confidence almost immediately.

"You've never tangled with a pain wraith before, have you Desmond? When we take over a vessel, the act of conflicting minds, gradually burns away the person within. Needless to say, once you have been erased from existence from within, if I will your body to die, then it will die."

"No, no, NO!"

Desmond leapt to his feet, and sprinted for the door, but as he reached the handle, from within, it was as if a switch had been flicked, and he simply dropped to the floor. Moments later, the motionless body reached its hands out on to the wooden floor, and began to push itself up, gradually rising until fully standing.

"On the other hand, perhaps there is a little usefulness left in this body. Thanks Desmond."

28

As Duncan placed the final shovel of Earth onto the make shift graves, the surviving members of the group stood back, heads hung to the ground. This series of events had cost them dearly. Grace was perhaps the one hit the hardest. She had taken so long to tell Max how she had felt, and then after just three months together, she had lost him.

Scarlett had become her best friend, and she was gone too. She thought she had lost her father, but then the joy surrounding his survival was replaced by the horror of losing her mother. And potentially her biological father, as much as she hated him now the truth was out, was also gone. She was feeling as though a huge claw had come down and tore her entire family out of existence and punished her with survival to endure the pain. Perhaps she would be suited to the realm of the pain wraiths. Kathryn cut another bleak figure on the side-lines. The level of guilt she was harbouring was immense. She was the one who had harassed Jack into coming to Wealdstone. She was convinced somehow that these interactions had caused the death of his fiancée somehow, and it was her and Daniella that had led this team, alongside Desmond. And now they were both gone, and Desmond all but lost. She had no idea where to turn next. How can they fight something so capable of tearing them apart with such ease? She glanced over to Deanna, who was redressing Kristin's wounds. She was out of whatever came next, that was for sure. Broken ribs, broken leg, and who knows what other injuries, and no access to a hospital. And now no home to shelter in. The mansion was gone, their street amongst dozens of others was now completely destroyed. It was time to face facts. Wealdstone was gone. Now it was up to them to ensure that it was the only casualty.

Deanna finished dressing Kristin's lacerations. They had tried to share some humour over the fact that Kristin had seemingly survived by being in the bathroom at the time of the explosion, but then they each dwelled on the imagery of Daniella's mutilated body, and the conversation ground to a halt. Ariella on the other hand was consumed. She sat on the remains of the kitchen, reading the note left by her mother over and over again. Annie was perched next to her, trying to reconnect, but her mother was now consumed. Everything that had gone before was now the past. She had one goal now, and that was to avenge all those that had been lost, and if it cost her life too, then that was the price she was willing to pay.

"Mom, how are you doing?"

Despite her daughter using the word 'Mom' for the first time in decades, Ariella was consumed by the contents of the note, which she was now reading for the twentieth time.

'My daughter,

You tried it your way, and all you did was risk our exposure. I tried to take you home, and you pushed me away. Now I'm going to tear you apart, just like your friend here. If she is the strongest you could put forward, then this fight is already over. These chains will soon be yours.

See you soon, daughter.'

As the fury peaked within her, the paper began to burn in violet flames, and Ariella's fists began to tremble, the sparks becoming more and more frequent and intense. Annie jumped up as the ground around her began to shake, something which the others noticed. The ball of hate within the chest of the pain wraith built and built, like a tumour, and Ariella tilted her head back, pushed her hands out to the side, and seemingly exploded in a massive four way projection of light, a deafening scream echoing around the entire town, through the empty buildings, and along the deserted streets. Kathryn, Deanna, Grace and Duncan watched on as the incredibly colourful display played out before them, Annie crouched next to her mother, shielding her eyes from the brightness. This was the first time they had seen the extent of Ariella's abilities, and while they were frightening to behold, Kathryn began to feel confidence growing within her. They just might win this fight. But they would need to get that blade away from Jasmine. As the light show came to an end, and Ariella fell forwards, gasping for breath, the group walked over to her, and Kathryn led the pitch.

"That's a nice light show you put out there."

Ariella looked up at her, with her chest still heaving as she tried to catch her breath.

"Thanks."

Kathryn knelt in front of her, and spoke directly to her eyes, flickering with lightning, and slightly mesmerizing.

"We are going to win this fight. And you're going to help wipe the floor with that crazy bitch you call mother. You're not just going to kill her, you're going to rip her to pieces, parcel her into a nice little box with a purple bow on it, and shove it up the asshole of that realm you come from."

A smile began to spread over Ariella's face, and this seemed infectious. A slight chuckle began to spread through the team, despite the death, despite the sadness, the anger and misery. Once more, even though they had never been down as much as they were now, the sparkle began to return to their eyes, and hope began to return also.

"And how do we do that, Captain?" asked Ariella.

With a smile, Kathryn looked around, and gave her reply.

"We are going to kill Deanna."

29

"I'm sorry, just run that by me again?"

Duncan looked at his daughter for clarification, but didn't find any, as Grace appeared to be just as confused as he was. Thankfully, Kathryn and Deanna reiterated their seemingly suicidal plan.

"Jasmine has taken over Desmond, because he has knowledge of all of us, our operations, and because she thinks she can use him to get between us and take us apart from the inside," Kathryn begun.

"Which she has done," interrupted Grace.

Kathryn brushed off the comment and continued.

"She has the elder blade which gives her a level playing field, with neither her or Ariella able to utilise their power, but she has the body of an immortal man with hundreds of years of martial arts and self- defence training, which gives her an advantage."

Deanna took over the explanation.

"By wearing my son as a suit, she thinks it will make us weaker. But thanks to Ariella, we know that Desmond is gone. There is no use dwelling on the fact that we can't change."

Despite what she just said, Deanna paused to try and contain her emotions, before continuing.

"So, our best chance is to remove that advantage by one of two ways. Ariella?"

Stepping in from the side line, Ariella held aloft the amulet of immortality, before explaining their two options.

"First option is to wait for her to come to Deanna. I think she will use Desmond's form to try and lure us into a trap. She has done it before, back in the olden days, I fully expect it's a tactic she would employ again."

"And the second option?" asked Annie.

"The second option is to flip that on her, and for me to inhabit Deanna's body, making the playing field even again. Two immortal beings, with no pain wraith abilities, fighting it out."

Grace did not like the sound of this plan. Deanna was like an Aunt to her, and she had already lost enough.

"Woah, but you just said that once a wraith takes over a body, the person inside burns away! That means Deanna would be gone!"

Duncan placed a hand on her shoulder, but he too expressed his concern over this idea.

"Grace is right. We've lost enough people already, we don't need to lose another, to put a plan into action that probably won't even work."

Deanna took the amulet and held it high, waving it at the group.

"You're forgetting that we have this. If Ariella is in control of my body, then she can contain Jasmine in the final fight. In the meantime, the rest of you will be flanking in positions around them both. Your goal will be to wound Desmond's body in such a way that a normal human would not survive…"

Deanna flinched at the thought of the next part of her sentence.

"… and stuff the amulet inside the wound."

Annie wretched at that idea, and the image of such violence brought back the image of Daniella's demise, and there were many disgusted looking faces across the board, including from Kristin, who was sat perched in the back of the pickup truck.

"So, you think one of us can catch her off guard and stuff her like a Christmas turkey? If she is as advanced and skilled as you say she is, then one flick of that blade and we are toast!" Kristin pointed out.

Kathryn stepped forward to once again reaffirm her position as leader.

"Look, she is clearly planning to take us all out. Ariella had already told us that her goals were always to keep their realm a secret and now it's such a widespread exposure, we have to assume the next goal is sterilisation. That means nobody lives. We know we can't leave the town, because of some sort of energy barrier, which means the fight is here."

Ariella stood beside her in solidarity.

"We have one shot at this. Hurt her, take Desmond's body out of the equation so she's forced out, and then dispatch her with the elder blade."

Deanna then moved to form a trio of powerful figures.

"If it takes my life to save the rest of you, that's my decision to take, and if it saves millions of others, that's a bonus I guess."

Duncan, Grace and Annie still weren't happy at the thought of losing yet another team member, but when they pressed each other for alternatives, they found nothing. The three of them moved to join the three women, and they nodded to each other that this was the only course of action they could take. Ariella spoke one last sentence of inspiration.

"We have to stop Jasmine at all costs. Whatever it takes."

Kathryn and Deanna nodded and agreed.

"Whatever it takes."

"Whatever it takes."

From the background in the pickup truck, the seriousness was broken by Kristin.

"So, who gets to say, '*Avengers Assemble*?"

The group began to laugh. And then came the question that had not yet been asked but was a crucial factor in the plan. Annie looked at Ariella with a puzzled face, having completely missed out on the *Avengers* joke, and spoke first.

"Just one thing. How do we find her?"

Ariella smiled and didn't seem to be concerned about that.

"We are going to lure her to the waterfront."

"And how do you plan to do that?" Annie asked.

Ariella paused for moment before answering that question.

"You know, I forgot how inquisitive you really are," she said to her daughter.

The bond was now beginning to show itself naturally, and both women could feel it.

"Just trust me. I have a plan."

30

The waterfront of Wealdstone was disturbingly empty. As the waves lapped at the shore, gently caressing the sand, the memories of the events that had occurred here over the last twenty years had left their mark.

The still fire damaged pier that had been closed for five years after the explosion the night of the first John Martin murder, had only seen a few of the units rebuild and reopen, with a new structure being built further down the beach, before the world went to shit. The car park next to the Exhibition Centre, where a man called James had been the victim of a pain wraith lightning bolt too and gone on a rampage killing four people before being arrested by Sam Greenwood. The tool store where Scarlett had become another wraith victim and murdered several people, windows still smashed to pieces, and the door hanging off its hinges.

The street on which Sisko's Bar had been located, where Kathryn and Kristin had met up with Grace and Daniella following their ordeal on board the *Sapphire Serpent*. So much death. So much suffering. And that was just in this one part of the town. But now this area had a new purpose. It was where everything would come to a head.

And yet looking around, Deanna could not help but feel

more frightened by how everything was portraying the death of what had come to be her home. As her eyes flowed from one battered building to another, she almost floated above everything, forgetting the reason she was there.

Her gaze moved over the shattered glass from the store fronts that had blown out during the high activity, the sunshine shimmering in the fractured fragments. In the reflections, she could make out the stereotypical letters hanging from the sign on the old cinema. She remembered seeing one of the last movies to be shown there before the place closed down. But she had come a long way since that eight p.m. showing of *Fast and Furious 9* two years ago. She took one last look around before taking a deep breath and closing her eyes. This was it. There was no going back. After hundreds of years of trying to find a way out of this life, and the dozens of meaningless ways she had tried to complete such an act, she was finally going to achieve that goal, but in a noble way, with an incredible purpose. All Deanna had ever wanted was to have a life with purpose, and these people she had come to know and love, had given her just that.

And Desmond.

Her son had come to be the most important part of her life and kept her going day after day. While they had not been very close in the last couple of years, she felt she had owed him a great debt. He helped her find the team, which gave her that very purpose. And now he was gone. Taken from her. She wanted more than anything to rip Jasmine apart herself, but she knew she had no chance. As she gazed across the water once more, watching the light glinting off the crests of the waves, shimmering in the movement, she closed her eyes once more. She had said her goodbyes to the others, and she had come to terms with Desmond's loss, as painful as it was. This was her time. Before too much longer, the time rift would absorb so much energy, it would tear the town apart. It had to be now.

"I'm ready."

From out of the darkness of the underside of the pier, a violet mist emerged, twisting in spirals slowly moving towards Deanna. It surrounded her, almost brushing her skin, before moving tighter like a boa constrictor, moving Deanna's hair and lifting her body a foot off of the ground. As the fog grew thicker and more vibrant, it left Deanna, still floating and moved away towards the water, before turning back, and launching at speed directly into her chest. The entire mass immersed itself within her, and as the last strand vanished within, Deanna's body fell to the floor. The merging was complete. And the battle was about to begin.

31

The scene reminded Grace of one of those old westerns she used to be forced into watching when she was a little kid. Duncan had always loved westerns. His favourite *Back to the Future* movie was the third one, purely because of the Old West setting. His favourite *Star Trek the Next Generation* episode was *Fistful of Datas*. Although to look at her father, you never would have guessed that was his thing. Her father. So much had happened in the last few days and weeks. Duncan *was* her father. Nothing would change that. He raised her, he loved her, and she loved him. But a part of her still wondered if she would have come to know Desmond as a father figure too. He had always been stern and decisive when it came to the action part of the job but was always locked away developing some new form of weaponry, or off into the past with Annie. Would have been nice to have gone back just once to see what it was like, she thought.

But with everyone now getting into their final positions, the modern Wild West showdown was about to begin. But this one, would change everything. Grace was sat on top of the now battle scarred *Holiday Inn* hotel, behind the giant green neon sign, weaponry in hand, and a bag full of ammunition at her side. They knew the silver and garlic concentration destabilised Jasmine's ability to concentrate her powers somehow, so hopefully, with her powers restricted by the elder blade, they might help stop her. This had to work. Everything was riding on it.

Grace had lost so much, and she feared that before this was over, she would lose a lot more. Her father, and her aunt were in this to the end, whatever it took. And so was she.

32

As he watched his daughter nestling down across the street on top of the hotel building, Duncan could not help but feel like he had been given a second chance with her. Something had told him when he lay on the table in the back of Herman's shop to take the amulet from Desmond. He didn't know why at the time, but he was proven right in the end. Maybe someone really was watching out for him. But Daniella was gone.

He would never get that image out of his mind. He had loved that woman through everything since they were in school together. Even during the times when their relationship took a violent turn into infidelity. He knew she was seeing somebody else, but his attention was so focussed on the toy store, and running a successful business, he had neglected her, and with a personality as strong as hers, he had always felt like he had pushed her away but was too scared to do anything about it.
It's strange how everyone was reflecting on what had gone before. Nobody was expecting to come out of this alive, and it was almost as if their lives were flashing before their eyes.

The biggest regret Duncan had though when it came to his wife, was the day he realised that Grace was not his daughter. He never let on that he knew, but he had seen

Daniella with Desmond on the day she had told him. That day had been like a dagger through his heart. And yet still, he stuck with her. That was love. Or blind stupidity. They often coincided. But Grace was his daughter. She had been through so much incredible trauma, and pain. He wanted to just take it all away and throw it into the sky to burn up in the atmosphere. The irony of fighting a being of pure pain was not lost on him. This fight meant everything. And if they lost, then the pain would win. He often thought back to the night of terror they suffered at the cabin up in Alaska. The night that changed everything. When Daniella revealed her true self, and the horrifying transformation of his body had begun. The emotions raging through him twenty-four hours a day of just pure anger, and hatred for himself and everything around him. The uncontrollable thirst for violence and blood.

As damaging as Desmond's presence had been to his marriage and his family, he did have to thank him for one thing. The experimental treatment that rid him of his vampire tendencies. He was free to live his life and protect the only family members he had left.
But in truth, these people were his family now. They had all suffered loss and heartache. And as he watched the purple mist of Ariella's true form enter Deanna's body in the distance on the beach, he reminded himself that the team would take a bigger battering before this all came to an end.

33

Annie was out of her time and out of place. She had not been in Wealdstone, or the modern day in fact, since she was a teenager. And yet although the majority of the damage was contained to this one little town, she felt like she had skipped the modern day era and gone straight to the post-apocalyptic wastelands of the future. She wasn't at home here. This was no longer where she considered she belonged. Too much time had passed.

Nobody had prepared her for any of this. She used to be a small child, obsessed with exploration and knowledge of wildlife and the environment, and mysteries of the non-deadly kind. And now she found herself the granddaughter of a deranged supernatural being, who was hunting down her mother, who was also a supernatural being, to potentially end the human race as they knew it. Seriously, she felt like she had read that in a book somewhere, it was that far-fetched. She looked across the main street leading to the waterfront, at her new found friends, scattered around the place in their various flanking positions, and wondered if she would be as close to them as they were to each other, if she had never fallen back through time. She had always wanted friends like them. Although she had now become knowledgeable in the likes of incantations, and potential ammunition against the paranormal and supernatural, which was a far cry from the young girl desperate to learn about African Mythology, she still had not amassed much of a friend base or developed a family of her own. And now before she had that chance, it could all be coming to an end. Ariella was her ray of hope.

As far as Annie was concerned, she had lost her mother the day she was pushed out of the way of that car outside Herman's Curiosities. She remembered watching the life fade from her eyes, and Herman taking her aside as the paramedics arrived and crowded her mother. She missed him. He was like the grandfather she never had. She'd never met her paternal grandfather as Arthur's dad had died before she was born, and she never knew if she even had a maternal grandfather. Did he exist in corporeal form before Ariella took over Caroline's body? Was he a pain wraith too? Did he even exist?
These were all questions that she felt she would never now get the answer to. She cradled the immortality amulet in her hand. It remained dark and empty. No injuries to heal, no power. But although Annie was fine physically, just like the others, she was reliving a lot of injuries on the inside.

34

Kathryn was perhaps the most relaxed of the group, given the circumstances. She gazed out at the deserted, and rubble filled streets, but did not feel the same kind of impending doom that the rest of the group were feeling. She, whilst losing some of those closest to her, including her sister-in-law, had gained so much more during all of this than she had lost. She had met her wife, during her confrontational experience with John Martin, opening up the haunted museum. Had it not been for the deranged pain wraith energy that took him over, it's possible they wouldn't have met. And even through the deadly sequence of events involving the *Sapphire Serpent* and its ghostly crew, they had both come out stronger, and still together.

The biggest challenge they had faced was the arrival of Jack. The more intense the workload became in Wealdstone, with all the activity, and unexplained behaviour, the more she had seemed to drift away from Kristin. Then when Jack showed up, it was like something dormant within her began to emerge on the surface. The afternoon she almost slept with him, she really began to think that it was over between her and Kristin. But the second her wife was in danger, it was like Jack became just another cog in the machine that was the team, and her heart beat only for Kristin. As she thought back to those moments, she began to think that perhaps she should have told her that more often. So many times, she thought she had lost her, and yet time and time again, she would survive the odds and come back fighting. Of course, this time, she was out of the fight. And to be honest, Kathryn was glad about that. At least this time, she wouldn't have to worry about her wife being in danger. But she did worry a little that she might not see her again. As prepared as the team felt they were, this was something on a scale they had never imagined possible. Only time would tell, but she suspected that if they did succeed, it would be at great cost.

Kathryn just hoped she would still be here at the end of it all to hold Kristin's hand again.

35

The rift on the site of Herman's Curiosities was now visibly glowing to anyone foolish enough to walk near it. It had absorbed so much energy from all around it and from the gateway to the realm of screams, that it had an ominous violet haze. Jasmine stood there admiring it. Too long had she been deprived of her true power. Too long had it been since she felt the combined energy of those five million souls rushing through her very being. She had become weak, not only by her own standards, but by those of any pain wraith. She had not wanted to admit it to herself, but she knew she was no longer a match for her daughter. And then she stumbled on this wonderful phenomenon.

It was not very often a scientific and a supernatural co-existence was possible, but here was an untapped source of energy, and Jasmine planned to utilise it. Desmond's body was simply an insurance policy if this should fail to work, but she was confident it would. When she slaughtered those five million traitors as she called them, she simply moved into their dissipating energy and absorbed it like a living sponge. And thanks to the rift absorbing the energy directly from her own realm, she believed the same would be true again. If it worked, then not even the elder blade she held in her hand would quench her powers entirely. As long as she didn't feel the tip of its blade across her throat. So much had led to this moment. When she first decided to conceive a child with the leader of the Council of Thirty-Two, her intention was to create the next leader of the pain wraiths. To strengthen their species, and take them into new territories, new dimensions, and truly make them a force to be reckoned with. Someone who could traverse the gateways and explore the universe unchallenged. But what she didn't count on was her daughter growing a human-like sense of curiosity and adventure. Their moral compass had corrupted her being, and she was becoming too righteous, every day growing in defiance.

It soon became apparent to Jasmine that her realm must be kept secret. Nobody must be allowed to cross the gateway but the wraiths. It was the wraiths who must remain the truly powerful, and Ariella risked exposing that link. As painful as it was, she realised that her daughter must be destroyed. Training her as she matured and grew was a highlight of her existence. Watching her learn to fly short distances, to manipulate matter on a small scale, and grow into her powers, was wondrous. She almost forgot her initial task and began to slowly slip closer to that human way of mothering her child. And then Ariella's defiance when she first refused to go back to the realm of screams snapped her right back to reality. She had chased her daughter across the centuries to bring her back. She genuinely felt she had gotten a hold on her when she had instructed her, she could not travel back through time to fix past mistakes. As she watched her daughter destroy the human race over millennia, finally, her dream of a unified mother daughter team, with the wraiths as the dominant force was beginning to come back into the realms of possibility. But for that one stupid human. Mace ruined everything.

By showing her, he was willing to sacrifice his life to stop her, even though he was now the last human alive, showed her that anything was possible. At the time of her entering the sun around Titan, she thought back to where she had been when it all started to go wrong, and when she found herself transported back there, that was when Jasmine truly knew she had lost her daughter. And it was then that she knew she must be destroyed.
As she stood before the now humming gap between times, she smiled to herself. She glanced down at Desmond's hands, wondering just how much punishment this body could take.

"I guess now is the time to find out," she said to herself.

As she stepped forwards, leaving the elder blade behind her on the ground, stabbed into the Earth like a tether, she could feel the hairs on Desmond's body rising. The ground began to quake slightly, the closer she got. Another step forward, and a bolt of lightning struck out from the rift and hit her in the left arm, pushing her shoulder back, before it retreated. Jasmine felt a jolt of adrenaline rush through her, and her smile widened. She stepped forward again, and this time two individual bolts

~ 339 ~

shot forward hitting her legs, forcing her to her knees. But again, a huge rush went through her. It was as if she was plugging herself into an electrical outlet. She was recharging. With a final roar of intent, she rushed forward, and was impaled by a huge beam of energy that shot right through Desmond's chest and raised his body up from the ground. The power surged through Jasmine, and she screamed through Desmond's mouth both with extreme pain, and ecstasy as she felt herself becoming reborn from within.

The whole area was pummelled with shockwaves of energy, rippling the dirt and the rubble on the ground, as wave after wave of energy was absorbed by Jasmine. Her eyes began to glow with such intensity that they too lit up the surrounding area. Desmond's skull seemed to become a glowing beacon, transmitting light through the skin. The scene almost resembled a *Doctor Who*-style regeneration. Beams of energy now erupted from every limb of Desmond's body. Wherever the beams struck was obliterated. Chunks of already ruined buildings, cars, anything that was in the direct path was turned to dust, if it wasn't already, and if it was, then that dust was turned to atoms. The power surging through the body was god-like.

As the power within Jasmine grew, the rift became smaller and smaller, its glow was diminishing. As she let out one final scream of triumph, Desmond's skin began to fracture. Cracks appeared on his face, and along the veins in his hands and down his neck. The energy was burning the body from the inside. As Jasmine's scream stopped, the rift closed up, all of its energy was absorbed, and Jasmine dropped to the ground, landing in a superhero pose, one knee cracking the ground with the impact. The time rift was gone. But the impact it had left was devastating.

As Jasmine rose from the ground, she took deep breaths through Desmond's lungs. His skin was now mottled and burnt, as if it were made of clay that had been scorched by the sun. But the smile was apparent. Jasmine held one of his arms out to the side, and the elder blade left the ground where it had been and moved to meet the palm of the hand. As she held the blade, the momentary euphoria of the power she had absorbed did decrease substantially, but not entirely.

Jasmine gripped the handle, and gazed around the area, spotting a car abandoned nearby, that had seemingly survived any type of damage. Not even a scratch, she thought to herself.

"Well, we can't have that," she said. "It doesn't fit the scene here."

With one thrust of her other hand, a beam of white and purple energy shot towards the car, and it exploded in a huge fireball that was far more devastating than it should have been, such was the power of the energy shot towards it. Across town, standing on the beach, catching her bearings, Ariella, now inhabiting Deanna's body, felt the shift in the air, and heard the screams and explosions. And as she watched, a mauve shimmer cascaded down in the sky, like a bubble being popped. It appeared the town of Wealdstone was no longer containing the effects of what was happening here. The energy barrier was gone. Now the rest of the world truly was in danger. The pit of her newly taken stomach sank. She felt that their advantage had now gone, and that Deanna's sacrifice had been in vein before they had even begun. But it was too late. They had no choice. It was Jasmine, or them.

Time to go to war.

36

The sky had darkened considerably, and the wind was now whipping up a storm. The waves were growing in the water, and as the waves crashed down onto the sand, the noise was growing with each impact. The atmosphere was now turning sour, and every member of the team felt a weight on their shoulders. But this was not a problem for their nemesis. Jasmine strolled down Main Street, each step forming a crack in the ground beneath it. Sparkles of white electricity shot out randomly as she moved along, striking brickwork, and sending little shards of debris scattering to the floor.

"Where are you daughter?" she shouted aloud as she moved.

Duncan looked across the street to Grace, with a newly installed case of dread. Duncan gestured with his head, and Grace followed his gaze to see that Desmond's hand was clutched around the elder blade. This was not a good sign. A demonstration of power despite holding the instrument which was meant to suppress it was probably the worst sign they could have wished for.

"Not willing to show yourself? Well perhaps an incentive is needed."

Without even looking in her direction, Jasmine threw out Desmond's hand to the right, and a beam of pure white obliterated the front of the old cinema, on top of which Annie was poised, and her scream was audible as she tumbled down the cliff of rubble, several boulders and bricks striking her as she fell. As the others watched on, Annie's limp body crashed to the floor, just feet from Jasmine's position. Grace covered her mouth, and began to well up, before she noticed that Annie was still breathing. She held up a hand to her father, signalling Annie was okay, and then attempted to refocus her attention. Jasmine was not impressed at the lack of response and began to grow angrier.

"ANSWER ME!" she bellowed, and swung her arms around in different directions, hitting the buildings where the rest of the team were scattered, sending them all running for their lives, as structure after structure began collapsing.

An up thrusted hand into the sky began to part the clouds until it formed a clear gap, from which a lightning bolt then flew down and struck the old pier on the beach, completely erasing it from the landscape, leaving not even a scrap of material intact. Knowing that an assault on Jasmine was now or never, Kathryn opened fire on her with everything she had, as she ran from rooftop to rooftop. The bullets struck Desmond's body with a thud after each impact, briefly lowering the intensity of the strikes Jasmine herself was dishing out, but not by the same margin they had previously.

Jasmine spun around and directed both hands towards Kathryn's position, narrowly missing her as she leapt through a glass window, into the next building, glass falling down behind her onto the street. She glanced down at the newly formed slice in her thigh but couldn't stop. The onslaught continued, and as Kathryn pushed her way through the building towards the ground, she felt the whole place falling above her. She raced down the stairs as quickly as she could, as the ones she had just used fell into nothing. She made it down the to the ground level as the last remnants of the building fell behind her, a cloud of dust encompassing her like a sandstorm.

As Jasmine lost sight of her target, she felt more bullets penetrating Desmond's back. His healing powers were not keeping these wounds regenerating at full power any longer. It seemed the amount of energy he had absorbed had weakened his capability. But still this body was a useful tool. Again, she turned and fired powerful beams towards Duncan's position, but he was much more agile than the others, and he leapt not only from rooftop to neighbouring rooftop but was able to leap across the street to avoid being hit. Jasmine had never been one for target practice and was becoming more and more frustrated at trying to get rid of these pestering little mortals.
She let out a little cry of pain, as she felt an arrow bury itself into Desmond's shoulder. She ceased firing towards Duncan, and pulled it out of the flesh, causing her to

wince. She examined the arrow. Pure silver. She growled with anger at how such a feeble element could destabilise her concentration so easily, snapping it and throwing it to the ground. Another arrow hit Desmond's left thigh, and Jasmine screamed in both pain and frustration. Tearing this one from her flesh too, she spotted Grace preparing to launch another arrow from her crossbow and reached her hand forward to direct an energy beam towards her and obliterate her once and for all.

But nothing happened.

A strange green ribbon of light began to wind its way around Desmond's wrists, almost like invisible restraints. Jasmine thrust her arms forwards again, but again she was restricted, only managing small sparks of energy. She looked around her frantically, until she spotted Annie, still lying in the rubble, mouthing words quietly.

"*Magic!*" Jasmine proclaimed. "I should have killed you when I had the chance!"

As more bullets were fired from Kathryn's gun, Jasmine dropped to her knees, and closed her eyes, concentrating as hard as she could, mustering all her power. She thrust the elder blade into the ground, and curled up into a ball, and as she began to make Desmond's body glow, she leapt upwards, and a huge ball of white light erupted from her form, casting away the green incantation energy, and sending a ripple so wide and powerful that it blew Annie clean out of the rubble she had been laying in and threw her a quarter of a mile through the air, tumbling like a leaf on the wind, until she fell from the sky and crashed into the water of the ocean with such force, she was knocked unconscious, but not before she felt at least half a dozen bones break on impact. Jasmine was now in a furious state, as if she hadn't been before. There was nowhere safe from the immense power being displayed. The street was now little more than mounds of shattered brick, glass and stone, and there was nowhere left for anyone to hide.

As she targeted Grace, Duncan and Kathryn, each one was blasted from their feet, and dispatched with ease. None could get close enough to enact any part of their plan. Duncan was sent hurtling through the side of an eighteen-wheel truck, and Kathryn was buried beneath what used to be a pharmacy. As Grace dodged the energy beams to help her aunt, it seemed to give Jasmine a new found source of entertainment.

"Maybe I do like target practice after all," she chuckled as she stopped chasing Grace, and blasted directly in front of her, causing her to spin through the air like a kite caught in an updraught, clattering to the ground, cracking her head as she landed.

She was out cold.

"Well, that was a bit too easy. I'm a little disappointed."

With her back turned, surveying the destruction of the town around her and the image of the team in pieces, she was not prepared for what came next. She was thrown forwards from a blast directly into Desmond's spine, of purple and violet twisting energy, launching her over the top of the now unconscious Grace and Duncan and landing hundreds of feet away. As she tried to force Desmond's now battered body to stand, she glanced up and saw Deanna marching towards her, fingers twinkling with energy, hair flowing in the breeze behind her. But this of course was not Deanna.

"Nice of you to finally join us," said Jasmine in Desmond's gruff, weakened voice. "Although I have to say, that is rather hypocritical of you Ariella."

As Jasmine stood up, Ariella stopped her advance.

"Deanna was a willing participant. Desmond was not."

Another deep chuckle from Desmond's lips followed.

"I killed your friend. And now you've killed another one of your friends. You're exactly the same. The sooner you admit it, the sooner you can embrace what you are!"

"I am NOTHING like you!" shouted Ariella. Desmond's head shook negatively side to side. "And that is why you will die here."

Jasmine reached out Desmond's arms and fired white beams of light towards Deanna's body, but as Deanna moved forwards and directed her arms to retaliate, she felt herself weaken, and nothing happened. She glanced down and saw the elder blade just metres from her, embedded in the ground, and looked up just in time to be hit full force by her mother's strike. She followed the in the footsteps of her friends by being tossed through the air like a ragdoll.

As Ariella forced Deanna's body to get back to her feet, she realised her fears were confirmed. Whatever Jasmine had done, had nullified the effect the blade had on her usage of power. A fact which her mother picked up on and acknowledged.

"You can't stop me, daughter. You are weaker than me, and you cannot fight the elder blade. I'm so glad you helped me stumble upon this little town. Your little time rift helped me no end."

Ariella could feel her anger building up again, and being slightly further away from the blade, she felt small doses of her energy returning, and fired shots towards her mother. Feeling confident in her strength, Jasmine allowed the blows to strike her unopposed, but they packed a bigger punch than she was expecting, and she too was knocked back. Ariella used this to her advantage and backed away from the blade more, step by step, and continued firing blows of energy at Jasmine, knocking her back with each one. But her mother was too stubborn to allow her to get cheap shots in, and as Ariella launched another bolt towards her, she counteracted with a blast of her own which not only blew straight through Ariella's shot but continued on striking her in the chest and once again sending her careering backwards, landing in the windscreen of a nearby Pontiac.

As she landed, the bones in Deanna's spine cracked, and Ariella felt a huge wave of intense pain. However, unlike Desmond's body which had been weakened and battered by the influx of energy, Deanna's had not, and began to knit the bones back together. As Jasmine advanced, she was hit on all sides by more gunfire and another three arrows embedded themselves in Desmond's back. Kathryn, Grace and Duncan were bruised, dusty and staggering their way forwards, but they were closing in. As Kathryn paused to reload, Duncan leapt into the air preparing to strike directly on Desmond's body, but as he prepared to deliver the blow, Jasmine flung Desmond's arm forward and grabbed him by the throat, stopping him in mid-air. She looked him dead in his eyes as she squeezed his throat tighter and tighter. Duncan fought against the grip but was not strong enough.

"You have courage. I respect you for that."

She glanced over at Grace, whose eyes were now wide with fear, and Jasmine recognised the bond between them.

"But as I will say goodbye to my daughter, say goodbye to yours."

She tore one of the arrows from Desmond's back with her free hand, and thrust it into Duncan's chest, piercing his heart. Grace let out a scream of agony as she realised what had happened. Duncan gasped for breath, but found none, and as he felt his body going limp, he spotted something in the rubble of the cinema behind Jasmine. As she released his body and he fell to the floor, he turned his head towards Grace, and nodded in the direction of the ruins. She momentarily forgot her pain and followed his direction until she saw what he saw. But as the life left Duncan's body for a second time, the final time, the pain returned. And then the anger.

This time, Jasmine had struck too deep, and Grace was done taking the brunt of it. As she leapt into the air, and her eyes filled with fury, Jasmine for a moment felt a hint of uneasiness for the first time. But the battle was not yet over.

37

The blows kept coming from all sides, nobody prepared to stand back. As often as Jasmine kept batting the mortals away, they kept getting back up and coming again. The only one she had managed to take down so far had been Duncan, which seemed to have struck one hell of a chord in terms of resistance. Ariella was limited in the effect she could have due to keeping distance from the elder blade, which despite all the action was still firmly planted in the ground. Ariella was also acutely aware that behind her, laying on the sand amongst the waves breaking on the shore, was a very badly wounded Annie, but she was having to direct all her attention on fighting Jasmine, who at this point was losing all control over the regenerating effects of Desmond's body. The hits from Ariella and the others were coming too fast to take effect.

As Grace lined up another barrage of silver headed arrows, Kathryn was scrambling for cover, having exhausted her supply of ammunition, Ariella attempting to provide cover, but taking dozens of hits in the process. They were a man down, and it was beginning to show. As Grace was once again swept aside, this time she fared worse. Much worse.

She sprinted around behind Jasmine as Kathryn became the target for more abuse and made a run for the elder blade. However, as she got within inches of the weapon, Jasmine grabbed hold of her left arm, swung her around and slammed her into the ground, hard. As her vision became blurred, Grace looked up in time to see the blade coming down towards her. She rolled quickly to the side, the blade hitting the ground instead. But she was not fast enough following the initial attack to leap out of the way, and Jasmine swung the blade upwards, and the tip ran across Grace's stomach, carving a deep laceration in her skin.

Watching on, Ariella threw caution to the wind and charged Deanna's body forward, screaming with rage, and firing violet energy on all cylinders. Grace clutching her stomach, blood pouring through her fingers, collapsed back, but tried to warn her friend to stay away. Her protestations went unanswered, and Ariella continued to charge forwards. As Kathryn made her way towards Grace, Jasmine continued to bat away her daughter's advances. She had remembered one fact that her daughter had forgotten in her rage induced sprint.

As Ariella got within a couple of metres of her mother, her violet bursts of energy began to weaken, until she could produce them no longer. She realised she had crossed the point at which the elder blade was effective but could not stop herself running. It was too late for that. A momentary panic set in, as Jasmine forced Desmond's arm to swing the blade towards her daughter, but she regained her composure long enough to duck down and slide beneath the swipe, coming out on the other side, where she leapt back to her feet and turned. The die had been cast, and with three of her friends now down and out, she could no longer keep the battle going from a distance. She had to try and outwit her mother. She saw something glinting in the rubble in front of her, and a faint smile made its way to her face. A smile which disarmed Jasmine slightly.

But only briefly.

As Ariella once again charged forwards, her mother held the elder blade in Desmond's right hand and directed her bursts of white fire with the right. Ariella's agility was impressive, but it had been a while since she had needed to be in combat in a human host, and misjudged a manoeuvre, crashing into the pile of rubble from the old cinema instead of sliding past it. As she grabbed the item she had been aiming for, she turned back and shouted to Kathryn to get her attention. Kathryn looked up and received a single nod. She knew there was no time to waste. She reassured Grace and moved to run toward the battle, but Jasmine was too alert for that, and a fireball was shot directly at Kathryn, sending her into the side of a discarded bus with such force, that her leg audibly snapped, the sound echoing around the empty, destroyed street. Ariella stood up, reaching out a hand towards her friend. But her reaction cost her dearly. As she felt the elder blade plunge into her back, she felt her mother's presence leering behind her. Desmond's voice whispered in her ear.

"You fought well, daughter. But you were never a match for a true pain wraith. You were a mistake. And now, that mistake has been rectified."

Ariella yelped, as Desmond's hand forced the blade further into the skin. With a swift push and pull, Jasmine pulled the knife out of Deanna's back, keeping her free hand on her shoulder. Ariella began to slowly turn as she felt herself being pulled from the corporeal form. As her vision began to destabilise, she spotted a slowly healing gash in Desmond's left side, now almost completely healed. With all her remaining strength, she shoved the twinkling amulet directly into the wound. As the cut healed up, it sealed the amulet inside, and the effects on Desmond's body began almost immediately. The internal damage it had taken from the initial absorption of the rift energy was now beginning to pick apart the previously immortal figure. The cracks in the skin were now becoming cavernous voids, and the burns intensified.

Each bullet was now feeling like it was penetrating the skin for the first time, and Jasmine found herself in enormous amounts of pain. She let the knife fall to the floor and staggered backwards. Deanna's body collapsed, and as her eyes closed for the final time, she smiled as she saw Desmond's body fall apart, and the final stage of her plan coming together. Deanna's body ceased functioning, and a thick purple fog poured from her chest, darkening in colour, as Ariella was torn away from the realm of the humans, and floated away into the sky, vanishing through the gateway and back to the realm of screams, for good.

With Desmond's body now dead, Jasmine was forced from the vessel in much the same way Ariella had been, and a dense purple fog erupted from the mouth of the body and began to reform her human appearance. It appeared at first as though the intake of energy had seemingly split itself between her and Desmond's form, as she immediately fell to her knees. She felt severely weakened and could not stand. Her head lifted, and she was able to see the carnage she had caused. Kathryn was in a broken heap, Duncan's dead body lay where it had when she killed him, eyes still open. Grace was still sat in her own blood, barely alive, and Annie was presumably still lying flat on the beach being battered by the waves. And Ariella was gone.

Sent back to where she came from. It had not gone according to plan, but her task was finally established. All that now remained was to wipe out the rest of the humans, much as her daughter had done in an alternative future. Nobody would ever challenge the wraiths again or know of their existence. As she stood, slowly, she felt herself recharging. She closed her eyes and took deep breaths, and she raised her arms to the side, flickers of white and violet light beginning to become visible once again. That wry smile she had displayed so often when feeling victorious, began to creep its way across her face.

"Pathetic humans. I knew you were weak, but I can't believe just how weak you were. I knew that werewolf bitch was your strongest weapon. I should have torn you all apart like I did her, whatever her name was."

But then she heard something. A shuffling noise. Much like a laboured walk. A staggering walk. Such as that exhibited by an injured person. Again, she looked around, and everyone was where she had put them. But her confidence and cockiness would this time be her downfall. As the shuffling reached right behind her, she span on the spot, and as the elder blade plunged itself into her heart, the lightning in her fingers was extinguished. Her throat could not muster her voice, and her body was paralysed by the blade. She looked down at the knife, and slowly back up and along the hand that was holding it.

Kristin leaned right in until she was face to face with Jasmine's now pain stricken, and still surprised face. Behind Jasmine, Grace looked over to the scene before her, and Kristin's eyes briefly met hers, before looking back into Jasmine's.

"Her name… was Daniella."

And with that, Kristin drove the blade, handle and all right through Jasmine's body, the tip of the blade poking out of her back, and Kristin's hand almost immersed in Jasmine's chest cavity.

She tore the blade out, and with one swift movement, swept the blade across from left to right, the tip slicing along Jasmine's throat, sending her spinning to the ground. As Kristin collapsed back onto the floor, dropping the blade, she and Grace watched as Jasmine's form began to break down into a dark mist. Much darker than the colour Ariella was when she was forced away, and rather than flowing into the air, she simply rose up to a height of about twenty feet and dissipated in the wind.

Over by the bus, Kathryn regained consciousness just as Jasmine's form floated away, in immense pain. Kristin turned to see a very broken Annie staggering towards the remainder of the group, managing to reach Kristin, and they both helped each other to get to Grace, who was in a very bad way.

"Nicely...done...auntie…" she stuttered barely able to speak.

Her temperature had plummeted, and her skin was turning clammy and white. Her usual healing abilities were not working well enough for wounds as bad as this. Kathryn dragged herself across the ground to reach her, in a pretty bad way herself, but they needed each other. She looked at her wife, who despite all her previous wounds, actually looked the healthiest of all of them.

"Where the fuck did you come from?" she asked with a smile on her face.

Kristin giggled but winced at the pain from her very much still-broken ribs.

"Well, I saw you were getting your asses handed to you, so I figured I'd do it myself."

The mood soon turned sour when Grace lost consciousness, and her hands fell from her stomach to show how bad the gash actually was. No stitches could fix that wound up, even if they had a fully working hospital and medical staff on hand. Kathryn felt her pulse. She was still alive, but barely. And then Kristin realised something. She saw what Ariella had done, and as quick as she could move, stood up and hobbled her way over to the elder blade, now lying on the floor. She picked it up and immediately headed for Desmond's body.

"What are you doing?" asked Kathryn, who had not been awake for the demise of Ariella.

"Saving our niece," was the reply.

With a swift swipe of the blade, she cut open Desmond's torso, and began digging around inside the wound, much to Annie and Kathryn's horror. That is until they saw what she was able to retrieve. The amulet began to pulse yellow, and Kristin began to feel relief from some of the pain she had been in. But there would be plenty of time for that later. She staggered back over to the others, forced open Grace's hand, and slipped it into her palm, closing it tightly around the gem. The three of them sat back and waited. It seemed an eternity had passed, but nothing.

"It has to work, it just has to."

Kathryn was now beginning to fall apart. She had lost her entire family up until this point, she couldn't lose Grace too. And then a gruff chuckle.

"I'm not dead yet Kat."

Relief swept over the other three as Grace opened her eyes once more. The colour began to return to her skin, and as they lifted her torn shirt to inspect the wound, they saw the edges very slowly closing up. Kathryn wanted to embrace her niece so badly but knew she would cause her pain with the wound still having a fair way to go, so she grasped her free hand instead, and held it tightly.

"I should think not. I need all the help I can get explaining what happened to the town!"

Laughter once again swept through the four women left behind, and for the first time in what felt like an eternity, sirens could be heard in the distance.

38

The grass had grown quite high since Grace had last visited. Almost to the point where it was knee high.

"I guess they gave the groundskeepers the year off," she said aloud to herself as she pulled up chunks of the turf.

As she sat down in front of her parents grave, she stroked the edges of the marble stone. She pulled out the dead flowers and replaced them with white roses. They were Daniella's favourites. Every time he had lost an argument, Duncan would run to the nearest florist and pick her up a bouquet. Grace always wished him luck when he came into the house with a bouquet of white roses.

"I hope you like your spot here, guys. We chose it for you. For all of you."

As she gazed around, between the long strands of grass, her eyes took in several other marble stones, one for each of their fallen family.

"We figured, you'd want to look out over the sea as you relaxed. I mean what's more tranquil right?"

A single tear slid down her cheek and was swiftly wiped away. She continued to speak to Daniella and Duncan, with Max's gravestone watching on in the background.

"Kat and Kristin are doing well. They're still chasing down ghosts and ghouls. Wealdstone wasn't the only place to be plagued by those pesky demonic forces, so they tracked a wendigo down to New Orleans. They got it, so should be back soon. They've started rebuilding the south quarter now. Of course, typical cover up type stuff. The government got involved and were convinced the Russians had blown up the town for some secret ops or some shit, I don't even know. The long and the short of it is that they went to great lengths to not accept beings made of pure energy levelled the place. I had money bet on them going with the good old fashioned gas explosion story, but they switched up their game, and went old school and pulled an excuse right out of the cold war."

As Grace looked up, the sun began to peak through the clouds, making her wince, and lifted her hand to shield her eyes.

"Hmm. Should have worn shades."

She looked back down and then up towards the stone again.

"We miss you guys. *I* miss you guys. All of you. I hope you know that we won in the end. That we *won*. To be honest, I figured with the levels of hauntings and shit in this town, that at least one of you would be back. I mean with your sense of humour, Dad, I figured you'd pop up while I was on the toilet or some shit!"

The laughing felt good, and Grace felt the sun warming her skin. As it did so, her mood seemed to become more optimistic too. This was only the third time she had been to the new cemetery since the town had started reconstruction. Five months had now passed, but every day she felt their loss. In total, over fifteen thousand lives were lost, but the media, with persuasion by the government, narrowed it down to five thousand to make it look like a smaller scale catastrophe. While they hadn't been able to locate every victim, those that they had managed to find, were now here, on top of the highest cliff on the coast, overlooking the ocean. Grace continued her news report to her family.

"Oh, did I tell you about Annie? She's been hired by the British Museum to do some research into a new set of artefacts they've dug up in Cairo. She finally gets to go back to what she loved doing as a kid and exploring ancient myths and legend. Of course, she still dabbles in the mystic arts. I mean once you start that stuff, it's difficult to quit. Personally, if I could magically clean my apartment without lifting a finger, I'd do it too!"

The cloud began to mass back over the cliff top, and there was a distant rumble of thunder over the sea.

"Well, I guess that's my cue to head on home. I promised

I'd have Kat and Kristin's place finished by the time they got back. It's a lovely little house. We built it on the site of the mansion. Kinda hoping if you guys had a place to go, you might come visit once in a while. They offered me a place there, but I just think it's time I made my own way. I know that they're there if I need them. Besides, I got a job! I know, me with a job? I'm the new manager at Sisko's. That place was the first building to be finished after the contractors rolled into town. Sometimes, you just need a place to hang out."

She glanced over her shoulder as the sound of construction equipment drifted on the wind. The roof was finally being lowered onto the new diner. Kathryn had insisted the new eatery should be named after Deanna. She had chosen to make the sacrifice for the final battle, and she shouldn't be forgotten. So as the roof panels were lowered, the truck rolled in with the new signage.

"Deanna's Place. The best go to stop for your pie and coffee needs."

Grace smiled as she said the slogan. There was to be a place or structure named after each of the fallen gang. Scarlett Park was next to be built, just down the road from Max's Arcade and Desmond's Army Surplus store. Customers were already visiting the newly built Herman's Curiosities, and Duncan's Toy Emporium was due to open in a couple of months' time.

"Well, I'd better head off. Looks like a storm. I'll catch you guys later. I love you."

As Grace pulled up her hood, she tucked the amulet necklace inside her shirt, and headed on down the hill. The wind picked up, and the long grass began to sway in the breeze. As Grace's head disappeared from view, Max stood beside his gravestone, leaning on the marble. A smile spread across his face as he began to disappear into the wind.

"I love you too."

EPILOGUE

The sound of applause echoed around Sisko's bar as the sound of plates crashing to the floor brought the inevitable embarrassment for the waitress who had dropped them. Luckily, she saw the funny side of it, and held her hands up and took a bow. Eliot turned back towards his date, and the smile across his face slowly grew smaller.

"You know, I used to be manager here. Well, the old here anyway."

"Really? What was that like?" his date asked.

He thought about it for a minute before giving a rather blunt answer.

"Bull shit, actually."

The two of them laughed, and their hands touched on the table. Eliot continued.

"It wasn't too bad initially, but then everything went downhill, literally, and then when they rebuilt it, they gave the place to new owners."

"What do you do now?" asked the woman.

"Now? I'm actually opening up a new restaurant in a town down the coast. You ever heard of Trinity Bay?"

The woman shook her head.

"Well, it was a town built specifically for the military families of the nearby base. But when the army moved out, the criminals moved in. They've had some serious drug and gang problems. And even gun running along the water. Don't ask me how, but they've managed to get some pretty serious funding to move in a private police force and bring the place back up to code. It's definitely the place to be."

The woman took a sip of her cocktail. Tequila Sunrise. It used to be Jack's favourite. She stared a little too long at the glass before Eliot woke her from her daydream.

"You okay…"

Her name escaped him.

"Kimberley."

"Sorry. Kimberley? You, okay?"

She took another glance at the drink and placed it back on the table.

"Yeah, just thinking about my ex."

~ 367 ~

Eliot looked down at the table.

"Oh, I see."

Kimberley grabbed his hand to reassure him.

"Oh, no, not like that. It's just, he died. I never got to say goodbye, and this was his favourite drink."

"What happened?" asked Eliot.

"I was… I left. Rather suddenly. Something I had no control over. When I finally got back, it was too late."

Eliot felt a tangible amount of pain.

"Where did you go?"

Kimberley was not sure how to phrase that particular scenario.

"Let's just say there was a case of mistaken identity, and I was sent away. It took me a long time to get back. I had to risk a lot. And I had a helping hand from a friend. But by that time, everything had changed."

Eliot wanted to know more, but he didn't want to push. In all honesty, he didn't see this going anywhere, especially as he was heading out in less than two weeks to Trinity Bay. He figured that he'd enjoy her company and have some fun and leave it at that. If more developed, then all the better.

"Well, I hope things look brighter for you. After all, Wealdstone is coming back to life pretty quickly."

Kimberley laughed.

"Yeah, coming back to life is the key word."

Eliot was a bit confused at that statement but shrugged it off.

"You wanna go get something to eat? I hear Deanna's Place has great pie."

Kimberley chuckled.

"I'd love to, but can we take a rain check? I have work tonight."

Eliot was disappointed, but as he was trying to keep it casual on a first date, he nodded, and stood to leave.

"Yeah, I'd love to. How does lunch tomorrow sound? I hear the cherry pie is to die for."

More laughter from Kimberley.

"Yeah, sounds great."

The two kissed on the cheek, and Eliot left the bar, turning around once just to wave as he opened the door. As soon as he was out of eyesight, Kimberley knew she probably wouldn't see him again.

"He wasn't your type anyway."

Kimberley rolled her eyes as she turned around.

"I have more than one type, Kristin."

"Yeah. She has at least two types. Cops, and Ex-cops."

The second interruption from Kathryn was as unwelcome as the first.

"You know I could blast you both through that wall."

"You are not blasting holes in my walls! It took forever to get those picture hooks in!"

Grace entered the conversation, swinging her coat around her shoulders.

"You know, I'm starting to think breaking out of my realm was a bad idea after all. Remind me why I stick around here?"

Kathryn pushed her towards the exit, and the others followed.

"Because you want to help us make sure nobody else ever follows you out. That's why."

Kimberley shook her head.

"No… I think it must be the cherry pie at Deanna's Place. It genuinely is to die for."

The four of them walked out of the bar laughing amongst themselves, leaving the rest of the clientele chattering away, the sport on the TV in the background. Manchester United were currently three goals up against Real Madrid in the Champions League. Not that anyone was watching a British game of 'football'.

At least, almost nobody.

Jack sat on a bar stool in the far corner, watching the match intensely. Nobody paid him any notice at all. Probably because they couldn't see him. But he was there. And he finally had the answer he had been looking for. Kimberley was alive, and he knew she would be safe with the others. As he relaxed and the game came to an end, he closed his eyes, and faded away, the stool spinning gently as he left.

AFTERWORD

And there we have it!

That brings a close to the Pain Wraith Saga, and hopefully you enjoyed the ride. When I started writing this book, my first full length novel, I was planning for it to be the potential ending to tales set in Wealdstone. But the more I wrote it, the more I realised I wanted to carry on.

This became much more apparent, when I lost my day job with no notice, and it was completely unexpected. I hadn't planned for this or been prepared for it in any way. I went into a bit of a spiral for several weeks, before picking up some courier work for Amazon. Needing to have somewhere to keep receipts and things for tax purposes, and my wife being cramped on her tiny desk in the lounge, I turned our gym room into a home office for the two of us and came across 100 pages of a story I'd started writing all the way back in 2015.

This story was not a horror or ghost tale, it was an action story set in a fictional purpose built town. It was kind of a cross between Baywatch and a cop version of Buffy the Vampire Slayer. Unexpected scenarios, pretty dark and disturbing, and more character orientated than pure action. And it was actually pretty good. While I'm not ready to pick up that story yet, it did confirm my feelings that I wanted to build out this particular universe, and, eventually, have another dabble in short stories.

There are still two or three ideas that might creep a few people out that aren't novel material! And I've always wanted to write a sci-fi tale!

So, I decided that I would close this chapter of the Dark Corner Universe, but continue to expand it in other directions. I've also had that sci-fi based idea rattling around in my head, and if I keep sheltering in Wealdstone, then I won't be able to get these ideas out of my brain, and I'll lose them.

Bear in mind, if you will, that the rough idea for the first story in the first Dark Corner book came from an idea I formulated way back in 1997! I was just a kid, but I knew I wanted to tell that story. I didn't expect it to take me over twenty years to actually do it! And I don't want that to happen again, so I'm pushing forward!

I greatly enjoyed writing this story. The ability to delve deep into the world of the pain wraiths freely, and to get in all the various elements from all the previous stories, and bring all the little Easter eggs together, and make them clear to the reader was an absolute pleasure. I wanted to make it clear who they were, where they came from, and what had led to this situation.

I found it really difficult to juggle so many characters as the stories began to merge towards the end of the second book, so I made the decision before I even started writing this book that I would kill off several characters. I didn't know how I was going to do that with the exception of Max. I knew I was going to have him killed by one of the other characters, to demonstrate the seriousness of the situation, but I didn't decide who it was until I noticed I wasn't writing Scarlett into many of my scenes.

I also decided before I started, that the main character would have to be a new character if I wanted people unfamiliar with the Dark Corner to be able to pick it up. However, as I started writing it, I noticed it was switching between the characters, and I was essentially writing the story as if it was a TV show, and we were switching scenes rather than sticking with the one guy.

I considered switching it back and having everything

told from Jack's point of view, but decided my writing style suited this better, and carried on, which eventually culminated in his death before the final battle. Some people will say that Jack was a wasted character, but when you're writing, and other authors will tell you this, you either fall in love with a character, or you don't. And when the realisation sets in, you have to make a decision. Although that decision was not as hard as the way Daniella was killed off.

That one made me uncomfortable for quite a while, but I resisted changing it because I needed to demonstrate just how powerful Jasmine was. If she could take apart the strongest member of the team so easily, and so brutally, it would put the reader in no doubt about any blurred lines. Jasmine was evil and there was no getting around it, and no redemption here.

And now I'm done, I find myself missing these characters already! But we shall see them again not only in the planned Wealdstone sequels I have, but across the new entries in this universe.

And I must say that while it seemed after Jack's death that the initial thread of his fiancée being killed looked like it wasn't going to be answered, I managed to sneak in the resolution into the Epilogue, which also set up the return to Wealdstone in the future, as I said earlier.

Quite a few people, including my wife Charlotte, have asked me in the past who my favourite character is. I really had to think about it, because I get attached to quite a few of my characters, but on reflection, I'm going to have to go with Kristin. I think I wrote a strong character there. I think when you're writing a supernatural or a superhero based story, if you can make your favourite character, a person who has no abilities at all, then you've written them well. It was part of the reason that I had her kill Jasmine rather than Grace.

It was almost a deal breaker though, because I seriously considered bringing the whole phenomenon of Kathryn and Kristin's seemingly unbeatable good luck to an end and killing one of them off. But it was pointed out to me that to have an LGBTQ couple surviving all of that and doing it together makes a much stronger statement, and I have to agree. I love them both, and I think they are a true power couple, each with their own unique strengths and qualities. If they can survive demons, ghosts, vampires, werewolves, pain wraiths, explosions, and a potential old flame, then they can survive anything!

As for the next project, well that would be my sci-fi story 'Resurrection' which will be with you all on 4th December 2021. This sees the Dark Corner Universe move into the far future and look at an alternate version of what happened in 'Galaxy of Pain' from the first DC book.

So, I just wanted to say thanks once again to everyone who has followed the Dark Corner Universe, through the short stories, the slightly longer and more developed stories, the rewrites, and now to the conclusion of this story, with this novel. It's been a labour of love and I can't wait to share what's next!

UPDATE

Now, with this being the updated version of the book, I was able to sneak in previews of what you have to look forward to. By this point, you will know that Resurrection was released, and I can tell you after a year of planning that the next book will be as I said at the start of this edition, Wealdstone : Crossroads.

But that's not all I can reveal...

COMING SOON...

WEALDSTONE CROSSROADS

–2023–

THE LAND BEYOND

–2023–

WEALDSTONE ORIGINS

–2024–

ACKNOWLEDGMENTS

I usually go off on a rant and a huge long list of who I'd like to thank and then list my entire family and all my friends, and everyone on planet Earth, but this time I decided to do something different.

In the last six months, particularly, I have received a huge amount of support from my parents, which led to me dedicating this book to them. They've always been supportive to me, but when I lost my job, they were backing me all the way to come out the other side and I did. They both encourage my writing, and they keep badgering me for the next volume, and I'm happy to oblige! They are just the epitome of what parents should be. I wouldn't swap them for the world. An extended autobiography is something I'm considering writing in the future, so I hope to get across to the world just how amazing these two are if I ever get around to writing it.

On an equal if not stronger level, I have to once again praise my incredible wife, Charlotte. She designed an amazing cover for this book, from scratch, but more than that, she has been my absolute tower of strength during all of the difficulties I've had recently. She has been nothing short of miraculous, keeping me from slipping into a dark place when everything seemed to be crashing down around me. Her love is the reason I keep going every day, and everything I do is for her. I hope she realises what an absolute treasure she really is.

Now I also feel the need to mention someone I thanked in the last book, but she has continued to spread positivity in me, and that is Karen Watson. When I lost my job, she kept in touch, sending me job adverts she thought I would be good for, and reassuring me that I could get over this, and always wished me and Charlotte well. So, thank you Karen. Being kind takes so little effort but has such an impact, and I'd encourage you all to do the same whenever possible, and we can truly make the world a much better place to be.

I'd like to thank Amazon at this point. Not Jeff Bezos, because let's just say I don't agree with his approaches, but the people behind KDP and the logistics department in the UK. Not only were they the source of my paperback and e-book publishing, but also the source of work for me when everything went wrong. Delivering packages for them through SCR, paid my rent and kept my bills in check, so overall they've given me a lot in recent times. That, and they're the ones that bring me *Star Trek Picard,*

Star Trek Lower Decks, and *The Grand Tour,* so they're pretty much the only monthly subscription service I'm never going to cancel!

And finally, thanks must go to the complete muppets who keep reading this crap! The majority of my readers come from the USA, Canada and Germany through the Kindle Unlimited program. So, I'll keep writing, for me, my family who keep pushing me on, and of course for those of you who keep turning those pages, digital or otherwise!

See you all soon!

Are you seeking support for your mental health, distress, or trauma?

Look no further! Flare Peer Support is here for you. We may not be professional counsellors, but we are a compassionate peer support group that believes in the power of connection and understanding.

Talk it Out Thursdays: Every Thursday, we host structured and activity-based sessions where you can share your thoughts and experiences in a safe and supportive environment.

Self-Care Sundays: Our relaxed Sundays are dedicated to practising self-care, having fun, and building a strong community. Join us as we create a nurturing space for relaxation and rejuvenation.

We understand that some individuals may require more personalised and regular support. That's why we offer one-to-one sessions for those who feel the need for a deeper connection.

Feeling the need for a trusted confidant? Our Key-Mentor Programme pairs you with a supportive mentor who will check up on you semi-regularly. Your mentor will be there to listen, offer guidance, and provide a private space for you to express your concerns, issues, or problems happening in your life.

You don't have to face your struggles alone. Join Flare today and become a part of a caring community that understands and supports you on your journey toward mental well-being.

Find out more about Flare at
ALLMYLINKS.COM/FLARECARES

Printed in Great Britain
by Amazon